A Mother's
Love

CAROLYN DAVIS CID

ISBN 978-1-916529-42-7 Paperback

ISBN 978-1-916529-43-4 Ebook

The Unbound Press

www.theunboundpress.com

WELCOME!

Hey unbound one!

Welcome to this magical book brought to you by The Unbound Press.

At The Unbound Press we believe that when women write freely from the fullest expression of who they are, it can't help but activate a feeling of deep connection and transformation in others. When we come together, we become more and we're changing the world, one book at a time!

This book has been carefully crafted by both the author and publisher with the intention of inspiring you to move ever more deeply into who you truly are.

We hope that this book helps you to connect with your Unbound Self and that you feel called to pass it on to others who want to live a more fully expressed life.

With much love,

Nicola Humber

Founder of The Unbound Press

www.theunboundpress.com

To my husband, the love of my life. You are on every page in every chapter of my story. I am so proud of our family and what we have achieved. Thanks for always being there.

To my mother, who supported me in all my endeavors. Thanks, mom, for your love and for always encouraging my writing.

1

Friday, April 17, 2020

"Positive," someone called loudly above the din to someone beyond Jeanette. Surprisingly, the white-clad person stopped alongside her gurney and spoke directly to Jeanette.

"My name is Alicia, and I'm your nurse. Your husband, Adam, completed the insurance forms. Due to COVID-19 protocol, no family members are permitted. He said to tell you that he loves you, and he'll speak to you soon, once we get you settled in. You're being admitted; you've just tested positive. We're preparing a bed for you now on the COVID floor."

What? It was so loud here and distracting, and she was so focused on breathing. Jeanette Lynn Remington barely registered the nurse's muffled words. Except that Adam wasn't here. A finger of fear began to poke, but Jeanette reasoned. She was in the hospital. They would fix her. She began to smile, thinking of Adam saying, "Here's my copay; fix my wife." More coughing and she remembered to focus on breathing. Tried to rest in between. Restless, she turned on her side and faced the wall. *How did this get so bad so fast?*

Monday, April 13 (4 Days Earlier) - Day #1

First, she heard the birds singing outside the bedroom window. Then, the water. *Was it raining?* No, Adam was taking a shower in the bathroom. *Morning already? It feels like I just laid down!* Tired and clammy, Jeanette rolled out of bed, dressed, stopped at the bathroom in the hallway, and went downstairs on autopilot to take care of Lucy. The cream lab was waiting in her kennel in the office for her morning ritual. "Hi, baby!" Jeanette crooned as Lucy bounded out of the room. "Let's feed you!" Momentarily distracted by the realization that she had a sore throat, Jeanette felt Lucy paw at her leg impatiently. "Alright! I'm getting it!"

Even at thirteen, Lucy was a puppy first thing in the morning. Still, age was affecting the labrador. Jeanette filled her bowl and prepared Lucy's medications. She retrieved the cream cheese and sorted through the three daily doses: fish oil, a pain reliever, and a nerve block. As Jeanette leaned over to feed Lucy the first dose, she coughed.

Just then Adam came down the stairs ready for work. "Hey, that doesn't sound good. I hope you don't have the COVID!" He'd been making that joke following every cough and sneeze since the pandemic began and closed down parts of the country last month. In New Jersey, the governor's executive orders related to the novel Coronavirus started on February 3, with a declaration of a state of emergency. The executive order was updated weekly, leading to the stay-at-home order that was released on March 21.

Adam greeted his dog as he let Lucy out the back door, "Good morning, beautiful. Go ahead; take care of business." He stepped out onto the deck of his suburban home, appreciating the bright sunshine, watching Lucy navigate the deck steps. The birds flew away from the feeders immediately, as if Lucy were a danger. He noticed how quiet the neighborhood had become, now that there were no school buses, and less traffic since many people were working from home. When he stepped back into the kitchen, Jeanette was speaking.

"So funny. I'm fine; it's just a cold," Jeanette sniffled.

Adam came in close for a quick hug. "Hmm. Looks like a beautiful spring day in the burbs. Maybe you can work outside a bit today. Don't forget; I'll be on a Zoom meeting tonight with other agents," he reminded her as he gathered his coffee and briefcase. "Call me later." A peck on the cheek and he was on his way to his insurance agency. Jeanette heard the garage door open, his BMW roar to life, and the garage door closing. Deemed "essential" by the governor, Adam had adjusted his hours and office protocols while he continued to run his business over the phone and internet. His brick-and-mortar office was located in a strip mall, where several other businesses were forced to close due to the executive order while restaurants remained open with the required modifications in place. Those businesses without the floor space to socially distance customers at least six feet apart continued take-out orders when possible.

She stood by the kitchen slider door, waiting for Lucy to return. The ornamental grasses in the yard were blooming, and every migratory bird had returned to join their hearty friends. She smiled at the promise of the day and enjoyed the squirrel's antics running along the top of the fence. Adam was right again: It did look like a beautiful spring day! No wonder her allergies were erupting! After letting Lucy back into the house, Jeanette finished dosing her pet. The lab waited patiently, sitting sideways and eagerly awaiting her treats. Putting the cream cheese away,

Jeanette steeped her tea, wandered into the office, turned on her laptop, and checked her email and the day's assignment she'd scheduled on Google Classroom last Friday. As a middle school seventh-grade Science teacher, she was also conducting business over the internet. All public schools began the new normal of at-home learning at the direction of Executive Order 107. She checked her notebook for her to-do list before heading upstairs for her turn in the master bathroom. Having several of her own Google Meets for the day, she showered, dressed, and made herself presentable. After teaching this way for a month, Jeanette had the basic makeup routine down pat.

Downstairs, her agenda on her mind, Jeanette fixed her tea and oatmeal. Still feeling a bit lethargic and clammy, she took a pain reliever for the sore throat. Thinking the cough was allergy-related, she debated about taking a decongestant. In the end, she decided the cough would get better with tea. "We're both dosed up for the day, Lucy," she said as the pooch followed her into the office. Although she didn't get sick often, being a teacher meant she was exposed daily to colds and viruses. Well, before the shutdown when they were all in person. "This is going to be a tough allergy season," Jeanette informed Lucy. Usually, in the spring she was in a school building with air conditioning and ventilation for the majority of five days a week. And she still suffered mild allergy symptoms. Being home this spring, she was sure to experience more allergens, between her open windows for fresh air and being in and out with Lucy. She returned to the kitchen to add Tylenol, Sudafed, and nasal spray to her ongoing shopping list on the counter and moved into the office.

The morning flew by as Jeanette tackled her remote learning Monday morning as usual. This entailed checking for missing assignments from the previous week, entering the grades online, and sending emails notifying the appropriate students that the grades were currently missing. When it was time for the first Science class's Google Meet, Jeanette inhaled deeply. Although she couldn't expect one hundred percent attendance, it was frustrating to have so few joining online. It was her only source of personal contact with the children. Jeanette was grateful to see ten join out of the seventeen in the class. Several boxes were completely black, with just the student's name showing. Several boxes were missing bodies but showed backdrops of bedrooms: ceiling fans spinning, neon strip lights along the ceiling, closet doors, unmade beds, etc. Four boxes were showing faces smiling directly at her.

"Good morning! How is everyone this fine day?" Jeanette asked enthusiastically.

Suzie unmuted herself and said, "Great!"

Bobby unmuted himself and said, "Tired!"

Reggie, Steven, and Cindy pushed the "thumbs-up" icon on the screen. The remainder did not respond.

Jeanette continued to smile encouragingly hoping that a stray student or two would join late. That did not happen.

Attempting to hide her disappointment, Jeanette overcompensated in her tone. "Well, I'm glad you joined the Science Meet this morning!" She cleared her throat and brought her pitch down a notch. "Thank you to those on camera; it's wonderful to see your faces. I'm glad you're all here."

The Meet was only 20 minutes, so Jeanette followed her agenda closely. She reviewed the assignment for the week, requested (but did not receive) feedback in the chat from everyone, and finally began the Kahoot game she had created on the water cycle. Overall, the class did well on the review, and Suzie and Bobby lingered on the Google Meet just to chat and talk about their pets. After the Meet ended, Jeanette saved the file that appeared in her inbox for attendance. She noted which students had not joined at all, so she could send them an email. She also noted which students either did not respond or did not appear on camera in her "handy-dandy" notebook. To what extent did they really attend the Meet?

Jeanette and her colleagues had been experimenting with more ways to engage students online since it became apparent at the beginning of the school shutdown that many students went missing. Some students literally did not answer emails, complete work, or join the Meets. The abruptness with which the executive order was enacted left everyone scrambling: teachers, parents, and students alike. She was happy to say that through her daily emails, assignments posted on Google Classroom, and occasional Google Meets, she was reaching about 95 percent of her students. The five percent, however, were a constant worry. Jeanette made phone calls and emailed parents weekly. Aside from the difficulty of assessing understanding, she was concerned about their welfare.

Then she went back and began grading the assignments before the next quick Google Meet. About half the students in each class joined the online meetings, just to "check in" on the current assignment and play the Kahoot game. Jeanette found these meetings both uplifting and draining. On the one hand, she enjoyed seeing her students' faces; she missed them! On the other, the Meets were optional, and Jeanette knew other students would still have questions. Remote learning was far from ideal, in Jeanette's opinion. Throughout the morning in between Meets, she continually ran into the kitchen for more tea to soothe her dry cough and sore throat. Each time, Lucy would get up and follow her from room to room, finally repositioning herself in the office with Jeanette.

By noon, Jeanette was drained and her throat raw, despite the tea. She took more Tylenol. Too tired to fuss, Jeanette ate a stale protein bar from the cabinet. As was her usual, she planned dinner during lunch. Deciding on salmon, she took out two pieces of the wild Alaskan from the freezer in the garage and placed them in the refrigerator to defrost. Rice and frozen broccoli would round out the meal. She took Lucy for a potty break in the yard, and they walked slowly together around the perimeter, breathing in the fresh spring air.

Feeling tired, they returned to the house. She decided to lay down on the couch in the living room for a brief nap before the Science Department Meeting at 1:00. "A benefit to working from home, Lucy. Let's take a nap." After setting the alarm on her phone for fifteen minutes, Jeanette was out. When the alarm went off, Jeanette dragged herself off the couch and back into the office with Lucy in tow.

Somewhat revived, she focused on the final meeting of the day with her colleagues. When she joined the Meet, she felt that surge of comfort to see everyone's faces. The first few minutes were composed of an easy-going banter about the beautiful day.

"Y'all look great! I've decided if I'm working from home, I may as well take advantage!" exclaimed Rachel. She looked like she was on vacation, sitting outside in her yard with sunglasses and the breeze blowing her hair. Always smiling, Rachel had to be the most positive person on the planet.

Jeanette smiled and used the same thumbs-up icon her student Cindy had used earlier.

"Okay everyone, I'd like to get the meeting started so we can *all* enjoy the day, like Rachel," smiled Paula Rice, the Science supervisor. "Before we begin, I know your most pressing question is when we'll be returning to school. We have no indication from the governor that it will be soon. As you know, he has been updating the school districts every three weeks or so. Any questions about that?" Paula paused to allow anyone to respond. No one said anything, but everyone (except Rachel) looked disappointed.

"At our last meeting," Paula continued, "we were discussing ways to encourage more student engagement. I asked you to complete the shared spreadsheet with your ideas, and they look terrific. Y'all are doing a great job! I'd like to first highlight a few of these ideas, and ask you to describe your lessons a bit more to the entire department. I'm hoping that you'll continue to think outside the box, or use some of these excellent ideas your colleagues have come up with. You can see that I've added a column to this spreadsheet for you to complete as a result of this meeting. Please indicate which new idea you'll be implementing over the next two weeks. It could be one from your colleagues or something brand new. Now, let's begin with Arthur." In his box, Arthur perked up. "Could you discuss your idea on how to have the students conduct and share their experiments at home?"

Smiling, balding Arthur pushed back his glasses and said, "Of course! So, I discovered this website, which I included on the spreadsheet ..."

Jeanette listened halfheartedly to Arthur's idea. She smiled woodenly in her box. Then conversation flowed to the remote learning procedures going forward and the possibility of returning to school before the end of the school year. Jeanette's frustration grew in direct relation to the length of the meeting. She was so exasperated! This entire scenario was untenable–even with everyone doing an outstanding job. How could everyone be sitting in these boxes on a screen and acting normal? Meanwhile, Paula confirmed that ongoing issues with student connectivity were still being addressed. Apparently, some students were having difficulty with their home internet. How could students participate in remote learning without the internet? Paula then ended the meeting but invited anyone to stay and ask questions or make comments. Jeanette waved goodbye and left the call. She'd jump out of her skin if she stayed another minute.

All of these meetings felt the same at the end for Jeanette: soul-crushing frustration at having absolutely no control. At-home schooling was an oxymoron. It did not work. Period. She exhaled a deep breath and read aloud the sticky note she placed on the office desk with one of her favorite quotes from Theodore Roosevelt: "Do what you can, with what you have, where you are." As always, it helped Jeanette concentrate on what was next on her to-do list. Any individual task was preferred rather than attempting to navigate the COVID reality right now.

"Great advice, Theodore." Jeanette made more tea and took another stroll around the yard with Lucy to relax. Her beautiful backyard always helped to shake off the frustration and focus on her work. In fact, she had moved the desk in the office so that she was now facing the window. She could look up at any moment and watch nature all day long. Having two classes mostly graded, Jeanette began scheduling the assignments for the remainder of the week. She stopped several times to answer student emails. While daily assignments were required, it seemed that the majority of students did not begin the assignments until late afternoon. This meant emails arrived in her inbox at all hours.

Jeanette was still working when Adam called at 4:00. "Hey! You were going to call me?"

"Oh, yeah! Sorry ... I was busy all day with Meets. How was your day?" Jeanette asked while responding to yet one more email.

"Good. Same ol'. I spoke with Jerry today," Adam informed her.

Jeanette immediately focused on the call. "Oh? How is he?"

"Good! We can talk about it over dinner. What will that be?" he asked.

"I'm defrosting salmon. Jerry's good?"

"Yep, our oldest is solid. Remember, I have a call later. Gotta go–looking forward to coming home."

They ended the call, and Jeanette realized she had to shut down for now. She figured she could check her emails later while Adam was on his call. She usually checked her email while watching TV at night, and often fell asleep these days with it open on her lap. Jeanette went into the kitchen to begin dinner and called her daughter.

She left a message on her voice mail. "Hey, Evie, it's Mom. You don't have to call back; I just wanted to hear your voice. Love you." As much as she wanted to talk to her daughter, Jeanette was *almost* relieved that Evie didn't answer. Moving about to put the rice in the pot and the salmon in a baking dish, she then left a similar message for her younger son, Alex. She didn't expect Alex to answer; she knew his working from home meant that most of his meetings occurred in the afternoon. She didn't call her oldest son Jerry since Adam had spoken to him earlier. "I feel like I weigh a ton," Jeanette said aloud, leaning on the granite countertop of the island.

That's where Adam would have found Jeanette when he returned home from work if she hadn't been alerted to his return by Lucy's exuberance at the garage door. "Is Daddy home, Lucy?" Jeanette teased the dog who obviously recognized Adam's car. This was, of course, their usual routine. "Better get dinner in the oven," Jeanette muttered as she placed the prepped salmon and broccoli in the oven and set the timer for the pot of rice on the stove.

"Hey. What's up?" Adam asked Jeanette as he walked into the kitchen.

His faithful companion sat the best she could with her tail wagging triple time. "Good girl, Lucy!" he said, rewarding her with a rawhide chew.

"Not much. I just put everything in the oven. How was the rest of your day?" Jeanette replied.

Adam didn't immediately answer. Then with a sigh, "We've lost another client to COVID. A lovely gentleman ..."

"Oh, I'm sorry. What a shame!" Jeanette replied.

"Yep." As an insurance agent, Adam's office was promptly notified by families when an insured passed. It was not his favorite part of the job.

She moved closer to her husband. "You know I find this remote situation frustrating ..."

"Yep," he responded as he turned away to place his keys and wallet on the counter.

"I keep forgetting that you have to personally deal with death. I mean you *know* these people ... I can't imagine having to do that ... I don't think I could."

Adam turned and hugged his wife. There wasn't much of a follow-up to that thread that either wanted to pursue, so Adam went upstairs to get changed while Jeanette continued dinner.

By the time he came downstairs, dinner was ready. Adam shared his short conversation with Jerry and assured Jeanette that both Jerry and his wife were well. Afterwards, Adam and Jeanette exchanged little small talk other than the usual discussion of when the restrictions might end. Jeanette, unfortunately, was caught unaware when the state-wide shut-down was announced a month ago. She was shocked when the toilet paper shelves were empty, and the rumors were confirmed in her school district-wide emails. Ever an optimist, she was hopeful that each week they would all return to normalcy. Today's department meeting confirmed, however, that was not imminent. Adam, on the other hand, kept telling Jeanette to get used to it. He diligently researched various news agency websites and could see that a true emergency was unfold-ing. In fact, he actually predicted in January that COVID would be a big issue. He referenced articles such as "China Orders Centralized Response to Virus Outbreak as Crisis Alert Level Rises" and "U.S. Hospitals Aren't Ready for the Coronavirus." How right he was!

When it came time for Adam's Zoom call with fellow agents, Jeanette announced she was tired and wanted to go to bed. Adam recommended a shot of whiskey for her throat, which was another ongoing joke between them. He contended there was nothing a shot of whiskey couldn't cure. Jeanette declined the whiskey and instead dosed herself with more Tylenol and grabbed a few throat lozenges to settle the random cough.

"No problem; go to bed. I hope you feel better, and I'll see you up there following my meeting," Adam said as he hugged his wife. "Oh, you feel warm. Do you have a fever?"

"The thermometer needs a battery, but probably not. I'm sure it's just allergies," Jeanette said dismissively. She kissed Adam, hugged Lucy, and went upstairs.

She took a quick shower and smeared menthol rub all over her nose hoping it would help her sleep. She needn't have worried; even the occasional coughing did not disturb the exhausted Jeanette. When Adam got in bed and pulled her close, she didn't even notice.

2

Tuesday, April 14, 2020 - Day #2

When Jeanette woke in the morning, the bed was empty, and there was no sound in the bathroom. *Where was Adam?* After her usual ministrations, she went downstairs and found a note on the kitchen counter from Adam saying he left for an early meeting. He had fed Lucy, hoped she felt better, and wanted her to have a good day. She *was* feeling just a hair better, even if she did have a low-grade headache. Her throat was still sore, and there was an occasional cough. *Must be allergies.* After greeting and dosing Lucy, Jeanette dosed herself with more Tylenol and added Sudafed, thinking the cough and headache were from sinus pressure. Although she still felt sluggish, the tea helped. She knew from past experience that some allergy years were worse than others. It was only mid-April; time would tell.

Jeanette struggled through another day of Google Meets, emails and assignments with Lucy. There was so much to do! Four weeks into the shutdown, Jeanette had exhausted the easy assignments and was into the next area of curriculum. Not being able to explain the lesson in person, and not expecting the students to be familiar with the ideas, she was amassing videos to embed into documents with practice labs to follow. If the lesson required using multiple websites, then Jeanette created a video to explain the concepts, how to navigate the websites, and how to complete the labs. So many steps! For a twenty-minute video, Jeanette would spend at least three hours recording and editing. She was essentially recreating the wheel.

She texted with Adam, told him that she was feeling a bit better, and they agreed on frozen pizza for dinner. Neither one of them wanted to deal with pick-up and/or delivery issues; the restrictions caused a backlog in both cases. In between Meets she spoke briefly with Evie.

"Hey, mom. Was that a cough?" Evie said immediately.

"Yeah, it looks like spring has sprung. Allergies are causing the usual sinus headache and a bit of a cough, but I'm fine. How's work going there? Do you have everything you need?" Jeanette was a bit worried about all three of her children in their separate lockdown locations. They were all adults, with jobs and partners, but it was a global pandemic! Adam and Jeanette immediately shared conversations and/or texts they had with any of their kids, so they both were always updated. Evie, the youngest, was working from home with her fiancé in their apartment in Miami, Florida. Both their offices had closed. Luckily, they had a two-bedroom apartment to work from. Despite being on call at inconvenient hours, Evie was happy with the "safer at home" mandate. As far as she was concerned, she was saving time and money commuting, enjoying the beautiful Florida weather by taking frequent walks, and petting her cat *all* day long. None of that was possible when she was stuck in the office.

Evie sounded upbeat. "Yep! Kevin and I masked up and did a bit of food shopping yesterday for the first time since the latest restrictions. We can still go out, and order pick-up or delivery from our favorite restaurants, which makes us happy. We never had any plans of joining groups of ten people anyway, day or night."

"Smart!"

"We just maintained our distance and finally stocked up on my favorite Cheez-Its. Thanks for the advice; 2:00 in the afternoon is the perfect time! We were in and out in about 40 minutes. We're set for at least two weeks! How're things with you and Dad?"

"Good. We're good." As much as Jeanette hated to end the call, she really did need more tea. Her throat was so irritated, and she was just tired. Still, she had much more work to do today.

"That cough does not sound good, Mom. Are you sure you're alright? Are you sure it's allergies?"

"Yep, I just need a little tea," Jeanette hurriedly reassured her anxious daughter. "What else could it be?"

"Mom, could you have COVID?" Evie whispered.

Jeanette closed her eyes. The last thing she needed right now was a daughter with an overactive imagination. "Absolutely not! Please, Evie, don't worry. It's just the usual allergies. You should see the backyard. Everything's blooming! I'll send you a picture," she placated.

"Oh, yeah, you've always had allergies." Perking up, Evie suggested, "Well, make some of your famous chicken soup!"

"Sure! Listen, I've got a class ... gotta go. Be safe; I love you!"

"Love you, too, Mom! Take care!"

Jeanette did make more tea and continued her day. Later, she exchanged texts with Jerry and Alex separately, who were also working from home.

JEANETTE: Hey, how goes it?

JERRY: In a meeting. Will text later.

ALEX: Hey. Busy. Working on a pretty important presentation for a meeting on Friday.

In response, Jeanette "loved" Jerry's text. Jerry and his wife Beth lived in an apartment in Chicago. They had just gotten married last October, but enjoyed only a short mini-moon because Beth had just started a new job. They expected to take a wonderful, extended honeymoon in Italy next October, and were unsure how or if the global pandemic would affect their plans. Now, with the city locked down and a stay-at-home order in place, they were both working from home and making the best of it. This was the child Jeanette was worried about the most, even though he was the oldest. The city had tighter restrictions than both New Jersey and Florida. Unrest in Chicago was reported daily, and no matter how much Jerry reassured her, Jeanette wished he would just come home. At the outset of the shutdowns in March, she had tried to convince him to rent a car and drive to New Jersey, but he and Beth were loath to leave their home. Jeanette respected his decision, and settled for frequent calls and texts to ease her anxiety.

In response to Alex's text, Jeanette answered with a thumbs-up and heart emoji. Alex and his pregnant wife, Sue, owned a home about 15 minutes away from Jeanette and Adam. Due to COVID, however, Sue was on "hiatus" from her retail job (the store was closed) while Alex was working from home. This was fine with Sue; she was happy to relax and bake bread. Being seven months pregnant for the first time, she did not want to take any risks with the baby's health. Alex was doing any of the necessary shopping errands. Sue barely left the house, and neither family wanted to endanger the first grandchild, so no one visited.

Later over dinner, Jeanette shared her conversation with Evie, and Adam shared the latest news of the restrictions put in place in New Jersey. When they were alone, they usually just ate at the kitchen island side-by-side.

"Mark my words; things will get even worse," Adam predicted. "There will be shortages of more than just toilet paper and Lysol."

"Oh, great. Things will get even worse?"

"Yep. One of the resolutions passed today will allow you to teach remotely for the remainder of the school year, as long as the schools put in the requisite number of days."

"It's only April! How could the governor decide that already?"

Adam reached out to soothe his wife. "I didn't say it was *decided* that schools would *stay* remote, just that he *approved* remote instruction for your school year."

Jeanette sighed, shook her head, and reached for her glass.

"By the way, I stopped and picked up more Tylenol. What a scene in CVS."

"Yeah?"

"Besides the crazy people buying out half the store, a customer was trying to pay with cash. She complained when the cashier requested credit card payment only. Apparently, there is a shortage of change."

"Change? You mean coins?"

"Yeah, coins. Then there was a man without a mask. The CVS manager was saying he couldn't shop without a mask, and the man was arguing. Where could that guy be living that he doesn't know he needs a mask? The manager kept stepping backward, because he was way too close."

"Ugh! I'm glad I wasn't there. It sounds stressful!"

"Oh, it was annoying. I had to wait in line."

"I guess staying at home is safer …"

Trying to change the topic, Adam inquired, "How are you feeling? You look tired."

Jeanette sighed. "Definitely. Thanks for the Tylenol. Keeping up the steady stream of tea and honey helps. The cough is getting better. It's just this annoying low-grade headache and sore throat today. After dinner I'll apply a compress."

He leaned over and felt her forehead. "You do feel warm. I think you may have a fever." Adam was beginning to look more closely at his wife. "And you've hardly eaten your pizza. I hope you don't have the COVID!" he joked with a smile.

"I'm fine. Really. I just told you ... I drank tons of tea! I'm so full!" Jeanette brushed away Adam's concern and joke with a bit of irritation. All of a sudden, she was overwhelmed. "Adam, I really don't know how I'm supposed to teach this way. I don't know how much longer ..." Jeanette choked up.

"Hey, hey," Adam said embracing his wife. "You're doing the best you can, Jennie."

Jeanette whined into Adam's chest. "I spent so much time recording a lesson. A lesson I already have the materials prepared for in my classroom and know forwards and backwards. Yet I have to find and explain new online sources that the students can access and use. It's so frustrating!"

Adam said nothing. They had had this conversation before.

After a huge sigh, Jeanette retreated. "I am super tired. Too much screen time! Mind cleaning up? I'm heading upstairs," she murmured walking away holding her head.

Raising his hands in surrender Adam called, "Sure, I'm right behind you." After he heard Jeanette going up the stairs, he lowered his voice. "Whatever, right Lucy?"

As he cleaned up the crumbs from dinner and tended to Lucy, he couldn't stop the feeling of uneasiness that crawled through him. She did take her job way too seriously; she always had. He also knew Jeanette was overly sensitive at times. But could this be more? It could just be the accumulation of weeks of remote teaching. Or ... no more jokes ... *could*

Jeanette have COVID? Sure, she'd been out to grocery stores. But she wore a mask and hand-sanitized regularly, even before COVID. In an abundance of caution, he knew that immediately upon return from being in public she went directly into the laundry room, removed her clothes, and placed them into the washer. She kept workout clothes in the laundry room so she wouldn't have to streak through the house, even though only he and Lucy were home to see if she did. And no one they knew was sick.

Adam turned on the TV and watched the news for as long as he could handle. While he felt obligated to stay informed, there was nothing reported save COVID and death. The ticker crawling along the bottom of the screen with the latest reported cases, hospital admissions, and deaths was incredibly upsetting. It substantiated his burgeoning fear about Jeanette. As he pondered this, he heard her walking between the bedroom and bathroom upstairs. As if on cue, she began coughing. *No, I must be wrong!* He consoled himself with the thought that her cough wasn't getting worse. And it had only been two days. It was April and so much was blooming outside. Besides getting outside to, as Jeanette would say, "breathe" as often as possible, she loved open windows. Pollen abounded, and she's always had allergies.

No need to get ahead of things. She'll be better tomorrow.

3

Wednesday, April 15, 2020 - Day #3

The sound of Adam's anxious voice roused Jeanette from deep slumber. "Jeanette ... Jeanette! Don't you have classes today?" a dressed Adam demanded, looming over his sleeping wife.

She blinked and focused on Adam. The blue quarter-zip pullover he was wearing matched his eyes. He was folding and unfolding the handkerchief that he would pocket for the day. Automatically, she said, "I'm awake ..." as she peered at her alarm clock on the nightstand. "What time is it?" Sitting up, she coughed and winced at the sore throat. So raw!

Concern etched Adam's face. "Seven. Jeanette, you should call a doctor and take it easy today," he said as he reached to feel her forehead.

She did not want to talk right now, but she knew her husband. She sighed and absently rubbed at the headache behind her eyes. "Sure. I've already posted all my assignments for today and don't have any meetings. I can sleep in a bit and take it easy. Are you on the way to your office? Did you feed Lucy?"

"Yep, and yep. How do you feel?"

Like crap! "Better, I think, but tired. I'll sleep in and take a hot shower. I'll text you later. Don't worry ..." she murmured as she pulled the covers over her head and willed her husband to leave.

Adam hesitated, but eventually left. He needed to open the office as his two employees would be arriving within the half hour. He'd come home for lunch to check on her.

The next time Jeanette surfaced, it was 9:30. She rolled out of bed slowly, so as not to bring the headache to life. She coughed and popped one of the throat lozenges she had brought upstairs with her last night as she shuffled into the bathroom. She took an extended hot shower, and the steam helped soothe and revive her body and spirit. The window was open a crack in the bathroom, and the birds were definitely enjoying the spring morning. Jeanette could tell it was overcast by the lack of sun shining through the bathroom skylight. After donning her jeans and sweatshirt, she actually did feel a bit better. Migraines had always been a part of her life, so the lingering headache was annoying, but tolerable. And allergies were definitely one of her triggers. Leaving the bedroom, Jeanette was met by a happy Lucy waiting at the bottom of the stairs. It had been several years since Lucy made the effort to go up by herself. While she could still ascend, she was absolutely terrified of going down. Her back always seemed to want to go before her front.

"Good morning!" Jeanette said petting Lucy. In her excitement, Lucy rubbed herself back and forth through Jeanette's legs. When Lucy was sufficiently greeted, they both went into the kitchen. Jeanette turned on the hot water kettle for her beloved tea and oatmeal. She then dosed both herself and Lucy for the day. She decided to switch it up by taking a different pain reliever with her decongestant. Hopefully that would get rid of the sore throat and mild headache plaguing her.

She and Lucy took a spin around the yard, enjoying another morning of spring promise. Although fall was really Jeanette's favorite time of year, she did love spring. Typical for New Jersey, it was currently about 66 degrees with a light breeze. It was still cool overnight, with the danger of frost lingering into May. It was what her mother would have called "sweater weather." The birdsong was delightful, and the mild breeze caused the buds to sway. Not for the first time, Jeanette was struck with the beauty of nature, and was glad to be home. Glad to be safe at home. *I need to make the most of this shutdown and enjoy this time.* Jeanette walked slowly, giving Lucy time to sniff and take care of business. She reminded herself to bring a bag out with her next time to pick up Lucy's remnants in the yard.

After tending to Lucy and having breakfast, she fired up the school laptop to check email and grade assignments. *I'm feeling better already!* Multitasking as usual, she called Adam.

"Hey! How goes it?" Jeanette asked her husband.

"That's what I should be asking *you*," he said. "How do you feel?"

"Actually, I feel much better. You'll be happy to know that along with the whiskey, I'm taking a decongestant for the sinus headache and cough and something for the sore throat. It helped; I'm actually hungry this morning!"

"I told you whiskey was the answer! Good, I'm glad! I was worried about you," Adam admitted.

"Aww, you're so sweet! I appreciate your concern, really! I'm better. Just tired, with this cough and headache. Allergies!" she coughed. "See? Any chance you want Chinese food for dinner tonight? Since I need to rest and all ..." she trailed off with a laugh that turned into another cough.

"Absolutely! I'd actually love that!" Adam's relief was palpable.

They bantered about his insurance business and how his employees were doing. Adam, of course, had his own separate office. Both insurance agents had moved to opposite sides of the floor (more than 6 feet apart) and were wearing masks. And since they were on the phone most of the day, and needed to occasionally remove their masks while talking, Adam outfitted each desk with a plastic barrier. Both agents were concerned about COVID–who wasn't?–so they maintained a locked office. Adam was pleased with how well these procedures were working to enable the essential agency to remain open for the customers.

Abruptly, Adam asked Jeanette to hold on. He must have carried his phone with him because she could hear him speaking, but not to her.

"How may I help you?" Adam asked loudly and authoritatively.

Less clear was the muffled, unfamiliar voice: "Hi, Adam. Remember me? I'm Sonny Verma. I have a few questions about my policy."

Jeanette could hear the tone change as Adam recognized his customer. "Hey, how are you, Sonny? And the family? Glad to hear it! Please give me a minute. Our office is closed to customers as per the shutdown; however, we will work with you. Our agent Fran will meet you outside to determine the best way to handle your issue. Then if it will take some time, she'll bring you in. Does that sound OK?"

Again, the response was muffled.

Adam's affable laugh came through loud and clear. "Oh, Sonny, Thank you! I really appreciate it! I just ask that you remain masked. Fran will be right out."

Jeanette could hear more rustling as Adam returned to his office. She assumed that Fran had heard the commotion, gathered the iPad, and was meeting Sonny at the door.

"Sorry about that. Are you still there?" Adam asked.

"Of course! Everything OK?"

"Oh, yeah. Sonny's a long-term client. It's good to see him. But I'd better get off in case Fran needs something."

"Ok. I'll get us the usual from Great Wall of China for dinner," Jeanette replied. "Coming home for lunch?"

"Nah, now that I know you're good, I'll just pick something from my stash." By his pause before he answered, Jeanette could tell Adam was either reading an email or listening to Fran and Sonny. His insurance agency office was located in a strip mall, where a few of the other businesses, like the nail salon and barber shop, were closed as per the shutdown. The Dunkin' Donuts, with its drive-through lane at the end of the storefronts, was thriving. It seemed people wanted to get out of their houses, and getting a donut and cold brew was fast and easy. Lou's pizzeria was also open on reduced hours offering pick-up for dinner only.

They disconnected as she also went to work.

Since schools went remote, Jeanette had been working at her desk in the office, which she shared with Lucy. Since she moved her desk, she overlooked the backyard, affording Jeanette a front-row seat as the birds and squirrels paraded along the railing of the deck. She cracked the window for fresh air and went to work. Once she opened her laptop, time slipped away. There were no student emails with questions about today's assignment. However, in grading the work as it was submitted, Jeanette discovered that while most students completed the assignment correctly, several students had misunderstood. This led to resetting the form, rewriting the assignment directions, and sending emails to students explaining how to correct and resubmit their work. She was so engrossed in the process that she paused only to make more tea with honey, and to let Lucy in and out. She kept the lozenges handy for her raw throat and cough, and switched to Excedrin in an attempt to alleviate that dull sinus headache.

Eventually, it was 2:30, and Jeanette realized she hadn't eaten since her oatmeal. Suddenly starving, she left the office in search of sustenance. After several minutes of deliberation, she opted for chicken bone broth:

fast, easy, and soothing. Filling a mug and placing it in the microwave, she turned to find Lucy waiting patiently at the kitchen sliding door.

"Need to go out? Me, too!" Jeanette said as she opened the door for Lucy. At the beep, she returned to the kitchen, removed the cup of broth, and carried it out onto the deck. She removed her phone from her back pocket as she sat at the chipped, faded green, wrought-iron patio set. Still overcast, it was a bit cool, yet refreshing. Sipping her broth, she surveyed the yard. The hard seat reminded Jeanette that she had yet to bring out the cushions from the garage. Watching Lucy wandering the yard, her eye was drawn to the garden area. Overrun with weeds and dead remains from last year, it needed work. Would she be able to buy her tomato and pepper plants for her salsa garden this year? Maybe she could start seeds now. Order online? Would she be able to buy flowers for her planters? Home Depot was open, yet they were limiting the number of people who could enter the store. Everything took more time, and there were shortages of many products as well as employees. It was stressful and exhausting to think of how complicated and strange everything had become due to this virus. All the things she needed to do were suddenly difficult. It felt like someone flipped a switch on her life. Outside and inside, Jeanette was overwhelmed.

Lucy was mesmerizing, her relaxed pace treading the bright green grass in perfect opposition to the constant knot of tension that was Jeanette's new normal. The ornamental grasses planted around the exterior of the yard had new, vibrant shoots emerging from the previous year's brown stubble. Small red-headed finches hopped from stalk to stalk on the hydrangeas that were beginning to sprout leaves. The birdsong was beautiful from a variety of species. Few cars or school buses interrupted the sounds of nature in this residential neighborhood. It was altogether quiet.

It seemed like such an ironic setting given the lockdown. The promise of new life afforded by spring contrasted sharply with COVID death rates skyrocketing. How could these be happening at the same time?

What was nature trying to tell her? She felt the familiar resentment rise toward the restrictions that had changed every aspect of her life. Yet, when her anger rose, she'd think of everyone else in the same boat. So many people had lost their jobs, were sick, in real financial or physical peril. Meanwhile, she was safe at home. All her children were safe at home. Not for the first time, she thought she had to make the best of the situation. Anyway, what good would it do to be angry? Yet, she felt defeated.

Her energy fading, Jeanette decided to share a picture on the Family WhatsApp of the yard bursting with new life. That was her way of having something to say when she didn't have anything to say. When she unlocked her phone, she realized she never did get a text from Jerry after his meeting yesterday.

Just then, Jeanette was distracted by voices. With her house situated on the corner, she could see the street beyond her yard. She looked over the fence to see people walking and talking on the street. Like many other suburban neighborhoods, the internet slowed a bit since so many were working from home. Increasingly, with the more temperate weather, people were drawn outside. At the moment, two families were speaking from opposite sides of the street. It sounded as though the parents and children were discussing school assignments, with the adults making comments and the children chiming in. Listening to their conversation, Jeanette wondered if her own students in another town were on some street at that same moment discussing her assignment. If so, what would they say? As her neighbors bid each other goodbye and walked on, Jeanette was reminded about when her own children were young, and she had taken years away from teaching to be a stay-at-home mom.

In those days, Adam had held various positions in different insurance companies, and he traveled frequently. Therefore, running the day-to-day household fell to Jeanette. Routine and structure were incredibly important to her children. Considering the shutdown, Jeanette wondered how she would have handled three children at home all day during a global pandemic had it happened all those years ago. Thinking of her past life as an active, young mother reminded Jeanette of her idea to text the family, so she posted a picture of the congregation at the bird-feeder on WhatsApp. Jerry had set up the Remington Family thread right after Christmas, which included Jeanette, Adam, the three siblings, the wives, and Kevin. This greatly improved the family group texting, considering they lived in three different states, and not everyone had an iPhone. She sat down once more on the uncomfortable iron chair on the deck and smiled as the comments appeared one by one. Everyone responded with a picture of something he or she could see out their window. Something eased inside her, enjoying the connections with her family. This was so tangible! Jeanette said a prayer of thanks to the angels and her own mother for watching over and keeping them all safe. Adults they were, yet a mother needs confirmation that her children are well, especially during a pandemic.

After another long hour on her laptop, Jeanette shut down. The overwhelming and quite frustrating transition to remote learning was hitting her hard today! The never-ending barrage of emails, posting, and grading was so time-consuming. What in the classroom could be assessed with a mere question and answer required a posted assignment and then each response checked. Because it was all new, Jeanette had to first learn the technology, incorporate the skill and/or lesson, and then roll it out to her students. There were so many technical considerations, yet the most important consideration was students' stress levels. Did her seventh graders really understand the basic concepts of solubility during a global pandemic? And did it really matter when faced with the turmoil and isolation of a shutdown? What a mess! They were only kids, after all. Her feelings continually vacillated between resentment and hopelessness.

Which brought her right back to the idea of doing the best she could for her students and her family. While she could not control COVID or the government's reactions to it, she could try to maintain some sense of normalcy. Recognizing that she needed a change, Jeanette thought tomorrow she would grab her laptop and a sweatshirt and work outside to break up the day. Even though the pollen was the culprit of her sinus headache and cough, the change of venue and fresh air would be positive. The only issue was that she had her desk set up with all the textbooks, notebooks, and resources she needed to post and grade her assignments. She'd have to lug it all outside. *Ugh! Maybe not!*

Later, while Adam and Jeanette consumed the Chinese food for which she waited in her car an additional 20 minutes, despite calling ahead 30 minutes, the conversation turned toward their children.

"I texted with Evie. She and Kevin are well. She's more comfortable with shopping and has been working poolside for part of the day. She says if more than three people in the apartment complex show up by the pool, she leaves." Looking up to see Adam nodding, Jeanette continued. "She feels like she's managing her situation a bit better. And she's happy saving the money she would be spending commuting."

"Good. I'm glad she had a frank discussion with her boss and set some timeframe boundaries. It was crazy for him to expect her to answer emails and phone calls at all hours," he replied. Adam had threatened Evie that if she didn't have that conversation, he would call her boss himself. Everyone believed that would not have ended well.

"Agreed. Meanwhile, her working by the pool gives her a change, and Kevin some breathing room. He's either attached to his office by laptop or out for miles-long runs, despite the heat."

"So, they're stable. I spoke with Alex, and Sue has a prenatal appointment tomorrow. She'll probably post any baby updates on WhatsApp as usual," Adam added.

"Yay!" Jeanette smiled. The birth of their first grandchild–a boy–was monumental! They were so fortunate that Sue was doing so well and actively posting updates on WhatsApp with the size of the baby in relation to food. It was so thrilling and made everyone feel connected to the pregnancy. No one really understood how COVID might affect the baby's birth in July. While no one expected issues, still Adam and Jeanette were concerned.

"Yes, I texted with Sue at the beginning of the week and she said she was feeling fine. And she sent me a recipe for cinnamon raisin bread," Jeanette said with a laugh. Everyone was stuck at home and so much cooking and baking (except for Evie, who would rather pet her cat) was going on in Remington households!

"Don't bother making that," Adam replied. "You know how I feel about cinnamon."

Jeanette smiled. *Everyone* knew how Adam felt about cinnamon.

"Jerry sounded busy, but I think he's OK," continued Adam.

"You spoke with Jerry? When?"

"Again today. He was talking about wrapping up his latest project," Adam confirmed.

"Hmmm. Jerry hasn't actually texted me directly in a few days," Jeanette confided.

She didn't need to continue. Adam immediately knew where she was going with this train of thought. "He's busy, hon. You know he and Beth are both working from home. It's a huge adjustment for them," Adam reminded her, "especially since Jerry is used to traveling every week. He only called me because he had a question about insurance benefits I could answer." Adam hoped this explanation would placate Jeanette. He knew that she had decided that Chicago was unsafe for Jerry, and she believed Jerry should pack up and bring his wife home to New Jersey. Adam also knew that would probably never happen.

"Yep, I know," Jeanette murmured.

Adam chose to ignore her disappointment. "Well, I'm so glad you're feeling better! You're still coughing, and you have a sexy deep voice, but you do seem better tonight," Adam joked. He hoped this would distract her from thinking about Jerry.

"Right, 'sexy'! Don't make me laugh," she chortled which led to a coughing fit. Despite her attempt at lightheartedness, he saw her grimace as she grabbed her throat.

"Ugh … you're right … nothing sexy about that!" Adam said with an exaggerated eye roll.

She tried to stifle the laugh, which was causing her to cough, and drank water while he patted her back. "Let's clean up and relax on the couch for a bit before bed." Adam watched as Jeanette went to the counter and took one of each of the medications waiting there for her. He noticed that she must have stopped somewhere and bought more when she went to pick up dinner, because there was a new variety of cough suppressants and lozenges. He thought of her in line at CVS and imagined everyone around her cringing when she coughed, regardless of the mask and six feet of separation.

After several episodes of *Love It or List It* on HGTV, Adam reached over and closed Jeanette's computer. She had fallen asleep on the couch, as usual, with her mouth and laptop open. He thought about her concerns for Jerry, and honestly, he shared them. But he couldn't tell her that. He would say whatever he could to ease her mind.

The quiet of the house that was once bursting with the daily accomplishments of their three children struck him as it sometimes did. They had been empty nesters for several years, yet the silence was deafening at times; it was unnatural. He welcomed Lucy's snoring on her dog bed, and looked at his wife of 32 years. *Where did all that time go?* The truth was that some memories were great, and some he had no intention of ever reliving. Right now, with the crazy, unpredictable COVID running the world, he was keeping it together for Jeanette and his children. *What would happen if I let myself unravel?*

Taking a deep breath and letting it out, Adam got up and walked around the house, making sure all was secure. He woke Jeanette, and she stumbled upstairs to bed, coughing the entire way. He took Lucy outside and stood on the deck while she relieved herself one more time. The mild evening's slight breeze caressed his face as he looked up. Gazing at the stars, Adam let his mind go blank and remembered the constellations. Out loud, he gave Lucy a mini-lesson about the Big Dipper, the Little Dipper, and the North Star. The constancy of the universe soothed him; there had been many plagues and diseases in the history of the world. He could imagine that there was another man, a husband and father, who looked upon the same stars centuries ago with similar turmoil and uncertainty going on around him. It comforted him to think that although that man was no longer here, his progeny still managed to live on and evolve. In the big scheme of things, all problems were temporary.

Entering the house, Adam put Lucy to bed. He took stock of his world: his wife was sick, his children in lockdown in three different states, his first grandson's birth was imminent amid a global pandemic, and his business was suffering financially from the shutdown. He had not shared his agency's negative cash flow with Jeanette. Adam prayed for all of it to simply go away. For a moment he indulged himself in a fantasy where that was possible. Sadly, he knew it wouldn't happen. COVID's impact on the Remington family, and the rest of the world, was real. *I will always do what I must to protect my family.* When he joined his wife in bed, he lay awake for a long, long time listening to her heavy breathing and occasional coughing on the other side of the pillow barrier she had erected. Adam couldn't shake the feeling that nothing would ever be the same again.

4

Lucy's hoarse barking woke Jeanette. She lay in bed blinking and waiting for clarity of mind. She was tired, that was for sure, with a persistent headache that had not gone away despite the Tylenol, Advil, or Excedrin. That was more proof that it was probably a migraine. Jeanette recalled waking up during the night coughing, and going downstairs to take more cough medicine. She brought more lozenges and water upstairs and left it on the bedside table. She was sorely tempted to add whiskey, but considering all the other stuff she took she was afraid of an adverse reaction. She wondered why Lucy was barking, when generally she just didn't. Then Jeanette heard Adam's footsteps coming up the hardwood stairs and into the bedroom.

"Hey, you're awake! Lucy was your alarm clock. Apparently, there's a dog across the street who managed to get off-leash. Our neighbors were running the collie down on our lawn and Lucy objected." Adam sat on the edge of the bed and leaned in closely. "How are you today, Jeanette? You were coughing *all* night!"

In answer, she coughed. Sitting up, Jeanette felt the tightness in her chest. She forced herself to breathe through her nose and drank from the water bottle on the nightstand. "Ugh! Today is definitely worse!"

"Hon, let's call the doctor. You need something for that cough. Remember when the kids were young? You used to say it was time for a visit when they coughed through the over-the-counter stuff." Adam was doing an excellent job controlling himself, as he really wanted to pick her up and do something. Take her ... where? The doctor's office? The hospital? He was struck with the realization that although she needed care, he was unsure. Were the doctor's offices or the hospitals safe? If one didn't already have COVID, those must be the best places to find it.

Jeanette managed to catch her breath and shook her head dismissively. "Don't worry! I'll be OK. The hot shower always helps. I'll call the doctor when I go downstairs."

"I want you to rest! Stop stressing over that damn computer! I'm staying home to take care of you."

Surprised by Adam's eruption, Jeanette also raised her voice. "Oh, hell no! Go to work!" She breathed as deeply as she dared through her nose and spoke deliberately to stifle the cough. "I'll let you know what Dr. Roman says. I'll take a shower now and call when the office opens. If you must, come home for lunch. I'll also schedule assignments for today and tomorrow and leave the students a message that I won't be answering emails until tomorrow." She grabbed Adam's hand. "Now stop yelling at the love of your life. I love you, too."

Adam stared her down; her attempt to deflate his anger did not seem to sway him. "I'll be waiting downstairs for you to shower and dress. I want to see you up and about."

She understood his warning. "Yep," was the only reply she could muster through her clenched teeth. She lay quietly, assessing her symptoms: headache, clamminess, tiredness, sore throat, chest soreness, and coughing. Panic gripped her, and her heart raced as she mentally tallied the odds. All channels had reported a non-stop litany of difficulties the healthcare system was experiencing in dealing with COVID, not to mention the death rate and impending shortage of medical equipment and supplies, including respirators. The horrific state of hospitals and overwhelmed medical staff was highlighted every night. *What if I have COVID?*

Her panic made breathing very difficult, and she fought for control. "Get it together, Jeanette!" she told herself roughly. "You have children and a grandchild on the way. You're fine! You'll be fine!" She refused to consider the alternative.

It had been 25 minutes. The crooked-sitting Lucy tracked Adam's agitated movements between the kitchen counter, sink, island, and laptop open on the table. Adam had made coffee, rinsed the pot, checked his email, and skimmed the *Wall Street Journal* online. Several times he moved to the bottom of the stairs and looked up expectantly before returning to the kitchen. "Lucy, if she doesn't come down soon, I'm going up to get her." Adam gripped the island's granite and closed his eyes in relief when he heard Jeanette coming down the stairs. Lucy wagged her tail.

Entering the kitchen, Jeanette exclaimed, "Here I am!" When she met his eyes, she knew her husband was wound up. "Don't you have to go to work?" she returned Adam's stare briefly, then looked away. She leaned down to greet Lucy before moving to the counter to turn on the electric tea kettle. "I'll call you as soon as I talk with the doctor's office," Jeanette announced.

"Good. You're up and about. Call the office now. You'll probably get the service and a call back." Adam stood his ground, and Jeanette reached for her phone. She spoke with the answering service who said she would receive a call back from a doctor shortly. Jeanette made her tea and oatmeal, and Adam drank more coffee (which was the last thing he needed considering he was already agitated).

When her doctor called back, Adam listened to the conversation on speaker. While Jeanette described her symptoms, Adam interjected, "And a fever on and off." She also confirmed that she did not have any medical conditions for which she was taking medication.

Dr. Roman told Jeanette to rest and specifically said, "Do not exert yourself." He prescribed an antibiotic and strong cough syrup so she could sleep. He told her to squeeze three doses of the antibiotic in today, and that he would follow up with her in 24 hours to see how she was doing. In the meanwhile, if Jeanette felt worse or suffered any difficulty breathing where she couldn't catch her breath, she was to go immediately to the hospital. She provided the phone number of the local pharmacy to call in the prescriptions.

Jeanette was sighing in relief when the doctor said, "One more thing, Jeanette: You should be quarantining. Please wear a mask and isolate yourself from your family members. You could have COVID." Then Dr. Roman disconnected.

Immediately their eyes locked. Fear and dread were reflected in both. As realization dawned and Jeanette's eyes began to open, he reached for her.

"Dr. Roman said *could*. It *could* be COVID," Adam hurriedly said to calm his wife. He took her hands and pulled her away from the kitchen counter into his arms.

The morning sun reflecting off the stainless-steel faucet momentarily blinded her, so she buried her face against her husband. Jeanette clung to Adam with her ear to his chest. She listened to his heartbeat going a mile a minute. At the same time, she could hear her own noisy breathing as well. She didn't even know what to think.

"Adam–"

"Jeanette, it's gonna be OK." Adam was all business. He took a breath and instructed, "Here's the plan. Take that damn computer and put it on the couch. I'll set up your tea and oatmeal in the living room. Get comfortable and stay there. I'll give the pharmacy an hour and then call to see when the prescriptions will be ready. When it is, I'll leave work, pick it up from the drive-through lane, and bring it home. Do what you have to with that thing," he gestured at the computer, "before I get back because it's going away after you get your prescriptions. Dr. Roman said not to exert yourself, and that means physically and mentally. Deal?"

"Oh, my God, Adam! Do I have COVID?" She pushed far enough away to look up into his face. "The thing that's killing everyone? Oh ... my ... God! Is that what's wrong with me?"

"Shh, shh ... No! We are not doing this! No good can come of this, Jeanette." Adam used his sternest voice and most threatening stare. It didn't work.

Jeanette clutched at Adam's shirt. "All those people ... on the news ... that are dead ..." Her voice trailed off before dissolving into another coughing fit.

He murmured comforting words as she struggled to control herself. She fought to get air in, let go of his shirt, and grabbed at her own chest with a grimace.

"Enough, Jeanette. You're making yourself worse," he chided as he led her into the family room. He sat his dazed wife on the couch and then returned with her computer and water.

Still coughing, she tearfully looked at her husband.

"C'mon, Jeanette. You heard me. Let's just take this one step at a time."

She took the water to sip while he placed the laptop beside her.

Looking at his watch, he said, "Listen, I want to get your prescriptions so you can feel better as soon as possible. And quarantining is absolutely ridiculous; I've been sleeping in the same bed with you all week." He kissed her cheek. Looking directly into her eyes and lowering his voice, he said, "Let's not borrow trouble, Jeanette. One step at a time," he squeezed her hands.

Her mind raced, but she stared at him and nodded. He was her rock. "Love you," she whispered intently.

"I know," he kissed her hand.

"Thanks," she called as he walked away into the kitchen.

"That's what I'm here for," Adam answered. "I'll be back as soon as I can."

Jeanette did as she was told. She handled her Google Classroom and turned the computer off. Now that they had called the doctor, she felt so much worse. Needing an antibiotic validated her illness. Her brain was scrambled. She had chills, a headache, and when she coughed, her already sore throat burned as she fought for air. Her chest felt heavy, and she was crying. Lucy, who always lay on her dog bed, awkwardly climbed up on the couch with Jeanette's help. She wrapped the blanket more closely around her and petted Lucy until she was in an exhausted trance. She heard a ping indicating a text on her phone, but it was in the kitchen, and Adam told her not to get up. *I only spoke with Evie this week; I wish I'd spoken with Alex and Jerry, too.* She cried because she felt like crap. And she cried because she was scared. *COVID is a killer! If I die of COVID, who will love my babies?*

Adam found a pathetic Jeanette zombified and sniffling on the couch. She was incomprehensible. Nevertheless, she took all the medication Adam gave her with water. He made her more tea and brought crackers, water bottles, and her cell phone into the living room. "I'm going in for a few more hours, and then I'll close the office early. Do not get up from this couch! Do you need anything else?"

"Adam, I'm scared!" she sobbed.

"I know," he said awkwardly leaning over to hug her. "The doctor said it was just a possibility. You probably don't have COVID. You'll feel better now that you've taken the medication." He lingered until her grip on him eased a bit. "Need anything else?"

"Please take Lucy out before you go," Jeanette replied between coughs, "and put on HGTV."

As Adam went out the kitchen slider with Lucy into the April sunshine, he grabbed at his clenching stomach. "Lucy, don't worry! She'll get better now." Adam slowly followed Lucy around the perimeter of the yard twice. Finally heading into the house, he hesitated. Lucy looked up at Adam as he took several deep breaths and steadied himself to face his wife.

Lucy ambled to her water bowl, and Adam went into the family room. He took Jeanette's hands in his. "Honey, I'll be back as soon as possible. Call me if you need me." Their eyes locked; Adam kissed each hand. He squeezed them slightly before letting go.

Jeanette leaned back and nodded, and Adam helped Lucy reclaim her spot beside her mom. Adam tucked the blanket around Jeanette. Lucy stretched out and laid her paw and head on Jeanette's lap.

After Adam left, she checked her phone and found a text from Alex.

ALEX: Hey. So busy with these meetings at work, but all is well. Sue said her appointment went well and the baby is big! He'll be arriving earlier than we thought! She'll be posting that info on WhatsApp by the end of the night. Love you!

JEANETTE: Keep up the good work! Looking forward to hearing about Baby Remington. Love you, too!

Not wanting to become nauseous from the medication, Jeanette shared a few crackers with Lucy and drank her tea. *OK, I'll feel better as soon as the antibiotic kicks in.* They both dozed in and out while *Fixer Upper* droned on. Her cough persisted, despite the prescription cough medicine, but she reasoned it would also "kick in" soon. Late morning passed into afternoon in a blur.

Sometime later, she received a text from Adam.

ADAM: I'm stuck here at the office helping a client with a serious problem. Take another dose of the antibiotic now. Be home ASAP.

JEANETTE: K

She took a few minutes just to think about getting up. She was warm and cozy; Lucy was snoring. More importantly, when Jeanette stayed absolutely still, she coughed less. The constant headache and sore throat were bearable, yet she wanted to get better. She sat up to take the medication Adam had left with the cold tea and water. Again, the resulting hacking cough shook her entire body, but for the first time, Jeanette struggled to catch her breath. She had been managing the coughing fits with a combination of nose breathing and suppressing her throat muscles. But immediately this feeling was different; it was alarming. This new feeling was a difficulty in drawing air into her lungs. Yes, she was coughing, but it was now accompanied with a pain in her chest. *Am I wheezing?* Her memory flashed with the picture of administering Ventolin in a nebulizer to one of her very young children suffering with bronchiolitis. *Oh my God! I can't breathe!*

5

"Hey, beautiful. Did you help Mom feel better today?" Adam asked Lucy when she greeted him at the garage door. He put the pizza on the counter, gave Lucy the usual rawhide chew which she immediately scampered away with, and then peered from the kitchen into the family room. HGTV was still on, and a couple were arguing over a kitchen renovation. Walking into the family room, Adam found Jeanette asleep on the couch. Her cheeks were red, and she was propped practically straight up in the corner with a throw pillow behind her head. He listened to Jeanette's heavy breathing for several beats before Lucy demanded his attention.

She pawed at Adam's leg, and he took Lucy out into the yard to do business. When they returned to the kitchen, Lucy went to stand by her bowl and stare at Adam. "Didn't Mom feed you, Lucy?" At the lab's continued stare, Adam decided to feed her. "Well, if you have two dinners tonight, more power to you!" But all doubt was removed by the way Lucy wolfed down the kibble. "Wow! You were hungry!" Adam watched her lick the bowl, and then went upstairs to get changed.

Adam stood in the doorway of the family room for several minutes holding two slices of pizza on paper dishes. Jeanette had yet to stir, but Lucy was sniffing the air. Instead of waking her himself, he put the volume louder on the TV. She immediately startled, and he lowered the volume.

"Oh, sorry. I hit the volume by mistake. How are you feeling?" Adam asked.

It took Jeanette a minute to respond as she took in her husband sitting on the chair across from her holding pizza. Although the smell was mouthwatering, she didn't trust herself to speak lest the coughing begin again. *Adam, where have you been?* She said "Mmm," and motioned for a piece.

Adam smiled and gave it to her. "You look better! I'm glad you're hungry. I cleverly placed this pizza order before I left the office. It's not piping hot, but I didn't have to wait in line wearing a mask six feet apart. I sat in the car and let them bring it to me curbside." Although he thought he was acting "normal" by making small talk, Adam was actually giving away his uneasiness; it was usually Jeanette who carried small talk until he had a chance to unwind from the day.

She took a few bites, and it was delicious, but when the coughing fit gripped her, she struggled for air. After the previous episode which sparked a panic attack, she stumbled to the kitchen sink as the coughing turned into gagging.

Momentarily stunned, Adam rushed to her side commanding, "Take a breath, Jeanette! Relax!"

The spasm continued for what felt like hours with Jeanette clinging to the counter and spewing spit and vomit into the sink while gasping for air. She turned on the faucet and scooped sips of water into her mouth. As the spasm subsided, she slid down the cabinet and sat on the kitchen floor. She registered that Adam was talking to her, wiping her face with the dish towel. This time she had been more exhausted than frightened, but Adam was obviously shaken. His deep, furrowed brow and stern expression was one of concern.

As she maintained shallow breathing to stifle more coughing, he sat down on the floor next to her and held her hand. Lucy, who had kept her distance from the commotion, came over to lick Jeanette's face.

"Good girl, Lucy," Adam crooned as he stroked the cream lab. "Do you think you can get up yet?" he asked Jeanette gently. At Jeanette's slow nod, he helped her stand and led her back to the couch. He tucked her into her upright corner.

After sitting quietly for a while, Adam made a few more comments about the current remodeling show. Aside from occasional smiles and nods, Jeanette said little. She refused more pizza but did sip from a cup of warmed bone broth Adam offered. He also made her peppermint tea. He listened to her labored breathing as she dozed on and off on the couch. Finally, he handed her the last dose of her antibiotic, Tylenol and cough medicine. She took it all slowly with little sips of water.

"Jeanette, if you're not better in the morning ..." Jeanette did not register Adam's words, and he didn't finish his thought. "You'll feel better in the morning. Let's go to bed, Jeanette."

"Nah ... I'll sleep right here," Jeanette whispered. "I'd rather not move. Adam, I'm cold."

"OK, then we'll have a sleepover. You, me, and Lucy," Adam announced with a forced smile as he wrapped another blanket around her.

"Oh no! I'm supposed to be wearing a mask and isolating from you," Jeanette said weakly.

Adam dismissed her concern by saying, "After all these years?"

He led Lucy outside for her final outing of the night, then went upstairs to take a shower. He stood for a few minutes, letting the water sluice over his body. *It's all me. She's depending on me. I have to take care of her.*

At different points throughout his life, Adam had been smothered with the weight of his responsibility as a father, a husband, and a business owner. Never had it been this heavy. He allowed himself to rage against the unfairness of it. His wife was downstairs, obviously very ill. Maybe with COVID. Obviously in need of more medical care than he could give. Yet he would not bring her to the hospital unless it was absolutely necessary. One of his clients, a nurse, had shared how overwhelmed and overworked the staff were, treating patients so numerous they were lined up in the hallways. She told how the hospital had turned any unused area possible into a room to accommodate the sick. And, he knew, family was not allowed. To think he would drop her off and ... and what ... leave her? *This is unproductive; Jeanette needs me.*

Adam returned to his chair in the living room and barely slept. Watching his wife, he relived their entire existence together: the courtship, the wedding, the birth of each child, events and milestones over the years. They came a long way from the awkward teenagers who met at a high school dance. Jeanette had been doing the Hustle with a group of girlfriends when he noticed her. She was having so much fun, laughing and bumbling through the steps. She was not the most graceful dancer, but her face radiated with pure joy. Adam was smitten and couldn't look away. At the end of that dance, she had agreed to meet him at Bruno's Pizza the next day for lunch. The rest was history.

They had their ups and downs, but Adam and Jeanette were blessed with mostly ups. Looking at Jeanette now, he wondered what his life would look like without her. Shaking his head to dispel the thought, he pushed deeper into the chair. He looked at Lucy peacefully snuggled against his wife. "Good night, you two." Adam closed his eyes and prayed.

6

Friday, April 17, 2020 - Day #5

In the morning, an exhausted Jeanette didn't protest when Adam loaded her into the car, headed for the hospital. Although she was truly frightened, they both knew this was the next step. He didn't bother giving her any of her prescribed medication; it didn't seem to be making a difference to that cough. She clearly had a fever and her strength was gone; she was extremely drowsy. Jeanette did respond to Adam's questions, but it was with as few words as possible. While her coughing may have decreased in frequency, her labored breathing now remained constant. When she did cough, it might be passing or a spasm that ended in her sputtering and fighting for air. On the way to the hospital, Adam kept up a stream of reassurances while Jeanette's head lolled toward the window.

"Are you ready?" Adam asked as they parked.

Jeanette took a minute, then turned toward him. "No. I'm terrified!" she sobbed.

Simultaneously, they reached across the console to hug and held on to each other for several minutes. Adam, used to giving orders, made himself clear. "Remember how much I love you, Jeanette. You'll be on my mind every minute. You do everything you need to do to get better." His voice softened with emotion. "I need you, Jeanette. I can't imagine life without you."

"I love you, too. You better think of me … text me … call me …" she sobbed once again trying to draw strength from her husband. It was no use talking about how scared she was; it only made it worse for both of them.

They masked up before leaving the car.

The Emergency Room at St. Peter's Hospital looked like a scene from a movie: staff completely covered head to toe in white or blue hazmat suits, and potential patients in awkward places due to social distancing. Sick-looking and injured people of all ages were sitting, standing, or leaning. The sound of the TV playing in the corner, ostensibly to divert those waiting, was drowned out by the announcements on the intercom for doctors and staff and people talking in low voices. Adam had called the doctor's office before leaving the house, so Dr. Roman had alerted the hospital that Jeanette was on the way. While they were waiting, Jeanette was clutching Adam's hand like a lifeline. Fortunately, or unfortunately, they waited only briefly before she was identified as a possible COVID-positive patient, loaded onto a gurney, and wheeled away to an isolated section of the E.R.

"I'm sorry," said the stiff voice that may have come from a white mannequin. It was loud and invited no response. "No family is permitted beyond this point, as per executive orders. Sir, please continue to complete the admitting paperwork with the patient advocate there."

Adam had only a minute to lean in close and whisper in Jeanette's ear that he loved her, and that she would be alright. She clutched at his neck and head with desperate strength. It broke his heart to peel her hands away, so he kissed both palms before putting her hands on her chest. They never broke eye contact. He removed her cell phone from his pocket and placed it into her hand and told her to hang on. Her tear-filled eyes held his as she was wheeled away.

In a haze, he provided their insurance information to another white mannequin so his wife could be treated. He was assured that there were phone chargers available in each room and vaguely wondered if Jeanette would need anything else from home. He was informed nothing could be brought into the hospital for the safety of all. After asking yet again, he was told he could not go with her or visit due to COVID protocols. The hospital instructed Adam to give the doctors a few hours for initial testing and diagnosis. Either Dr. Roman as the attending physician (who was on his way into the hospital) or one of the residents would call Adam as soon as they had information; however, they were currently close to full capacity. Everyone was busy. So, if he wanted to call the nurse's station, they would provide him with whatever update they had to give. Adam was told that pending his wife's COVID test, he was possibly exposed. He could not stay in the hospital as he may be contagious himself. He should go home or wait in his car until the doctor either confirmed his wife's admittance or was ready to release her. If she tested positive, he would need to quarantine due to his exposure to his wife, and monitor his own health for signs of infection.

After confirming his cell phone number, the statue never took her eyes off her computer screen as she said, "Mr. Remington, we'll call you as soon as we know if your wife will be admitted or going home. If she's going home, please park in the Emergency Room waiting lot and call us. Once we've completed your wife's discharge, an orderly will bring her out to your car."

"And if she's admitted?" he prompted.

Still typing, she replied, "As I said, Mr. Remington, you will be notified either way. You'll be given further instructions at that time."

The Emergency Room exploded into frantic activity as a group of three mask-wearing older folks stumbled in together. Adam stood abruptly and asked, "Do you need me for anything else?"

He ripped off the mask as soon as he was beyond the sliding doors. Alone in his car, Adam sat. He placed his phone on the passenger seat where his Jennie had been, which was still warm. Either from her or the morning sun he didn't know. Eventually, he lay his head on the steering wheel. He stole occasional glances at his phone and touched the screen to bring it to life. No calls. The constant flow of people and traffic in and out of the Emergency Room was agitating him, so he moved his car to a quieter place in the parking lot. There he put down the windows and laid his head against the headrest. His wife's name swam around his mind along with pictures of her through their years together. He watched the clouds move across the beautiful blue sky through the open sunroof.

His phone startled him out of the reverie. Swiping his sleeve across his dripping face, like he'd done as a child, he fumbled and answered quickly.

"Mr. Remington? This is Dr. Roman."

"Yes, how's my wife?"

"Ah, Jeanette has tested positive for COVID. I've admitted her to the COVID floor. I've ordered a battery of tests to determine her current level of infection. However, it's clear that her oxygen levels are low. I'll have more to tell you when the test results are in."

"How long will she be here, doc? And please, call me Adam."

"Adam, I have no way to determine that right now. I need more information. But Jeanette is young and in good health, which are two advantages in her fight against this virus."

Adam closed his eyes and nodded through the remaining information. Dr. Roman must have given this speech before, because he continued as if he could see Adam's assent. The hospital staff were busy, almost at capacity, so if Adam didn't hear from them, he should call the nurses' station anytime day or night. They would do their absolute best for Jeanette. Unfortunately, no visitors or belongings from home can come into the hospital. It would be futile to mention that the E.R. patient advocate had told him that already.

Honestly, Adam was relieved. Relieved that Jeanette would receive the medical care she needed. He knew when he was in over his head, and there was nothing he could do to help her. It was best to let the professionals do their job. But did they know how to fix COVID? The news reports were both alarming and confusing. He had no choice but to believe in the system. At the same time, he was bereft. He felt her absence deep into his soul. What was the longest time he was without her? Perhaps a long work trip? Two weeks? He was very rarely home when Jeanette was not; he couldn't even remember that happening. It would be so strange in the house. He allowed his mind to run wild for just a few minutes with all manner of possible scenarios. Then he decided there was no reason not to expect a positive outcome. His Jeanette would be home again, and soon.

Throughout his life, Adam had faced many challenges. He was successful because he knew just how far to let the crazy go. The uncertainty and fear of the global pandemic seeped into his consciousness. Then he reigned it in and thought about his next steps. He must quarantine, so he would run his office from home. As he exited the hospital parking lot, he considered how best to relay this news to his children.

7

"Relax, Mrs. Remington. You're here at St. Peter's Hospital, and we've got you. Dr. Roman has ordered a few tests. First things first, Mrs. Remington; I'm putting a nasal cannula on you now due to your low oxygen level. It'll help you breathe." As the white-clad figure leaned in, Jeanette caught a glimpse of brown eyes behind goggles over a blue surgical mask. The bright overhead fluorescent light reflected off her clear plastic visor. Jeanette closed her eyes against the glare as blue-gloved fingers adjusted the cannula over her ears. "Also, I'll replace your mask with this surgical mask. Can you lift your head a bit?" In a matter of seconds, Jeanette's face was covered again. Immediately, the coldness of the oxygen stung her sinuses, so she breathed through her mouth which caused more coughing. "Almost done. Now this clear hood, like my visor, which must be worn while in the hallways of the hospital. This is procedure for everyone's protection." The cold, gloved hands pulled Jeanette's hair a bit adjusting the band around her forehead. A smudge of something on the right side of the clear visor blurred the clock.

"We're very busy, but we'll let you know as soon as the results are in." The clearly enunciated, confident words were spoken slowly and close to her head to be heard amid the chaos. Gasping through her quick breaths, alternating between her mouth and nose, Jeanette focused on breathing and clutched the blanket. Another coughing spasm, and she struggled for air. *Just breathe!* Weakness gripped her as she attempted to calm herself. *Where was Adam?*

Jeanette knew she was on a gurney in the busy hallway of the Emergency Room. She could hear so much coughing and some moaning. A few people, presumably patients, were calling for nurses or doctors. Hospital workers covered head to toe in white, looking like so many astronauts, squeaked and rustled quickly and efficiently by her on their missions. Nurses, technicians, and assistants were constantly calling instructions and confirmations aloud to each other. Jeanette felt so exposed! She had remained where she was parked along a wall, across from a large room with curtains partitioning six more gurneys. Needing something to ground her, Jeanette was drawn to the second hand moving ever so slowly. She had been waiting here at least an hour, according to the huge clock on the wall, watching the astronauts carrying their tools navigate this alien world of sick bodies. Immediately after she was stationed here, someone stuck a long, nasty swab up her nose so far that Jeanette was sure it touched her brain. It didn't really hurt, but it was startling and extremely uncomfortable. Not to mention it brought on another exhausting sneezing fit and coughing spasm. If Jeanette didn't pass out, she came blessedly close. The spasm made her throat burn and the headache explode. She couldn't stop the hot tears and muffled sobs.

Minutes ticked by. Jeanette moved her head a bit this way and that to see the clock clearly around the visor smudge. Zoning in once again on the ambient coughing, including her own, Jeanette wondered how effective all these masking precautions really were.

"Positive," someone called loudly above the din to someone beyond

Jeanette. Surprisingly, the white-clad person stopped alongside her gurney and spoke directly to Jeanette.

"My name is Alicia, and I'm your nurse. Your husband, Adam, completed the insurance forms. Due to COVID-19 protocol, no family members are permitted. He said to tell you that he loves you, and he'll speak to you soon, once we get you settled in. You're being admitted; you've just tested positive. We're preparing a bed for you now on the COVID floor."

What? It was so loud here and distracting, and she was so focused on breathing. Jeanette barely registered the nurse's muffled words. Except that Adam wasn't here. A finger of fear began to poke, but Jeanette reasoned. She was in the hospital. They would fix her. She began to smile, thinking of Adam saying, "Here's my copay; fix my wife." More coughing and she remembered to focus on breathing. Tried to rest in between. Restless, she turned on her side and faced the wall. *How did this get so bad so fast?*

"Mrs. Remington, please relax. Your husband completed the admitting forms and we have your medical history. Do you currently take any medication other than what was prescribed by Dr. Roman this week?" the nurse asked.

Jeanette did not shift her position, but shook her head no in response.

"I see from your chart that you've given birth to three children."

Jeanette nodded yes.

"Do you remember during labor and delivery how you were told to rest and breathe in between contractions when you could?" Alicia paused again for the positive response. "Well, rest now. You may need your strength later. Meanwhile, I've got to take your other vital signs. Then I'm going to take a blood sample, and set you up with a saline intravenous drip for dehydration while you're waiting for your room to be ready. Dr. Roman has also ordered a chest x-ray. As soon as you're on the floor, a technician will do that. You're in good hands." As she was talking to Jeanette, Alicia noticed that she was shivering. Alicia retrieved another blanket from a nearby cart. Gently, she covered Jeanette and said, "Here's a blanket from the warmer, Mrs. Remington."

Immediately, the warmth and weight of the blanket soothed Jeanette. Too much was going on. "Wait," she struggled to turn toward the nurse who was rushing away. Up on one elbow now, Jeanette could see Alicia was actually eye level. A low ponytail of brown hair shifted slightly when Alicia hurried back toward Jeanette. Between coughs, she managed, "What did you say about COVID?"

Nurse Alicia leaned in close and spoke loudly and clearly. "Mrs. Remington, you have COVID." The nurse laid a gloved hand on Jeanette's shoulder, gave a gentle squeeze, and walked away.

Her elbow gave way, and Jeanette once again curled up facing the wall on the gurney. She closed her eyes as the tears fell freely. She sobbed uncontrollably, and her heart began to race as she had to accept that her greatest fear was real. *Two months ago, I didn't even know what COVID was, and now I'm in the hospital! I have the virus that has shut down the world and killed so many people! I have* that *coronavirus!* The oxygen did help her breathe easier, but it didn't help her process this life-changing fact. Jeanette felt cold move through her sinuses and into her blood. She kept her mouth closed and breathed shallowly trying to avoid coughing. Unfortunately, her sobbing made it even more difficult to catch her breath and she endured another spasm.

Alicia performed her tasks efficiently, all the while calling loudly to a nearby nurse throughout most of her ministrations. The nurses went from patient to computer to enter the data they were collecting. She spoke to Jeanette only to repeat her advice about resting when possible. The astronauts seemed to be moving at light speed while Jeanette felt frozen. Frozen in time and space.

Alicia was hanging the IV bag from the pole on the bed when another white-clad figure appeared.

"Hi, I'm Frank," a booming voice announced. "I'll be transporting you to your room, Mrs. Remington. Good, you have your mask and hood on; it's protocol until we get to your room. Can you verify your birthdate?" yelled the short, stocky figure clad in all-white personal protective equipment as his gloved hands adjusted the plastic contraption on her head.

Jeanette had to repeat the information several times before he could understand her. Finally, he checked it against his clipboard, and they were on their way. Although they passed other patients in the hallway, the effect of the mask and hood was isolating and unreal. So much was going on, yet it was hard to reconcile this foreign terrain with the statistics she had seen being bantered about daily on the news. Well, she was a statistic now. A sad statistic of infection.

She wondered again where Adam was, and what he was thinking. Did he know where she was? Jeanette sucked air involuntarily when she realized she may have infected Adam. It was one thing to joke about it at home, but now that she was a confirmed case, it was a real possibility. Jeanette's brain replayed that loop as Frank moved the gurney through the noisy hallway and into the stark grey elevator. She couldn't stop her tears, and Frank did his best to stand behind the gurney out of her line of sight during the awkward elevator ride. From behind her, he maneuvered the bed into the hallway through several double doors onto the startlingly quiet floor.

Compared to the cacophony of the E.R., this area was devoid of sounds of chaos. She could see that all the doors were closed to the individual rooms. As Frank rolled her down the hallway, she checked the names written in black marker on the whiteboards: P. Monroe, J. Smythe, R. Wilson, A. Cruz. *Now my name will be on a whiteboard, too!* Eventually, Frank came to a room with an open door, and Jeanette was wheeled inside, bumping against the door frame, where a blue-clad figure was putting the finishing touches on the bed. Like Nurse Alicia, this woman was wearing a surgical gown, gloves, booties, and a white N95-type mask (reported to be the best, and thus hard for non-healthcare workers to purchase) covered by a surgical mask. She also wore a face shield similar to the hood Jeanette was wearing and a hair cap.

Frank said loudly, "This is Mrs. Remington," and he repeated her birthday from the chart.

The tall, thin figure looked over at Jeanette and then lowered the bed. "Oh, good, you're here, Mrs. Remington. Hi! I'm Patti, your nurse; we just finished getting things ready for you." The floor was so quiet; Patti seemed to be yelling. Yet her voice was upbeat. It occurred to Jeanette that she might have to yell to be heard from behind all those masks. *Adam, where are you?* Jeanette shivered anew as she watched Patti move around the room. The clean-looking room was stark, with just the TV on the wall and the bed. There was a chair in the corner, a small cart, and a food tray along the wall. Jeanette could see sunlight streaming through the blinds, but little else from her angle.

"Mrs. Remington, Frank and I will help you move from that gurney to this bed. Can you sit up?" Patti asked as Frank removed the transport hood at the same time that she grasped Jeanette's upper arm to help her sit up. "Perfect. Now swing your legs over. Good. Frank, bring the IV bag over here, and connect Mrs. Remington's cannula to the wall-mounted oxygen. Yes, disconnect it from the portable tank. OK, Mrs. Remington, you're going to stand and take one step. That's it. Sit on the edge of the bed. Perfect. Wow! You're good at this; have you been here before?" Patti joked with a short laugh.

"No!" Jeanette said rather abruptly. Not wanting to sound harsh, she corrected, "I mean, no."

"I didn't think I recognized you," Patti laughed. "Thank you, Frank. Please return the gurney to the E.R. Don't forget to sanitize," she instructed.

Jeanette sat precariously while Frank left, closing the door behind him.

"Now that he's gone, let's slip into something more comfortable," Patti suggested holding up a standard hospital gown. "Blue and white is your color!"

Overwhelmed, Jeanette burst into tears and covered her face. Patti, her PPE fluttering with each movement, somehow relieved Jeanette of her clothing, replacing it with a hospital gown. Normally, Jeanette was a modest woman. But the practiced Patti worked so quickly and methodically that Jeanette had no time to react or recoil. Patti spoke kindly to Jeanette as she carried out her tasks, explaining what she was doing and why. All of Jeanette's discarded clothing was deposited in a hospital bag, sealed, and placed in the bottom of the nightstand drawer. Almost the minute Patti laid her into the bed and covered her with a blessed blanket, a knock sounded on the closed door.

"Come in!" Patti called.

Another white-clad figure entered. "I have an order for a chest X-ray," a slow voice said, pushing a large cart ahead of him. Jeanette could tell by the only body parts showing—the bald head and eyes behind the goggles—that he was an older man. As Patti explained how the portable X-ray machine worked, both she and the technician gently lifted Jeanette to position an X-ray film behind her. His work complete, Patti helped him retrieve the X-ray. He left as quickly and quietly as he entered.

Meanwhile, Patti continually asked questions. Interspersed with the innocuous were serious questions like, "How long have you been coughing like that?" and "How long have you been wheezing like that?" She demonstrated the TV remote and laughingly mentioned the ten channels to choose from on the cable, otherwise known as "the only games in town." Fortunately, there was a cell phone charger in the room, and Patti plugged in Jeanette's phone and placed it within reach immediately next to the remote. Several times Jeanette noticed that Patti, too, was struggling to breathe behind the mask. However, there was no coughing, only exertion.

Incrementally, Jeanette relaxed into her situation. She could do nothing else. Nurse Patti and the other aliens here seemed to be so confident and self-assured. None of them seemed overwhelmed or uncertain. In fact, they executed their duties effectively and efficiently. That led Jeanette to fold inward. The effort to breathe seemed a Herculean task, whether from exhaustion or the heaviness in her chest, she didn't know. The coughing spasms alternated with what she now confirmed, thanks to Patti, was wheezing. Jeanette had to face it: she was really sick. She needed them to make her better.

While Patti continued to minister, eventually Jeanette closed her eyes to focus on breathing and praying. Patti received a buzz on the device clipped to her suit. She spoke to someone through the device, told Jeanette she would be back, and closed the door as she left the room.

Alone, Jeanette grappled with her reality. Her eyes scanned the stark room and tried to think of it as home. Her home for the next ... how long? How many days would she have to stay here? *What if I never go home again?* Panic surged and stole her breath as if trying to make that fear come true. Coughing, coughing, crying, spitting and coughing, Jeanette struggled to stay positive.

8

Lucy, lounging by the slider door, rested her head between her paws. She followed Adam with her eyes as he paced the kitchen with the phone in his hand. Adam was talking gibberish to the dog, agitated and nervous. "What is happening to Jeanette? Why doesn't she call?" Simultaneously, Lucy's head snapped up, and Adam lurched when the phone rang.

"Jeanette! I've been waiting for you to call. How are you?" puffed Adam as he momentarily leaned against the counter and placed his hand over his eyes.

"Adam, where are you? Are you coming?" Jeanette whispered to prevent a coughing spasm.

He did not expect those questions, and he was momentarily stunned. "Jeanette ... oh, honey ... you know I'd be there with you if I could! I wasn't allowed to stay; they made me leave. How are you?"

She couldn't answer. She closed her eyes and squeezed her free hand into a fist. The tears were flowing freely once again.

"Oh, Jeanette … don't cry … don't cry … talk to me, honey. Tell me," he begged.

She had a full-blown meltdown. For long, tortuous minutes she cried and blabbered and coughed and wheezed into the phone. It broke his heart. Lucy came over to lean against Adam as he bent over the kitchen island and cried along with his wife.

"Shhh, shhh, Jeanette," he soothed, "honey, you'll be OK," he reassured and cajoled. "Just breathe, honey."

"I have COVID," she whined. She lowered her voice, "COVID!"

"Yeah, I puzzled that one out," he said sarcastically.

Jeanette was running out of steam. "I'm so scared, Adam," she whispered. "Adam, what … what if … what if I die?" Her last two words were barely audible.

"Jeanette, you are not going to die. I forbid it!" Adam announced. "Don't you even think about that. I won't let it happen!" His strong, confident tone was ridiculous, yet soothing.

"Adam …"

"Nope. That train of thought won't help you."

"But …"

"Honey, it won't happen."

"How can you stop it?"

"Trust me."

She was completely emotionally spent. After a few long minutes, she answered. "You promise?"

"I absolutely promise. Have I ever lied to you?"

"Hmmm."

"Hey! You know I haven't!"

"Adam, what if I gave it to you? How do you feel? Are you sick?"

"Nah, I'm fine!"

"No symptoms?"

"Nope. It's the whiskey," he joked.

Jeanette gave a small chuckle before sighing deeply. "I'm cold. I'm tired. I have a headache. My throat hurts. My chest hurts. I miss you. I want to be home."

"I know, honey. That's why you're there. They'll fix you." After a moment he added, "Then you'll come back home. I miss you, too."

Shattered, she succumbed to another coughing spasm.

"Hang up, honey. Rest; then call or text me whenever you want. You just concentrate on getting better."

"Kids?"

"I'll let them know you're in the hospital. I haven't called them yet; I was waiting to hear from you. Should I tell them they can text or call you?"

"Uh, sure. Can't talk too much. Maybe I should text, except I don't have my glasses ..."

"Huh! Should I bring them to you?"

"Only if you can come in."

"You know I can't."

"Never mind. I'm way too tired to pay attention to anything anyway."

"Jeanette, I love you. You know you're my whole world."

"I love you, too. I hope you don't get sick."

"Don't worry. You know I'm God's other son. Nothing can happen to me."

He could almost see her smile. "Yep. Adam–"

A knock interrupted Jeanette. Another white-clad worker entered her room with a tray.

"Mrs. Remington? I have your lunch tray."

"K. Honey, gotta go. Call me; don't forget" Jeanette whispered.

"I could never forget you. Eat your lunch," Adam instructed as they disconnected.

Jeanette coughed and picked through the tray. The cafeteria worker had explained it was available for a late lunch. Jeanette was given a menu request for dinner, which was a tough choice between meatloaf and baked chicken. Judging by the lunch of cottage cheese on a bed of lettuce with tomatoes, the food was typical for hospitals. A decaffeinated tea bag with lukewarm water and a small container of juice was also included. In the end, the only food consumed was the vanilla ice cream that did wonders to soothe her burning throat. Spent, but not sleepy, she arranged herself on the bed in the lonely room. So quiet! Although there was a curtain and space for another bed, she was all alone. There was a slight whistling noise from the oxygen connection on the wall. She looked over her head and saw the red ball floating in the glass. From her vantage point, the window view between the slats of the blind was the roofline of another part of the hospital and blue sky. Jeanette was clicking through the channels when Dr. Roman entered her room pushing a cart with a laptop.

"Hey, Jeanette. I came in as soon as my office would let me. How are you feeling?" Dr. Roman asked as he closed the door behind him. He was also covered head to toe in white.

"Oh, doctor, I'm so glad to see you! They said I have COVID! Am I gonna be OK?"

Dr. Roman looked up from logging onto the laptop to look directly into her eyes. "Yes, Jeanette, we're all going to do everything we can!" Although he was wearing two masks, she could tell he was smiling by the crinkling of his eyes behind his plastic visor. Jeanette teared up again as she clutched the blanket tighter.

"Tell me how you're feeling," Dr. Roman asked again. He was typing on the laptop as Jeanette spoke.

"I feel tired and sore, cold with chills. My throat is on fire, and I have a constant headache. Sometimes I can't stop coughing. My chest hurts, and sometimes I can't catch a breath. It's frightening when I can't breathe."

Dr. Roman waited for her coughing to subside. "Got it. When we talked on the phone yesterday, you said these symptoms started four days ago?" At her assenting nod, he continued. "Those are the typical symptoms of COVID, Jeanette. Let's take a look at your test results to see what we know. Your PCR test was positive for COVID-19. Your oxygen saturation level when you were admitted was 90%. That's why you're so tired. The nasal cannula is delivering oxygen–4 liters–to help your lungs produce what you need in your system. According to your chest X-ray, and I'm reading from the report, 'results indicate left right lower lung lobe basal hazy ground glass and consolidated air space opacities.' In other words, you have COVID pneumonia," he looked up and paused to give Jeanette a chance to take all that information in. "That's why you're coughing and having difficulty breathing."

Jeanette just stared at Dr. Roman. A man covered head to toe so he doesn't catch her germs just told her she has COVID pneumonia!

"So, to treat your condition, I've prescribed antibiotics and steroids which will be administered intravenously. We'll continue the oxygen and monitor your oxygen saturation level with that device on your finger. I've also prescribed several medications and inhalers to help alleviate the cough. In addition, we found vitamin D and zinc are useful in fighting against this virus." Dr. Roman took a deep breath. "We'll be taking a chest X-ray every day or every other day to monitor your lungs for changes.

"Listen, Jeanette, you've probably seen the news, and you're nervous. It's understandable. We know that your body heals better without worry. Just rest and let your body heal. I promise we'll do everything we can." Dr. Roman signed out of the laptop and began to push it out of the room.

"I'll get better, right?"

He stopped, turned, and replied, "Jeanette, the good news is that you have no chronic health issues, and we have no reason to believe that you won't make a full recovery."

"How long? I mean, how long till I go home?"

"Hard to say, Jeanette. I promise, as soon as you are able to go, I will send you home. You just have to do your best to get better; I can't do it all. Deal?" he queried as he extended his gloved hand toward her.

She grasped it. "Deal." And she relaxed. Dr. Roman would never shake hands with a woman who was dying, would he?

Once more alone in the room, with HGTV renovating, Jeanette was introspective. E.R. Nurse Alicia's reminder about labor and delivery breathing brought Jeanette's children to mind in a welcome diversion. She gave birth a long time ago ... Jeanette really had to think to figure out how long. It was thirty years ago to Jerry, twenty-eight years ago to Alex, and twenty-six years ago to Evie. In some ways, the details of each experience were as clear as if it happened yesterday. In other ways, the details were such that as soon as she thought she remembered something, she immediately questioned herself: Did that happen when she was giving birth to Jerry, Alex, or Evie? It was usually Adam who confirmed the details when needed, having been there for all three. In fact, Adam was in all her memories.

Remaining as quiet and still as possible, Jeanette lay listening to her loud breathing reverberating in the room and thinking of her children. She and Adam were married several years before they had Jerry. Yet it was always their plan to have children. Adam had a corporate job and she was a teacher, and they waited until after they bought a house before starting a family. Pregnancy agreed with Jeanette; everyone said so. She never suffered from the debilitating nausea some women experienced. Still, Jeanette realized that no amount of planning could really prepare her for having a baby or anticipating how that baby would change her and their lives. Despite all the advice from family and friends, Jeanette could never imagine how very different she would become. After she gave birth to Jerry, there was a sense of a rip in time. At this thought, Jeanette realized that at this moment she also felt time standing still. A definite lack of clarity in thinking, a slowness, along with a sense of waiting. Back then, it was waiting for herself to return to "normal," which of course never happened. Having Jerry changed her at a cellular level; she later thought of the suspension of time as an adjustment period. She went back to work, and dropped Jerry off at daycare as they planned, but she was not the same employee. And although she and Adam shared Jerry's care when he was not traveling for work, she was not the same wife. Both her career and her marriage still existed, but Jerry superseded everyone else. As fate would have it, untenured Jeanette was downsized during a reduction in force due to budget cuts in her small school district when Jerry was nine months old. She hadn't thought to be a stay-at-home mom, but once she was, she embraced it wholeheartedly.

Certainly, as an inexperienced mother, she doubted herself and what she should do, especially when Jerry cried with colic. That was part of the new parent magic: you may not know what to do, but you don't give up. It's hard to say what the true dynamic is—does the mother or father discover the secret of what works, or does the baby just get used to what the parent does? Either way, a bond forms. Jeanette remembered Jerry's baby cry, his toothless grin, his favorite Elmo, and her favorite blue outfit covered with cars to put him in. Mostly, though, she remembered just holding Jerry, the way he fit in her arms, the way he would snuggle and hold on, the smell of him. One of her fondest memories of Jerry was when he was two years old and she was very pregnant with Alex. On Mondays, they would sit with the Sunday newspaper comics and read them. This would take hours because Jeanette would point to a panel and ask leading questions like, "What do you think he's doing?" or "What do you think will happen next?" Toddler Jerry was a talker, spoke very clearly, and had a terrific imagination. Today, her Jerry was a tall, handsome man with gentle eyes and the same warm, outgoing personality. When you talked to Jerry, it was like you were the only person in the world. He gave you his full attention; he made you feel heard. *When was the last time I spoke with Jerry?* Try as she might, she couldn't remember. *Is he OK?*

Jerry, Alex, and Evie will be worried about her. That would only add to their own difficulties right now. *Was I going to call each one? Will Adam tell them?* She had difficulty recalling what Adam had said. *How will they react? The news around COVID is absolutely terrifying…*

Panic roared back to life, and the cycle repeated as Jeanette began to cough and struggle for air. Fortunately, Nurse Patti came in at that moment. Distracting Jeanette, she injected medications into the IV. Patti also gave the raggedly breathing Jeanette several pills and several puffs of an inhaler, spooned some ice chips into her mouth to soothe her throat, and suggested she rest. Completely worn out, completely stressed out, Jeanette catnapped, replaying the details of a life she lived many, many years ago: helping little bodies into and out of her Honda Accord littered with car seats, pretzels, baby rattles, stuffed animals, and matchbox cars. The little legs kicked in time to the nursery rhymes playing on the cassette tape as she retrieved the urgently needed item from the ever-present over-stuffed diaper bag. Those days were filled with relentless movement, a stark contrast to the prone middle-aged woman in the hospital bed. It was like watching an old, favorite, comforting movie.

She opened her phone and texted her husband:

JEANETTE: 🖤

ADAM: 🖤

His responding heart, sent within seconds, made her smile.

JEANETTE: XO

ADAM: XO

He made her smile. Damn, she loved that man. *Where are you, Adam?*

Just as she began to well up again, her phone indicated a new posting on the Family WhatsApp. As she read the messages coming through, her sobbing turned from fear to relief and pure gratitude.

EVIE: Mom, you're in the hospital?! Do your best to get better! 🩺

JERRY: How do you feel, Mom? 💗

ALEX: Sending you healing thoughts, Mom! 💚

JEANETTE: Thanks! I'm here to be fixed! Lol XO

KEVIN: How's the food? 🍽️

JERRY: Do you have everything you need? 🍴

JEANETTE: Typical and yes! XO

SUE: The baby says hi, everyone! 👶 He's the size of an eggplant 🍆

EVIE: So big!

JEANETTE: Keep growing, Baby Rem! 🌱

ALEX: He needs a bit more time! ⏳

JEANETTE: Me, too haha

BETH: Get better, soon! 😌

JEANETTE: I'm working on it. I love you all! 🖤

EVIE: Love you, Mom! 🖤

JERRY: Love you, too! 🖤

ALEX: Love you 🖤

ADAM: Get better already! XOXO

JEANETTE: 🖤🖤🖤

Jeanette clutched the phone and her family to her chest. *I will not let go! I will not let go!*

9

Lucy snored softly beneath the kitchen table, prompting Adam to absentmindedly reach down and brush her ear. The table had become his at-home office. Jeanette had turned the real office, also known as Lucy's room, into her classroom since the lockdown. Her school laptop, books, and notebooks waited patiently for her return. Instead of disturbing her set-up, he adopted the kitchen table while quarantining. Handling the needs of the agency from here was easy; he monitored everything online as usual. He had sent an early morning text to his senior agent to open and close the office today. That arrangement could continue indefinitely. If needed, however, he could close the office, as many other small agencies have already done during the shutdown. He would see how this played out and reassess mid-week. As usual, he seamlessly toggled between his Mac and work computers.

Before anything else demanded his attention, he drank water as he began an internet search for flowers. A dozen roses would cheer Jeanette up for sure. He googled Little Shop of Flowers, the local florist he used on Jeanette's birthday and their anniversary. When he dialed the number, he automatically went to voicemail. He recognized the owner's voice saying, "Thank you for calling The Little Shop of Flowers. We're closed due to the executive order. We hope to reopen soon. Stay safe and be well!"

"Huh! Lucy, I guess flowers are not essential," he said aloud. She briefly lifted her head, then resumed her nap.

Adam continued to search, but after checking two other local florists, he decided to take another tack. He googled the phone number to the hospital. After pressing the required digits to get the operator, Adam was connected with a disembodied male voice.

"How may I help you?"

"Hello. My wife is currently a patient, and I'd like to send her flowers. Can you connect me to the gift shop there?"

"I'm sorry, sir, but the gift shop is closed."

"When will it open?"

"Not sure; it's shut down. Also, we are not accepting any gifts for patients at this time."

"Excuse me? No gifts?"

"No, sir. Due to the pandemic, the hospital has restricted all deliveries. Out of an abundance of caution, no items will be brought into patient rooms." Leaving only a few seconds for Adam to process that information, the voice said, "Stay safe," and ended the call.

Adam looked at his phone in bewilderment. Then he shook his head at the sheer absurdity of the current situation. His wife was in the hospital, yet he couldn't visit her or send her anything. Meanwhile, he was virtually a prisoner in his own home. Ridiculous! If someone would have predicted this scenario, he would have laughed.

"Lucy, this is no laughing matter."

Never one to dwell in the moment, Adam stood to brew a fresh pot of coffee and deftly moved about the kitchen. Lucy followed, then waited patiently for Adam to settle. In anticipation of the upcoming Zoom call with his children, he considered the words that he would need to reassure them. He had called each to tell them individually that Jeanette had been admitted this morning with COVID symptoms. After speaking with all three, and repeating the same information several times to each child, he realized the enormity of the news and decided there may be a better way to keep them all informed. Having an agency account, Adam arranged a Zoom call for later in the day. Adam thought it prudent for several reasons.

First, he would be disseminating the same information. Hopefully, that would alleviate giving the same child the same information twice, while not telling another entirely. That had been known to happen, especially once they started asking questions. Then different details emerged that he hadn't previously thought to share. Adam also needed, and knew that his children needed, the comfort of family right now. He knew how terrified he was that Jeanette was sick; he laid his hand over his upset stomach. The acid churning in the pit was a constant reminder. How do they feel? Considering it was their mother ... he could relate.

Except his own mother's terminal illness had been slow and painful, and utterly heartbreaking for all members of the family. That experience, he vowed, was not being repeated. The early evening call would also give time for Jeanette's test results, and the critical update from the hospital. Hopefully, he could provide good news. Adam was patient enough to wait only 30 or so more minutes before calling the doctor. Meanwhile, he was relieved and heartened to have some contact with Jeanette. Alternating heart emojis and "xo" arrived via text, probably ten each already, which he responded to in kind. Leave it to Jeanette to find a way to be wordy without saying a word. For once he was thrilled.

Lucy ambled over to the slider. She waited patiently for Adam to notice she wanted to go out.

"Lucy, it's raining. You don't like getting wet," he said as he moved toward her. When he arrived, he could see that it was indeed not raining, just overcast, and he complied.

"OK, do your business!" He watched as she wandered slowly to the steps, looked back at him to see if he was joining her, and then went down the stairs to the yard. That backward glance had him feeling guilty, so he grabbed his phone and a poop bag and followed her out.

The showers were forecasted to continue on and off, curtailing Lucy's deck sleeping. Adam followed her gingerly, avoiding the puddles pooling around the concrete patio below the deck, which Lucy didn't seem to notice. He stood for a while surveying the yard by turning in a circle. Everything he saw reminded him of Jeanette. Over the years she had planted much of the landscaping. Some greeneries were already returning to life, but some had yet to sprout. There were her wine and roses bushes which delighted her with their pink flowers. Still sticks, her prized strawberry hydrangeas were her favorite. There were several clematis plants weaving across the wooden fence which provided both privacy and dainty white flowers in late summer. Around the deck and patio were multiple pots which she usually filled with annuals. Would she be able to plant those colorful pots this summer? He couldn't imagine the yard without them. Completing his circle, he came to the garden. Her garden. Currently a mess with last season's detritus, he wondered about this year. Would there be tomatoes? Would Jeanette make her salsa? He closed his eyes against the possibility of loss. *Please, God, don't take her away!*

Lucy's nails clicked on the concrete as she came to lean against him again. They walked together toward the house. Suddenly exhausted, Adam tied the empty poop bag to the arm of one of the wet chairs on the deck and dried Lucy's feet with the towel waiting on the floor inside the house. She leaned against Adam so she wouldn't fall over, but obediently allowed his ministrations. Again, here was Jeanette, because she had taught Lucy to allow her paws to be dried so as not to make a mess in the house. Overcome, Adam grabbed hold of his Lucy, fell to his knees, and cried. "What would we do without her, Lucy?"

He wasn't sure how long he and Lucy sat on the floor when his cell rang. Caller ID said "Saint Peter Hos" and he fumbled with the phone to accept the call.

"Mr. Remington, it's Dr. Roman. I'm calling with an update on your wife."

"Yes, doctor." For the second time, he wiped his wet face with his sleeve like a schoolboy. "Tell me. How is she?"

"Mr. Remington, your wife is very sick. Jeanette's test results are in, and I just reviewed them with her. Her PCR test was positive for COVID. Her oxygen saturation level when she was admitted was 90%. That accounts for her lack of energy. She's wearing a nasal cannula delivering oxygen–4 liters–to help her lungs do their job. The chest X-ray shows that she has COVID pneumonia." He paused to allow Adam to assimilate that information.

"Pneumonia?" Adam repeated.

"Yes. You could tell she was struggling to breathe; that's a result of the way this new virus attacks the lungs. We confirmed that with a chest X-ray. I could read you the report, Mr. Remington."

"Yes, please do." Adam would google all this later, but now that he had the doctor on the phone, he wanted as much information as possible.

"I'm reading from the report: 'results indicate left right lower lung lobe basal hazy ground glass and consolidated air space opacities.' This is exactly the picture we are seeing with all COVID patients." Again, Dr. Roman paused. He knew what was coming next.

"What are you doing to treat Jeanette?" Adam asked. It came out harsher than he expected, but so be it.

"So, to treat her condition, I've prescribed antibiotics and steroids which will be administered intravenously. We'll continue oxygen and monitoring her oxygen saturation levels day and night. I've also prescribed several medications and inhalers to help alleviate the cough. In addition, we found vitamin D and zinc are useful to fight against this virus." Dr. Roman took a deep breath and repeated the same information for the umpteenth time. "We'll be taking a chest X-ray every day, or every other day to monitor her lungs for changes." Dr. Roman moved his glasses up and wiped his eyes with his ungloved hand. His eyes drifted toward the whiteboard on the wall with all the patients' names. He realized two names were crossed out and two new names added since this morning.

"What can we expect now, doctor?" Adam asked.

"Well, Adam, what we're experiencing here is that COVID patients spend a few days at the reaction level where Jeanette is currently. Then, it's up to her body. I'm sure you see the news, Adam, and I don't want to mislead you. Your wife, as I said, is very ill. Jeanette will get better if her body can deal with the inflammation this virus causes. We're using all the medications we can to control her body's reaction, but ultimately, it's up to her. Time will tell." He began scrolling down the patient list on his laptop.

Adam's reluctant grunting noise confirmed he heard Dr. Roman. When he spoke, his voice was low and demanding. "Listen. Do everything you possibly can for my wife, Doctor Roman. I don't care about the other COVID patients. I'm telling you that my wife must make it. You just figure out what you need to do to make that happen."

Dr. Roman's attention fully returned to the telephone call. Updating family was never easy, especially with COVID, and reactions ran the gamut. He was reminded that behind all the responses was usually pure fear. "I assure you, Mr. Remington, that I will do just that."

"When will you have another update for me and my children, doctor?"

"Tomorrow. Remember, you can call the nurses' station at any time. If they can reach me or the resident on duty, they will. Otherwise, they'll update you with what they know."

Blowing out a tense breath, Adam relented, "Doctor, I appreciate everything you're doing. I look forward to your report tomorrow. Is there anything else I need to know about Jeanette?"

"No, that's it."

"One last thing ... Is there any way I can visit my wife? I know about protocol ..."

"I'm sorry, Mr. Remington, but according to the state of New Jersey, that's simply not possible at this time. Meanwhile, I'm your doctor as well. How are you feeling? Are you quarantining?"

"I'm fine. And, yes, I'm quarantining."

"Any COVID symptoms?"

"None," Adam confirmed dismissively.

"Good. We'll talk tomorrow."

When Dr. Roman hung up, he left the station and went toward Jeanette's room. He peered through the window and saw her sitting up in the side chair surrounded by pillows. She was watching TV, holding her phone in her lap. She scooped a few ice chips from the cup into her mouth, leaned her head back, and closed her eyes. Thinking of Adam's words, Dr. Roman fervently hoped he would be able to deliver good news. With renewed purpose, he moved to check on his other patients.

Lucy had settled her body wrapped around the legs of his chair at the kitchen table. Once everyone was present on the Zoom call, Adam looked at all the worried faces on the screen: Jerry and Beth, Alex and Sue, and Evie and Kevin in their separate boxes. He heard their strained greetings and banter. As he listened to them, he wondered if they missed being together. Missed being children cared for in this house together, with two parents to support and share the complications of life. Especially during this crazy COVID lockdown. Especially with their mother in the hospital. Adam knew how worried Jeanette was about them in their isolated locations, and wondered how they really felt. He had told Jeanette that they were grown and responsible and capable, which was all true, but his wife being infected undermined his confidence and caused his own fear and doubt to rear up. *Ah, Jeanette, I understand now ...*

"OK. So, I spoke with each of you individually, and you know Mom has COVID. We have no idea how she caught it; she doesn't know anyone who has it. They said she will probably never know where she got it from. That's how contagious COVID is.

"She was admitted this morning into St. Peter's, like I told you. Unfortunately, I can't be with her; it's driving me *crazy*. By the way, great job on the WhatsApp texts. We are *all* in contact with Mom *all* the time—she has her cell phone. You can text her as much as you'd like. Mom doesn't have her glasses, which might make texting more difficult. Talking makes her cough, so conversations may be short. Still, call or text. She'll answer when she can. I know you're all worried, but so far so good. And I'm absolutely positive she wants to hear from all of you.

"I've talked to Dr. Roman and one of the nurses, Patti. Any one of us can call the nurse's station for information if you're unable to talk to Mom. But you can imagine how chaotic the hospital is right now. They may not answer, and if they do, the nurse probably won't have much time."

Adam paused to allow any comments or questions. None came. All six faces continued to stare expectantly at him. *It's all on me!*

"I do have the latest test results and update from Dr. Roman." He paused. "Your mother has COVID pneumonia." Intakes of breath occurred in every box. Clearly, this was a bad sign. Each sought support by reaching out to their partner.

Adam rushed on. "Well, this is what COVID does. But they are treating her with antibiotics, steroids, and other medications. She's on oxygen to help her breathe. You know how much your mom loves you all; she's a fighter. Also, you know how stubborn she is," Adam said trying to relieve the tension. "She'll do her best to get better, even if it's just to come home to tell me what to do."

Evie broke in when Adam would have continued. "Dad, when you called before, I was stunned. I'm still stunned. How can I help? Should I come home?" Evie said sitting forward. Her voice began to rise. "I want to come home! I want to help ..."

"Evie, it isn't going to help Mom if you get all worked up," Adam reasoned. "I know how you feel. I ... know ... how ... you ... feel," he repeated slowly, emphasizing each word. He looked in each box to see the stricken faces of his children and their partners. He noted that in each case, the couples were sitting practically on top of each other. Their closeness warmed his heart.

"Dad, how sick is Mom?" Jerry asked. Even though he spoke in his low modulated voice, his question was heard by all. His wife, Sue, reached for Jerry's hand.

"Well, again, she has COVID pneumonia. She was admitted because of her difficulty breathing. She's on oxygen, and they're treating her right now with heavy-duty antibiotics and steroids. Your mom is in great health and does *not* have any underlying conditions. We all know what's happening with this virus ... how it's spreading and people are ... dying

... that's why this country–the world–is shut down. I know you're worried, but she doesn't have to be a statistic on the bottom of the screen during the news tonight or tomorrow. Your mom's chances of getting through this are excellent," Adam enthused. He felt a pang of guilt at Evie's sharp intake of breath ... was he giving Jeanette too much credit? Was he giving Evie false hope? He sincerely hoped not.

"Dad, people are *dying* of COVID ..." Jerry continued. "Dad, really ... tell us ..." he implored.

Adam took a deep breath before replying. "OK, you want to know what this looks like," he began. Adam had struggled before the Zoom call with how many details to give. Just now, looking at his children, he decided not to sugarcoat Jeanette's condition. They were all adults. "Yes, Mom is very sick. She's having trouble breathing; COVID attacks the lungs. She coughs and it's hard for her to catch her breath." Evie was full-out crying now and shaking her head. Kevin was holding her hand and listening. Adam continued on, "She's liable to go into coughing fits if she speaks. So, she's limiting her words. Not only that, but she's exhausted. I don't think I ever saw your mother this tired, even when she was running after the three of you kids. And believe me, you were active! So, she dozes on and off." Everyone was silent for a few minutes trying to assimilate that information. Jeanette's sons and their wives wore stricken expressions. Although not as emotional as Evie, they all were obviously frightened.

Alex said, "Dad, what can we do? Can I come over or go to the–"

"Absolutely not!" Adam practically yelled. "I'm quarantining, and you cannot expose Sue. I know as the only one of you kids here in New Jersey you feel obligated, but no!" Adam lowered his voice, "Thank you, Alex, for offering."

Alex looked at Sue, and she wrapped her arms around him as they touched foreheads. No one could hear Sue's whispered words but Alex.

"Really, what can we do?" Jerry repeated. "I mean, can anyone see her?"

"No, no visitors are allowed. You should text her, call her, FaceTime. That's what we have right now by way of communication with your mother," Adam sighed.

"Dad! We have to do something! Maybe we should drive to New Jersey," Evie cried.

"Honestly, that's not a good idea. You're safer where you are, all of you, for now." Adam repeated, "Stay where you are. We can schedule regular Zoom calls, and any of you can call or text me or your mother—or each other—at any time, day or night," Adam said.

"How are you feeling, Dad?" Alex asked.

"Good. No symptoms so far. I have a few more days of quarantining before I'm officially in the clear. So again, no one should plan on coming here. Not yet, anyway," Adam conceded. Depending on what happened, everyone may need to return home.

There was a long pause before Jerry inquired, "What can we expect, Dad? When will you have more information? And can we call the hospital, too?"

"The doctor informed me he will update me every 24 hours while she's in the hospital. In the meantime, they'll continue the protocol they started and add measures as needed. As soon as I receive the call, I'll pass on the update to all of you. Jerry, could you set up a new WhatsApp account without your mother on it?" Adam paused and watched as Jerry nodded yes and immediately picked up his phone to set up a new group. "Although everyone should continue to post on the WhatsApp she can see, she doesn't need to be bothered with our notifications. That will be the fastest way for me to alert you when I have news. Also, I'll put the phone number of the nurse's station on that account so you all have it. However, they did request that only one family member call for updates and relay that information to the rest of the family. Remember, they are busy, actually almost at capacity. It's crazy at St. Peter's right now."

The subdued and anxious group talked a bit more about the state of affairs in Chicago, New Jersey, and Miami respectively. All were experiencing stay-at-home orders and shortages of various foods and household items. As unnecessary and extreme as this pandemic seemed yesterday, Jeanette's hospitalization brought tangible fear to her family. Now a Remington *was* a COVID statistic. When everyone was quiet, Adam realized they had all reached their limit for the day.

"Hey, I know you're all upset. But let's stay positive. Let's give your mom a chance," Adam asserted. "You know how much I love you, and never, *never* doubt your mother's love. If you care to, pray," Adam said with a smile. Looking at the somber faces either crying or on the brink of crying, Adam added, "Do *not* underestimate your mother." He looked away from his children on the screen and at Jeanette's favorite flowered mug still sitting on the kitchen counter where she left it. His voice broke. "I would bet on her any day."

"I can't believe it," Jerry told Beth as he closed the computer. "I'm shocked; I had no idea she was even sick."

"Well," Beth reminded him, "your dad did say it came on quickly. When was the last time you spoke with your mom?"

Jerry took a few moments to answer. "Not sure," he responded curtly.

He did know; the last time he spoke with Jeanette was more than a week ago. Jerry groaned inwardly. Really, Mom always called at the worst possible moment! She regularly forgot the time difference (even though he himself was always mindful of that when calling her) and either called too early or too late. True to form, Jerry was in the middle of a project whose deadline was fast approaching when she last called. Still, he answered; she was his mother, after all. In fact, Jeanette was fond of joking, "Jerry, we have a *personal* relationship. I gave birth to you!" They exchanged pleasantries before she suggested, yet again, that he and Beth escape the city and drive to New Jersey. She must have seen another report on the news about the upheaval in the streets of Chicago. He did not have the time for that conversation, and he told her so. Frankly, he was busy and generally short-tempered. Everyone he knew was either annoyed, depressed, or anxious; just look at what was going on!

Jeanette had said she understood and let him get back to work. Since then, they had texted and each posted on the WhatsApp. He was remembering when he was away at college, and she had executed her bad timing regularly. Jerry actually suggested, and then encouraged, her texting instead in an attempt to eliminate the problem. Texting would satisfy Jeanette for a while, but eventually she still called. He must have listened to a million messages saying, "Hey, it's only me. I just wanted to hear your voice." There was one time in college when he answered the phone, and she immediately said, "What's the matter?" He was behind in a class, and certainly didn't want to tell her he forgot a paper was due and had been working on it hurriedly. It was unnerving and somehow made him feel ten years old. At the time he believed his mother was being needy; after all, she still had two children at home. As the oldest, everyone in the family knew his going away to college had been a difficult adjustment for her. Back then he had resented that. Who was all alone in a new place, adjusting to living with others, working hard in a difficult school and worrying about the future every day? Jerry or Jeanette? Remembering this incident and looking back now, Jerry realized his mother's exasperating texting and calls were–and still were–a sign of her love. Well, if he had called her back and heard *her* voice this week, would he know how sick she was?

"Listen, Jerry, you've been busy, preoccupied. We've all got so much to deal with right now trying to carry on through all these changes. Don't beat yourself up." Beth waited for Jerry to look up. "Hey, we have to believe your mom will be alright," Beth said putting her arm around him. "Tell me what you're thinking; don't go through this alone."

"I'm thinking about how many times I've been annoyed by her texts or calls," Jerry confessed. Quietly, Jerry asked, "Beth, my mom's in the hospital with COVID. *COVID*! I've never thought of my mother as mortal before. What if ... what if ..." They embraced. There was no need for Jerry to articulate his fear; Beth understood.

10

Exhausted. Jeanette was exhausted. Besides the sheer terror of COVID causing her alternate coughing and crying fits, Jeanette missed her husband, her home, her Lucy, and her life. Evie and Adam had Face-Timed her last night on a three-way call. At first, she was appalled at the sight of her wan self on the screen. Realizing her children would be thinking the same thing, she smiled a lot and contributed enough to the conversation to put Evie at ease. Adam, thankfully, kept it short. Both Jerry and Alex FaceTimed separately as well, their conversations also short. She wanted to see them, and she hoped it was a comfort to speak to her, but Jeanette was wiped by the end of it all. The more she talked, the more she coughed. It was that simple. Even with all the medication she was taking, which was brought to her religiously at all hours, breathing was difficult and the head and throat aches lingered on. In fact, her whole body ached now, and Jeanette breathed as shallowly as possible in an effort to alleviate the heaviness in her chest. She was grateful that everyone was texting her today and not expecting her to speak.

The grey walls were good enough. There was not much to look at, besides the channel constantly tuned to HGTV. Jeanette felt quite alone, and was clutching her phone to her chest, her lifeline to her family. And although drained at a cellular level, Jeanette found sleep elusive. Oh, she napped. She rested her eyes. But the deep, relaxing sleep of home escaped her. Not that it was too loud on the floor; on the contrary, it was eerily silent with the door closed. So silent Jeanette imagined she heard COVID flowing through her veins, taking over her body. She was watching the now familiar aliens bustling about past the rectangular window in the door, when one knocked and entered her room with a rolling cart.

"Hello, Mrs. Remington. I'm Annie, your respiratory therapy nurse. How are you feeling this morning?"

Jeanette waved hello as she took in Annie, a large black woman with thick, red-framed glasses beneath her plastic face shield and tomato red hair sticking out of her cap. An oversized crucifix was pinned to her chest.

"Mrs. Remington, can you speak to me? How are you today?"

"Fine," Jeanette replied and then coughed.

"Why are you still in bed? Let's get you in the chair, so you can sit up and watch TV," Annie suggested pleasantly. Annie moved the bedside commode a bit farther away and began peeling back the sheets on Jeanette's bed.

Jeanette looked at the blue-gloved hands that grasped her own. Annie had a strong grip and eased her into the chair. Jeanette felt weak by comparison and appreciated Anne's strength.

Effortlessly, Annie had Jeanette ensconced in the comfortable chair, with blankets tucked around. As she carefully arranged the nasal cannula tube and IV so Jeanette wouldn't get entangled, Annie said conversationally, "So, Mrs. Remington, are you married? Do you have any children?"

"Yes!" Jeanette exclaimed. "My husband is at home, and I have three children." Even though she wheezed and coughed, Jeanette was thrilled to talk about her family. Her phone remained clutched to her chest.

"Oh? Sons? Daughters?" Annie asked.

"Two married sons and an engaged daughter. My daughters-in-law are lovely. My middle son and his beautiful wife are expecting their first child, and my daughter's fiancé is wonderful."

"Tell me more," Annie entreated, pushing her red frames back up her nose.

Jeanette talked about each child in turn, and Annie proceeded to monitor her oxygen levels and take notes.

"Wow! You must be so proud, Mrs. Remington."

Her emotionally-fueled enthusiasm waning, Jeanette just nodded her head.

"It's important, Mrs. Remington, that you try to strengthen your lungs at this critical time. We know that COVID affects your breathing. Your oxygen levels are OK, but we need to practice some breathing exercises. It's very easy; I'll show you what to do."

Jeanette appreciated the company, and raised the yellow ball on the spirometer as Annie directed.

"Let me just update your file here while you continue. Ten more times, Mrs. Remington. You're doing great!" Annie swiped her card and added a note that Mrs. Remington was initially reticent, but became enthusiastic when discussing her family. The patient was responsive and cooperative. Annie also noted the number of repetitions Jeanette had completed on the spirometer.

Jeanette suddenly stopped the exercises and announced, "It's COVID," amid more coughing.

"Yes, I know," Annie said softly, repositioning the reds once again.

Jeanette deflated and fell back against the chair.

"Mrs. Remington, I see that you're Catholic from your file. Would you like me to pray with you?"

After agreeing, Jeanette bowed her head, and Annie recited familiar, comforting prayers while Jeanette mouthed along. Following the sign of the cross, Jeanette reached out, touched Annie's arm, and said, "Thank you."

Annie covered her hand with her own gloved palm and said, "Anytime, Mrs. Remington. Hang in there. I have to move on to my next patient." She patted her hand. "I'll come back and check on you tomorrow. Remember, at least ten more sets of ten on the spirometer. OK? We have to stay strong, Mrs. Remington. For your family ..." They nodded in mutual understanding as Annie pushed her cart out of the room.

Jeanette felt deserted as soon as Annie left the room. *Will I die here alone? When will I see Jerry, Alex, or Evie? Adam? Lucy? The baby?* Agitated once again, Jeanette was managing shallow short breaths when another knock sounded.

"Hi Mrs. Remington! Remember me? Nurse Patti?" she said as she breezed into the room with her cart. "I'm back with your medication. It's also time to take another chest X-ray. The technician is on his way. How are you feeling?"

When Jeanette burst into tears, Patti stopped in her tracks.

"Oh, Mrs. Remington! Don't cry! Tell me what's wrong," the nurse crooned. "Are you in pain?"

"I'm afraid I'll never go home," Jeanette stammered between the coughs.

"Now, you can't think like that!" Patti crouched down in front of Jeanette's chair so she was closer to eye level. She spoke softly, but with strength. "Mrs. Remington, we're all here to help you fight this thing! Don't give up! Please stay positive!"

Patti continued in the same vein until Jeanette quieted enough to breathe easier. Patti noted the shallow breathing and the way Jeanette was clutching the phone to her chest. She placed the oximeter on Jeanette's finger and waited for the result. "Annie said you did a great job during therapy. Was it tiring?"

Jeanette nodded her assent.

"Well, your oxygen level is a bit lower now; it's 88. That happens sometimes after therapy. I'm increasing your oxygen flow to 7. That should make it easier to breathe."

Jeanette closed her eyes and relaxed on the chair as Patti moved about the room. She could hear the flush in the bathroom as the commode was emptied.

"How's that?" Patti asked expectantly.

Although Jeanette could not determine a difference in the oxygen level, she still whispered, "Better."

"Good. Just relax. I'm going to let Dr. Roman know how you're feeling. Meanwhile, we can take the chest X-ray here with you in your chair."

Jeanette hadn't noticed the other alien standing by the door with a separate cart, but when he came further into the room, she recognized the same bald head as yesterday. Jeanette leaned forward to allow the device to be placed between her and the chair back. Like yesterday, he silently shuffled from the room with his film.

"Here's your medication."

Jeanette focused on the gloved hands. "Patti, aren't you worried–about this?" Jeanette indicated herself with her hands.

Patti understood that Jeanette was referring to contracting COVID and took a beat before answering. "Well, of course." She paused as their eyes met. "My family worries, but I'm a nurse. This is what I do; I'm as careful as I can be. Look at me covered from head to toe!" she joked in an attempt to alleviate the seriousness. "You know we're here for you, but we do limit our in-room exposure time to 15 minutes." An awkward silence befell the room as Jeanette dutifully swallowed the medication and sipped from the straw Patti presented.

An alarm on her wrist sounded at the same time as Jeanette's phone. "Sounds like a text, Mrs. Remington," Patti announced as she moved away and updated the record on the computer.

"Hmm," Jeanette agreed as she looked at her phone.

"Later," Patti waved goodbye as she left the room.

The text was from Alex.

ALEX: Hey! What's up?

JEANETTE: Not much ... Anything new with you and Sue?

ALEX: Sue is good. Tired. Baby Remington keeps her awake all night.

JEANETTE: Future soccer player?

ALEX: Yep! He's getting warmed up! 😊

Jeanette loved Alex's reply.

ALEX: How's the food there?

She smiled at Alex's question. When he was in elementary school, Jeanette used the food tactic to get him to talk to her about his day. If she just asked how his day was, she got nothing. But when she asked about his lunch and followed up with more specific questions, he unraveled. Did he expect her to do the same? She squinted to see the tiny letters on her phone.

JEANETTE: Good ice cream

After a pause, he continued texting.

ALEX: Thinking about you, Mom. Can I do anything?

JEANETTE: Yes! Take care of yourself and your wife and your baby

ALEX: Will do! How do you feel?

She began to text a few words, deleted, and settled on one word.

JEANETTE: Wiped

ALEX: Mom, hang in there. We love you 🩶 🩶 🩶

She loved his text and added her own heart in return. Her arms dropped to her lap as her head lolled in the chair.

Picturing her son, Jeanette's chest heaved, and she struggled to maintain her shallow breathing. As a child, her Alex was a hurricane. He was a bundle of nonstop movement and constantly in action, except when he was sleeping, which he did like a hibernating bear. Adam used to say that Alex had two speeds: on and off. Two years and six months younger than Jerry, the brothers were friends from the first and played for hours together. Jerry and Alex would lay out the Thomas the Tank Engine trains, fight with the Batman action figures, build houses with Legos, or race the Hot Wheels cars. Jerry would be talking, and Alex would be laughing. He still possessed that engaging smile and compelling laugh. It was like he knew a secret no one else knew; his whole face lit with his joy.

When he was sleepy, Alex was her snuggler. Much more so than the other two. As a toddler he would whine at her and lean into her until she picked him up and sat on the couch with him. Then he'd suck his thumb and twirl Jeanette's hair until he fell asleep. During those years when Jeanette was a full-time mom with three young children, she fondly recalled those welcome short breaks on the couch. Alex's warm, wiggly body was tucked against her right side; usually Jerry was on the left side holding the book she would read aloud to them both. After

Evie was born, Alex and Jerry made room for Evie and her bottle on Jeanette's lap, so long as Alex could still reach Jeanette's hair. Today, like his brother, her handsome son Alex was almost a foot taller than Jeanette, and the idea of him on her lap was ridiculous. Within a few months, Alex and his lovely wife Beth would welcome their own son into the world. She swelled with pride that her sons were stable, family men, like their father. Jeanette couldn't imagine how it felt to have this crazy COVID adding even more stress to the already challenging experience of parenthood! *How will the pandemic affect my grandson? Will he be just like Alex? Will I get to meet him?*

Later, Jeanette's buzzing phone in her lap startled her awake. Her neck protested as she shifted in the seat. Looking around, she recalled where she was and why. A food tray was on the adjacent overbed table and the light cast by the TV playing almost inaudibly was the only illumination. She fumbled with the phone and saw Adam's face.

"Hey! I thought you left the building! I was just going to put out an APB," Adam joked.

"I wish," Jeanette whispered.

"It looks dark there. Why don't you put on a light?"

Jeanette lowered the phone, found the remote, and pressed the red light-bulb icon.

"That's better. Now I can see you." Adam paused and added quietly, "How do you feel? You look exhausted."

"Well, you woke me up ..."

"Sorry! Want me to let you go back to sleep?"

"Nah. Hold on." Jeanette adjusted the pillows surrounding her on the chair to be more comfortable. "What's up?"

Adam didn't remark on her shallow breathing, clipped words, or closed eyes. "Well, I'm running the agency just fine from here. Makes me wonder. And Lucy requires petting 24/7. She's my new full-time job." He was rewarded with a smile, so he continued. "Of course, the laundry still needs to be done, and the house is a wreck. Dishes piled up in the sink and dog hair everywhere. I was thinking to leave all that until you got home."

Jeanette's smile grew into a full-blown coughing spasm. The phone dropped into her lap. When she was able to capture her breath again, she retrieved it and whispered, "Don't make me laugh!"

They exchanged smiles in suspended animation for several minutes.

"Hey, get better and come home already, will ya?" Adam quipped.

"Working on it," she returned. More quiet minutes passed. "Kids?"

His teasing tone grew serious. "Worried about you, but otherwise OK." Adam gave a brief account of all three. "Don't fuss about them, Jeanette. Just get better."

In response, she rolled her eyes and gave him a thumbs-up.

"What the hell, are you an emoji now?" he laughed.

She grinned and changed her hand to a peace sign.

Adam smiled and fought sudden emotion. "That's my girl. I love you, Jennie."

In response, she blew him a kiss. Their love spanned the radio waves as they lingered silently on the call.

Eventually, Jeanette used the commode and struggled back into the bed without dislodging the IV or tripping on the cannula. She didn't touch the food, but the cold, melted ice cream was balm for her burning throat. That reminded her of when the boys had their tonsils out. They were five and three. Jeanette scheduled it over the summer so they could stay home and eat ice cream and ice pops all day. She did all she could to manage their pain and watched her boys like a hawk throughout their recovery. That's what she remembered: the responsibility, the hypervigilance, the relief when it was over.

She turned on her side, using the pillows as she'd been shown to prop herself. She thought of Adam, her children, her home. She was in pain and felt so far away from everyone and everything she loved. *Is this it? Will I ever go home? Will I die here?* Jeanette stifled her sobs and had to flip her wet pillow several times. She stared at the grey wall, seeing instead snapshots of her beautiful children over the years playing in her memory. Awkwardly, she posted to the WhatsApp.

JEANETTE: I love you all 🤍 🤍 🤍 🤍

Immediately, Adam loved the post. Moments passed, as one by one her babies loved her back. She clutched her lifeline and fell into a fitful sleep.

11

Sunday, April 19, 2020 - Day #7

Déjà vu. At the kitchen table, with Lucy at his feet, Adam was peering over his computer to Jeanette's tea mug still perched by the tea kettle that he did not have the heart to put away. In a few short minutes, his family would be assembled again on a Zoom call for the latest information about their mother.

Earlier, Dr. Roman's call confirmed that Jeanette's COVID was progressing. Her latest blood test showed her carbon dioxide levels increasing; she was officially in acute respiratory distress. They had boosted the oxygen flow and "continued to monitor her condition." Most distressing to Adam, however, was that Dr. Roman reported that Jeanette was anxious, which exacerbated her breathing difficulty. Therefore, the doctor added Xanax to Jeanette's medications to help with her feelings of doom and to calm her breathing. This, too, was apparently protocol for treating COVID.

Adam had to absorb that. No one knew Jeanette like he did, and she was arguably the strongest person he knew. Sure, she felt sorrow and definitely suffered adversity over the years. If he were honest, there may have been a few times medication may have helped her. But her method of dealing with life's troubles was to double down and try harder. *That won't work with COVID!* It upset him to think Jeanette was despairing, and all he could do was text or FaceTime. He couldn't even hold her hand! *Do any of us have the resources we need to fight COVID?* Praying for the worldwide medical community to quickly discover lifesaving treatment seemed, well, woo-woo. What could he, Adam, physically do to help Jeanette? Nothing. He could do nothing. This thing attacking Jeanette and changing his life spread from across the globe ...

Lucy yelped when Adam's abrupt movement sent his chair sliding backwards. Her frightened cowering immediately invoked regret and returned his anger to its slow simmer. "It's okay, Lucy, it's okay," Adam consoled. He lay down on the kitchen floor with her.

His dog licked his face, and he accepted her loving balm. "Ah, you're the best, Lucy! I love you, too!"

The news from the doctor wasn't all good, yet he was relieved Jeanette was still fighting. This all still felt so surreal. The disbelief and numbness were recently replaced with anger. Anger that he had nowhere to put. This was so unfair! If he spent any time at all thinking about COVID, he was lost in a dark hole. He pictured his wife as the weak, coughing mess he handed over to strangers. Where was *his* Jennie? The Jeanette that he knew and loved all these years. He was an intelligent man; he logically understood the extreme situation this virus unleashed upon the world. But his heart was connected to her. *His* Jeanette. Why did *his* Jeanette have to suffer? He wished it were him lying in that bed, surely frightened and alone. But, no, he didn't even have a sore throat. For some reason, he was reminded of Billy Joel's song "Only the Good Die Young."

He stilled and realized his train of thought. "Whoa, Lucy! No one's dying yet!"

Adam took a few extra minutes to compose himself before he initiated the call to share Jeanette's latest condition. He knew they were all worried and desperate for news. Despite calling and texting their mother, everyone needed reassurance. But could he give it? Well, he would fake it. Until he knew otherwise, he would not let the fear take over. Better to live in the anger.

They exchanged greetings and Jerry and Evie explained that Beth and Kevin were on work calls that would end momentarily. Alex and Sue remained silent. *Keep it together!*

"How are you feeling, Dad?" Jerry asked.

Unhinged. "Fine," he lied. "No COVID symptoms, although I have to quarantine for a few more days. I'm running the agency from home for now. It's good to stay busy," Adam said.

Then he remembered who he was talking to. They were all in the same boat. "I hope you're all doing the same. Even if we can't all join on these Zooms, this is still a better option than texting the updates after the doctor calls. I feel like at least we're all together. It's so crazy not to be there with your mother." Adam had to take a deep, calming breath before continuing. "You may have some questions. If I don't know, I can ask Dr. Roman on the next call, or even call and ask Mom's nurse." Adam was speaking slowly, giving Sue and Kevin a chance to join.

"*Please*, Dad, just tell us! How is Mom?" Evie practically begged. She was much more composed than the last two Zoom calls, and Adam knew how difficult it was for his emotional daughter to remain calm. He knew exactly how difficult it was.

"Dr. Roman reports minimal change in your mom's condition." There was no way he would tell her children that she needed Xanax. "I'm sorry, baby, but Mom is not better ... yet. This virus causes inflammation in the lungs which is causing her breathing difficulty. Getting sufficient oxygen throughout her body is the main concern right now," Adam shared. To his own ears, he was talking about someone else. This couldn't be his Jeanette …

"Dad, can Mom *stay* like this? I mean, if this is what COVID does, what's the long-term damage?" Alex asked. Sue sat quietly by his side, looking down at her hands.

Beth joined the call, waved at everyone and took Jerry's hand as she sat beside him.

Adam waved back at Beth as he answered Alex's question. "Well, COVID hits hard and fast, Alex. Right now, we're worried about keeping her stable. Dr. Roman assures me that Mom is displaying typical symptoms. Still, this is a new virus and there is no 'usual' go-to treatment option. Obviously, the worldwide scope of this pandemic means many, many scientists are working to find a treatment, if not a cure." Another deep breath.

"Well, what can they do to help Mom?" Alex persisted.

"They've increased the flow of oxygen to help Mom breathe. They are using the standard protocol for her body's inflammatory reaction," Adam shared. He sounded so matter-of-fact. Did he sound hopeful?

"Dad, everyone, has Mom seemed even *more* tired to you?" Jerry asked.

Evie quickly agreed, "Oh, yes. When I FaceTime her, she has her eyes closed sometimes, and she drops the phone. Like she can't hold it up."

"And even her texts are shorter," Alex agreed.

Adam nodded. *Yes, I'm afraid that your mother is slipping away.*

"Dad, is that normal? What can we expect next?" Jerry inquired.

Adam took a deep breath. "I'm not sure. Dr. Roman is monitoring Mom's condition and doing what they can." He scalded his tongue with a sip of the too-hot coffee instead of talking. *I can't do this.* Totally overwhelmed in the moment, he could say nothing. Seeing his children was not a comfort; it was more pressure. He wanted desperately to end the call. Lucy licked his foot.

"I remember," said Evie, "when I was in third grade and could *not* learn my math facts. Mom practiced with me every day and never gave up. Look at me now; I'm an accountant!" Wiping her eyes with her tissue Evie said, "I'm not giving up on Mom!" She picked up her cell phone and texted as she said aloud, "You've got this, Mom. I'm with you, and I love you!" Evie's smile was radiant, if somewhat strained. Tangibly, the atmosphere on the call began to change.

Nodding, Jerry added, "When I was in middle school, I really wanted to be in the band. Mom brought me to lessons and encouraged me, but learning how to play the guitar was tough." Jerry paused looking down at his hands. "I just couldn't move these fingers the way the instructor was telling me to. The real breakthrough came when Mom suggested I learn how to play Christmas songs." Adam and Evie were nodding to indicate they remembered. "Because I knew the rhythm of those songs, I played them in my head and in my hands." Jerry was smiling, thinking of how awesome it felt to make music with his guitar. He pictured Jeanette listening as he played her favorite Christmas song. He picked up his phone. "I'm sending her an acoustic guitar version of 'Oh Come, All Ye Faithful.' And I'm reminding her that I have faith in her." He texted as everyone looked on.

"Great idea! Your mom will love that!" Adam was letting their enthusiasm carry him. "I remember how you struggled with the guitar. But you didn't give up," Adam pointed at Jerry smiling. "You really practiced! And your mom loved hearing you play. We both did!" Adam was thinking of all Jerry's concerts and events they attended together. Jerry had made the middle school band and then went on to play in several bands throughout high school.

"I know you don't play anymore, but you were so good!" Evie chimed in with a smile.

Alex was also nodding. "You were, Jerry. Guys, I can think of a few times Mom encouraged me. You all know how important soccer has always been to me." As Alex paused, he thought about all the teams and positions he had played over the years, including the adult league he enjoyed, currently postponed by the shutdown. "Besides the support at every practice and game, I'm thinking about when I couldn't play. During the injuries," he paused and smiled at Adam, "I'm sure Dad remembers. When I was hurt, I sat on the sidelines. Mom knew how I hated that and would keep reminding me that I could play again soon." He thought about his irrational fear that each injury was career-ending; her comments had alleviated that. He picked up his phone and smiled as he texted. "This is just a time-out, Mom. It won't last long. Then you'll be back in the game." After he sent that message, he sent another. "We need you!"

Jerry and Evie chimed in with their agreement.

Pride and love split Adam's face. *Jeanette, you are right—our children are fantastic!* "Guys, that was great! Your mom will *love* those texts." Everyone had shared hope; unfortunately, it was short-lived. In a few minutes, the smiles began to wane.

Jerry asked, "What more can we do, Dad? I mean, it's so hard to think straight and carry on with 'normal' when Mom is in the hospital fighting. This is all just so surreal ..." Jerry's heartfelt words articulated everyone's feelings. Evie was crying again, and Alex was visibly fighting tears. "It's like Mom on FaceTime and texts exists in some alternate universe ..." Beth put her arm around Jerry as he choked on his emotion.

Adam absorbed the waves of distress flowing through the ether. *Oh, Jeanette, we need you here! What could I possibly say to alleviate their pain?* "Keep sending Mom your love. That's all we can do. At least she knows she's not alone." *Or does she feel abandoned?* Her constant talking was a running joke in the family. She had, on occasion, been asked to "dial it down." For all of them to notice that she wasn't talking as much as usual was disturbing.

The group was again subdued. What a roller coaster of emotion! They agreed to meet via Zoom the next day, regardless of updates from the hospital. Everyone's anxiety eased after seeing each other. Adam reflected on the first positive takeaway from Jeanette's illness. Going forward, having achieved this closeness via Zoom relieved his concern about his children being spread among three different states. This last call proved that although they were now adults living independent lives, they were still close.

The minute the Zoom call ended, Evie called Adam. "Dad, is Mom going to die?" Evie whispered.

"Oh, baby, I hope not," Adam answered. He listened to his daughter cry and his heart broke. He heaved a huge sigh and put his own feelings aside. In total Dad mode, he responded, "You know, Evie, it does no good to imagine the worst. We have no control over what happens to Mom. All we can do is try to stay positive. Think about it, Evie, what would Mom's advice be for this situation?" he asked.

She took a minute. "She is a very positive person. She would want me to stay positive."

"Absolutely. You know she's fighting this thing with all she's got."

"Yeah, but Dad, we're talking about COVID ..."

"Evie, I know. *I know*. But she hasn't given up yet, and neither should we."

She drew strength from the conviction in his voice. "You're right, Dad," Evie admitted. "Thanks," she sniffled.

"That's what I'm here for," Adam replied. "I assume Kevin was delayed on the work call. Is he finished yet?" Adam asked.

"No, he's still on the call. But it's OK. Where can he go?" Evie joked.

"That's right; we're all hostages! Love you, kiddo. Call anytime," Adam reminded her as they disconnected.

He immediately laid his head on the table. He knew he gave Evie great advice; all he had to do was follow it. But fear prevailed and hijacked his thoughts, which went round and round. He was utterly spent!

When Lucy went to the kitchen door and scratched for relief, Adam discovered it was a different universe outside the house. It was a beautiful spring day! He decided to take Lucy for a short walk, staying away from any neighbors. Staying at home meant individuals and families were walking throughout the day. He grabbed his cell phone just in case he got a call from the hospital and left the house via the front door. The outdoors was refreshing, and Lucy was so happy! It eased his anxiety somewhat and put a small smile on Adam's face. "Mom's going to be OK," Adam reassured the pup as they walked. At the end of the walk, Adam realized he had repeated the words at least a dozen times. He was trying to convince himself.

After the Zoom call ended, Alex and Sue sat quietly at their kitchen table. "Are you ready to talk yet?" Sue asked. She knew her husband, and Alex preferred not to talk about problems upfront. Especially big problems. He liked to analyze the situation and then deliver his commentary.

"I think so," Alex surprised her by saying. "I'm so scared we'll lose her," Alex swallowed hard. "I'm scared our son will never meet her," he confirmed. Sue immediately hugged her husband.

"I totally understand," Sue agreed. "First, it's only been a few days. I believe your mom will pull through." She paused, gauging how much she should say. His open look urged her to go on. "But think about this: *if* she doesn't make it," Adam's eyes flew to hers and she hurriedly added, "that's a big *if*." When he nodded, she continued, "Your mom will always be with our baby through us–through you. *If* you have to, *you* can bring her to him. *You* can tell him about her." They shared a quiet moment while they both wiped at tears.

Finally, Alex sighed and replied, "Yes. I can do that. We can do that," he said smiling slightly at Sue. "Thank you!" He placed his hand on her protruding stomach, and at that very moment, the baby kicked. "Oh, that was definitely a goal, soccer player!" Alex joked as they both laughed. He realized that he did want his son to love playing soccer as much as he did. He could imagine them sharing sports together. That made him think about his mother and how much she supported Alex and his siblings in their sporting endeavors. She never played organized youth sports and admitted she wasn't an athlete. She had said repeatedly, "I like playing games, but I was never good at anything." She was, however, an excellent spectator. In fact, she'd say, "Anything you three do is much more exciting than what I do." And she did love attending as many games as she could and cheering on her children from the sidelines.

Thinking of all the games he played, Alex recalled when he was younger and his father was the coach of one of his travel soccer teams. He always thought his dad was cool, and so did his teammates. Following a win, Dad, not Coach Adam, would meet Alex at the halfway line and flip him. Sure, the wins were exciting. However, it was the losses that haunted Alex. He had long since learned how to handle defeat, but when he was young his mother's attitude bothered him. While Coach Adam would shake his head at the team's performance, his mother would espouse some cliché like, "You win some, you lose some," and it was supposed to be better. Oh, she supported him in every way, only to let him down by not understanding how *important* each game was to him. Worse, she gave one of her disappointing placating lines while hugging him. When it was a playoff or championship game, her attitude downright annoyed him. If he lost, he would avoid her just not to hear her useless advice. It hurt his feelings to think his mother didn't understand him.

Watching Sue knead bread at the counter, Alex thought about Jeanette's game advice. He'd always been a passionate player. And while it may have been a childhood fantasy, he was not a professional soccer player; he was a financial manager. What sounded so flippant when he was a child in the moment, at some point sounded both rational and circumspect. Alex realized now that she had been helping him manage his expectations. Especially considering she was right; none of those games actually changed his life. At this point he could admit that sometimes he blamed himself far too much after a loss. Her hugs and adages, given one at a time and seemingly insensitive, had eventually sunk in. His mother had helped him learn that competition was healthy, self-recrimination was not. Those words of wisdom were born of her love for him. As an expectant father, Alex realized he would be telling his own son (God willing) similar sage advice. As Sue covered the bread for proofing, Alex picked up his phone and sent his mother another text. "Thanks, Mom, for helping me to celebrate all the wins and the losses along the way. I love you. Get better!"

"Who are you texting?" Sue asked.

"Just sending another text to my mother," Alex replied.

"Good. Let's send her as many healing thoughts as possible," Sue agreed.

When Alex continued to stare blankly at his phone, she prompted. "What?"

"Sue, I'm scared," Alex whispered. "What if she doesn't text back?"

Quiet. Again. Annie, the bundle of energy, had seemed even larger today than yesterday. Respiratory therapy was exhausting. Reclining on the chair with HGTV playing without volume, Jeanette recalled this morning's conversation with Dr. Roman.

"How are you feeling, Jeanette?" Dr. Roman had asked while typing into the computer. For some reason, today his head-to-toe white PPE reminded her more of Mr. Clean than an alien.

"A bit better. Not coughing as much all the time." It was the first time she thought something had improved, and she was eager to share.

"Still experiencing coughing spasms?" At her nod, he continued. "How about the heaviness in your chest?"

"Still there. Still sore," she placed her hand on her throat, "and still have that headache."

Dr. Roman nodded as he updated her file. "Nurse Patti told me that you were upset yesterday?" he asked. When she didn't immediately answer, Dr. Roman stopped typing and looked directly at her.

"Well, yes. It's upsetting to be here–" she gestured toward him, "no offense to any of you–but I'm terrified!"

He remained quiet until she added, "Doctor, I'm afraid! I'm afraid COVID will kill me!" Admitting her darkest thought was like pulling the ripcord. The sobbing tears flowed freely. Then came the coughing spasm.

Dr. Roman patiently waited. He poured more water into the cup on the table from the plastic pitcher and offered her the straw. Finally, she sipped and fell against the back of the chair.

She could see his breath expelled beneath his surgical mask as he moved away. "Jeanette, it's perfectly understandable that you're upset. You are very ill. You can see that the medications are working on the cough somewhat. That's good. Your being anxious makes it more difficult to breathe, and can induce those wracking coughing spasms. Have you noticed that?" he asked gently.

Jeanette nodded.

"I'm adding another medication to alleviate some of your anxiety and help you breathe easier: Xanax. Have you taken it before?" he asked.

"Nope." Her head and heart were pounding, but she couldn't get a handle on the reason for it. *I'm taking so many medications now; most of the time I don't even know what it is! Yet, if Dr. Roman thinks it can help ...*

"Let's try it, Jeanette. It should ease your racing thoughts."

Shortly after he left, she had been given her first dose. Jeanette did feel calmer. A bit tired and detached. She immediately slept, and then Annie, the respiratory therapist woke her. Reaching for the buzzing phone which had been plugged into the wall, Jeanette realized that she had missed many posts on WhatsApp. She smiled and let gratitude and her family's love wash over her. She appreciated their positive vibe, and she wanted to return the favor.

JEANETTE: You're the best! I love you all so much! Had a busy morning with therapy and napping, but feeling better now! Coughing has improved!

She watched as one by one her family loved her post and responded with even more words of encouragement.

Maybe it was the Xanax, but the rest of the day flew by quickly. Jeanette accepted the hospital routine and even found an appetite to pick at the crusty, lukewarm macaroni and cheese for dinner. She spoke with each of her children and felt an overall drowsy tolerance for her situation.

After climbing back into the bed, Jeanette spoke with Adam last. Noticing her sagging efforts to hold the phone up during FaceTime, he suggested that she arrange the phone on the overbed table instead.

"There you go again," she laughed, "solving all my problems."

He laughed, then turned serious and said, "Jeanette, I'm so sorry that I can't fix this. You have no idea how much I wish I could."

She laughed at the audacity of the love of her life. "Adam, everyone knows you can't fix COVID." He swallowed hard and looked away. She reminded him of how she felt. "Adam, we've had a wonderful life together. Whatever happens, *you've* given me a wonderful life, including three fantastic children."

He had heard that before. "Yeah, I know. But why? If one of us has to be sick, why you?"

For the first time, she recognized the depth of his despair. "I'm so sorry, Adam. I wish ..." What could she say? How could she help him? "Hey, neither of us is responsible for this nightmare. I'm here, so you have to be there. You *have* to be there; the kids need you." He just stared at her. "If it were *you* here, what would you tell me?" She tried unsuccessfully to stifle a yawn. "You're going to have to tell that to yourself." He grunted a reply, and she added, "Besides, I feel better. I'll be home soon."

He reached out to touch the phone and nodded, they blew kisses to each other and ended the call.

Jeanette was drifting off to the light of HGTV when another coughing spasm struck. Unlike the usual dry cough, this time she felt mucous in her throat. She wouldn't realize until the morning the seriousness of this new symptom.

12

Monday, April 20, 2020 - Day #8

Harry, Evie's orange tabby, purred loudly on her lap while she petted him. When Kevin came into the living room carrying two glasses of iced tea, Harry protested loudly and jumped away. He tolerated Kevin, but it was plain that Evie was his momma. Generally, both Evie and Kevin ignored Harry's indignance.

"Oh, really," Kevin remarked lightheartedly.

Taking the glass from his hand, Evie blurted, "I feel guilty."

"Huh?" Kevin questioned wondering what he missed.

"Mom talks so much. Sometimes *too* much. We've *all* thought it," she admitted.

"And you feel guilty for thinking that?"

She nodded and sipped her tea.

Before she could answer, Kevin's phone rang. "Oh, the call from the client I've been waiting for. I'll be a bit … are you OK?" he asked as he stood with his tea.

"Yeah, go ahead. We'll talk later," she smiled.

Kevin walked into the bedroom, which served as his office, answering the phone and closing the door behind him. Harry returned to her lap, and she absently petted him while Evie continued her train of thought. Evie was thinking of all the times she tuned out her mother while on the phone with her. Mom was always talking about the dog, school, her students—topics that were mostly unexciting to Evie. While that was true, Evie tried very hard not to come across as disinterested. She had cultivated a few phrases like, "Oh, yeah?" and, "Uh huh," that were totally noncommittal. Sometimes her mother would say, "It sounds like you're busy." Mostly Evie would jump on that excuse to end the call.

Really, it wasn't as bad as it used to be. Evie remembered when she was in high school, and she would totally avoid her mother if she could. It annoyed Evie that her mother wanted so many details of her life; consequently, Evie was always extremely careful because inevitably the conversation would get too personal. As a result, there was a time when she just didn't get along with her mother. Luckily, neither Evie nor Jeanette liked drama, so the verbal assaults Evie's girlfriends claimed with their moms never happened in the Remington household. At its worst, there seemed to be an underlying tension, like a low-grade fever. Also, Evie had two older brothers to divert Mom's attention, not to mention a job and a husband. Oh, there was no doubt that Jeanette wanted a closer relationship with Evie at that time, and Evie was well aware.

As the memories flooded back of her high-school life, Evie recalled the daily routine of classes, the faces of teachers and friends, and the angst of an unknown future. That reminded her of the incident that literally changed the landscape of her high-school existence. As long as she could remember, Evie played soccer; it was in her DNA. She played with her brothers in the backyard before she was old enough to join recreational teams. From there she progressed to a travel team. As a freshman, she battled her way onto the varsity soccer team roster, finally earning playing time toward the end of the season. As a result, she spent all her time with the team; they were her friend group. When they weren't playing, they were fundraising or gathering for pasta dinners. Her identity in that school was as a soccer player. As a sophomore, on a beautiful fall day in early October, Evie was fouled and broke her arm during the fall. Her mom was on the sidelines, and they went immediately to the Emergency Room. Coincidentally, it was the same hospital Mom was in right now, St. Peter's. At the beginning, the team rallied around her, especially since the foul resulted in the game-winning penalty kick. But as time went on, the injury distanced Evie from the game, and another player filled her position. The backup was also good, took the opportunity to shine, and the coach and teammates readily embraced her. Unfortunately, Evie's break was complicated and slow to heal. As a result, the season and team moved on without her. Little by little she no longer fit in among the group.

At first, Evie was devastated and felt at odds. She fully intended to rejoin the team, so she was in a kind of limbo. Drama unfolded when certain members of the team liked the backup player more than Evie, and she became the target of gossip. Other teammates felt the pressure, and where once they invited her to join at lunch or after school, Evie was left out more and more. She felt like she lost her identity and struggled with her new reality. She worked hard to get her soccer skills back up to speed with her travel team to be ready for tryouts as a junior. Yet as time went on, she mourned the loss of the varsity team and her position among them.

When she tried out over the summer for the upcoming season, she didn't feel the same. Being with the girls, she experienced snide comments and clique behavior. Evie came to the conclusion that she no longer wanted to be involved with these girls and play at this level of competition. She still loved to play soccer, which she did with her travel team. So, she resigned from the varsity team, which the coach did not agree with. The team took it as a snub, and she suffered even more drama. However, Evie discovered more time for homework, herself, and reconnected with a few former middle school friends. That was the end of her high school soccer career.

Her mother's insidious questioning during this period exacerbated the issue. She couldn't accept that Evie would give up her hard-won position on the team. Not that her mother cared about the popularity aspect, just that Evie understood the impact of her decision to quit the team. Her mom also believed soccer was in her DNA. This played upon Evie's own doubts about relinquishing her spot. Once Evie opened up about the way the girls had treated her, she had Jeanette's full support and understanding. She laughed as she remembered Jeanette saying, "But those girls seemed so nice!" As if a teenager showing polite manners to a parent could be trusted!

If Evie struggled with her newfound free time at home, her mother made her stop looking at her phone or computer and play board games. At the time, Evie thought Jeanette to be intrusive, clingy and out of touch. With her two older brothers away in college, Evie was the last sibling at home. Board games were for middle schoolers. Further, she was stressed about her own grades and future college plans. What made her mother think playing Scrabble would make everything better? Evie was convinced that her mother needed a hobby.

Well, they played Scrabble, Life, Skip-Bo, cards, and many other games. On long weekends when her travel team was not playing in a tournament, they completed puzzles. When Evie leaned into it, those turned out to be the relaxing moments of respite from the stress of growing up. Sometimes they'd clean up together after dinner, and cajole her dad into joining them. He'd insist that he wasn't interested in games, but always had a good time. There had been many stressful situations since where Evie applied the same concept; she and Kevin often enjoyed a game of chess. Looking back now, she realized her mother was helping her to slow down and relax. Further, Jeanette had always encouraged and supported Evie no matter the goal.

It had been a long time since she thought about high school, but she recognized now that her mother's love and acceptance facilitated Evie's transition. Oh, Evie knew that her parents had given her a stable childhood that enabled her to focus and excel in school, thereby ensuring a top college choice and subsequent career. And she was grateful for that. However, Evie didn't always have time to chat. On the daily, Jeanette talked a lot! That was the way her mother stayed connected and demonstrated her love. For once, Evie thought of herself and her love language. What kind of mother would Evie be? How would she demonstrate *her* love for *her* children?

He returned so quietly she didn't see Kevin until he was standing in front of her. "You're smiling now. What are you thinking?" Kevin asked smiling himself.

"I'm thinking about our family one day, about being a mom when the time is right."

Kevin sat down facing her, sending Harry scurrying away, and took her hands.

Her smile faded. "I do feel guilty that I didn't always want to talk to my mom when she called or texted, and now, I mean, if she doesn't make it—"

"Evie, don't think like that. Believe me, everyone thinks their mom calls too much!" For emphasis, he repeated, "*Everyone!*" He was rewarded with a return of her grin. "And remember, we agreed with your dad to stay positive."

"Yep. Positive thoughts only," she agreed. "Kevin, I still need my mom —" she trailed off.

"Of course, you do!" Kevin soothed Evie as they embraced with Harry scowling at him from the floor. There was nothing else to say.

The buzzing of the phone continued from seemingly far away as she struggled to consciousness. Recognizing the reruns on HGTV, she knew it was late morning. By the time she lifted it from her lap, the phone was silent. Besides the missed FaceTime from Evie, there were new notifications on both her texts and WhatsApp to read. She tried to make herself more comfortable on the beside chair by moving the pillows when another coughing spasm erupted. Coughing into the tissue in her hand confirmed her fear; the red-stained mucous appeared again. *I thought I was getting better.*

At that moment, Dr. Roman rustled into the room with the cart.

"Good morning, Jeanette! How are you feeling today?" he asked brightly while logging onto the computer.

Mr. Clean immediately came to mind again. *Can doctors clean COVID?* She quickly held out the tissue in her hand for him to see. She held her breath waiting for his reaction.

Dr. Roman looked serious as he approached the bed to check the red-smeared tissue and his patient. He nodded as he asked, "You coughed up blood?" At her nod, he asked, "When did that happen, Jeanette?"

"Just now," she replied, complying with his examination. "What does it mean?"

Aside from her breathing and the crinkling of his PPE, they were both quiet while he listened to her lungs and checked her pulse. He moved away to make notes on the computer. "How's the anxiety?" he asked.

Uh-oh. He didn't answer my question. "It was better until I saw this ..."

Finishing his typing, he stepped closer, grasped the tissue between his gloved thumb and forefinger, leaned toward the small trashcan between the bed and chair, and dropped it inside. He placed his hand on her shoulder as he spoke. "Jeanette, coughing blood indicates the presence of blood clots in your lungs. This is not uncommon; we are finding that blood clots in general are a symptom caused by this coronavirus. I'll be adding a blood thinner to your medications to decrease the possibility of large clots forming. That could pose a serious complication. However, coughing up a small bit of blood is not wholly unexpected, Jeanette," he said reassuringly.

She focused on processing his words. His tone and answer were calming, but she still wasn't sure. "OK, what does that mean? Am I getting worse?" she asked.

"Well, your latest chest X-ray and blood work still indicate your body is actively fighting the virus." As he was talking, the pointed mask beneath the clear visor was moving in and out with his words. She was hyper-focused on that movement and thinking about how slowly and carefully he was speaking.

"Jeanette, you're in acute respiratory distress. The oxygen your body needs can be delivered through the hi-flow cannula, and we're giving you all the medications we can to reduce the inflammation in your lungs and help your body heal."

Huh? "Yes or no, doctor," she demanded, "am I getting worse?"

He deliberated behind his glasses, blinking rapidly at least five times before responding. "Yes, Jeanette, this symptom indicates a progression of the virus."

All the pent-up breath expelled from her damaged lungs. She looked down at her phone as another text from her loving family arrived. *I would be crazy if one of them were here. Should I tell them about this latest development? Is it kinder to be honest or keep their hopes up?*

"What next, Dr. Roman? Be honest." Her eyes and voice were flat.

"Well, Jeanette, your body will continue to fight the mayhem this virus is unleashing," he said returning to the screen. He was logging out of the system and obviously trying to wrap up his visit.

"Which means what?" Using her finger, she pointed to herself. "While my body is fighting, what will you do?" The quaver in her voice compelled him to turn back toward her to see her pointing directly at him.

"Jeanette, we still have a few more treatment options available. Let's not get ahead of ourselves. I assure you we are all doing our best here, and new protocols are being developed. Scientists around the world are working to fight this infection." His sincerity was obvious. He reached up beneath his clear face visor to scratch his forehead with a gloved finger.

His gesture looked absolutely ridiculous to her and made him seem a bit confused. *OH MY GOD, he doesn't know ... he doesn't know ... If I will survive ... or not.*

A peacefully sleeping Lucy yelped from beneath the kitchen table at the sharp tone. "Finally! Where have you been?" he fumed when Jeanette joined his FaceTime. He didn't try to hide his exasperation. She hadn't answered several calls, forcing him to call the nurses' station for help. When Nurse Patti reported Jeanette was indeed in her room and awake, his worry intensified. Patti volunteered to check on Jeanette and her cell phone, and she suggested he call Jeanette back in five minutes unless she called him first. Apparently, that worked.

He stared intently at his wife and knew immediately something was off. Instinct told him to hold it together, so he gave her space to respond. Lucy belly-crawled inch by inch from under the table. Eventually, she made it to where Adam was standing against the kitchen counter and laid her paw on his foot.

"Right here," she responded woodenly. She was absently adjusting the nasal cannula over her left ear and squinting at the phone. Jeanette was audibly breathing in and out of her mouth in short puffs.

"Honey, shouldn't you be breathing through your nose? That's where the oxygen is," Adam reminded her.

She nodded, closed her eyes and her mouth.

He waited, but no other response was forthcoming. "How are you feeling?" he inquired.

Jeanette did not open her eyes. "Same."

Frustrated and slightly annoyed, Adam demanded, "What's wrong, Jeanette?"

She opened her eyes. "Huh? You mean besides the fact that I'm in a hospital with COVID? That a virus has hijacked my body? That everything hurts and I can barely breathe? Adam, it's *ALL* wrong!"

Even with the uneven gasps taken in between the words, her sudden vehemence startled him. His Jeanette, when pushed, did not get angry; she grew quiet. But his Jeanette had never been so sick. Adam immediately regretted his harsh tone. "I know, honey, I know. It is so wrong," he appeased.

"You have no idea," she whispered brokenly, closing her eyes and turning her head away.

"Jeanette, please, talk to me. What's going on in your pretty head?" he entreated.

She scoffed. "Nothing pretty here. I'm getting worse, Adam. It's getting more and more of me every second–" she was interrupted by a coughing spasm. Feebly, she reached for the cup beside the stationary phone and sipped the straw. "I gotta go," she whispered with tears running down her cheeks. He watched as they hit the cannula and traveled toward her nose. She looked totally beaten.

Adam took off the kid gloves. "No, you can't go!" His demanding tone brought her eyes back to him. He spoke quickly and firmly to keep her full attention. "Jeanette, you listen to me: I love you. We all love you.

You must fight. I know it's hard; I know it hurts. Don't give up. Please, I'm begging you, don't give up. We *need* you ..." He wiped at his cheeks to gather his composure.

Adam's heartfelt emotional appeal appeared to reach through her despair. Dabbing with a tissue from the table, she took several deep, painful, hitching, sobbing breaths like a child after a tantrum. They both held the line as they grappled individually with the hand fate had dealt.

"I'm so afraid!" she murmured.

"I know, honey, so am I." He instantly lamented admitting that to her. He was supposed to be her pillar of strength.

But she continued as if he hadn't even spoken. "I feel so alone ..."

"No, you're not alone. We're with you. We're all with you, Jeanette. Just answer our texts and calls, would you?"

"I feel alone ..."

"Well, that's because you didn't answer our calls and texts. If you did, we would have told you that we're *all* here for you. We love you, Jeanette."

Lucy stood and barked her raspy bark at that moment.

"See, Lucy loves you, too," Adam confirmed and turned the phone so Jeanette could see her lab.

Her eyes smiled as she whispered, "I love you both, too."

Adam sighed. "That's my girl. Hang in there. We've overcome many obstacles over the years, Jeanette. Don't forget!" Even though he was wagging a finger at her, his relief was evident in the lighter tone.

"Yep," she confirmed.

"Remember the year after we bought our first house? Mortgaged to the hilt when we discovered we needed to remove the oil tank to the tune of

$6,000 dollars?" he reminded her. She grunted and he continued. "Or right after we had Evie, when my mom's health started to go downhill, and she had to move in with us."

By the look on her face, he knew he had broken through. Bringing out the big guns by reminding her of the most challenging six months of their marriage diffused her and reminded her she was not alone.

"It's always been the two of us, Jeanette."

She nodded. "You're right again; you know I hate that," she admitted as she smiled and closed her eyes. Her outburst had visibly cost her, yet she did have a bit more spirit.

"That's how I roll," he quipped. "You look wiped. Is that why you're in the bed today and not the chair?"

She nodded and closed her eyes.

"Go ahead and take a nap. Would you mind if I stayed on the phone?"

She shook her head no. "Creepy. Call later."

"Promise you'll answer?"

"Yep ... sorry ..." she was fading fast.

Adam held onto the phone for long minutes after they ended the call. For the first time since she'd been admitted, he saw defeat. If he was scared before, now he was downright terrified. Adam wasn't stupid; he realized being in the hospital with COVID was precarious at best. Still, his Jeanette of the past was a quiet warrior. He thought of how stalwart she had been through her pregnancies. At the time, he was amazed at how she could bear the massive changes in her body. She wasn't always thrilled–especially during childbirth–but they were together; they drew strength from each other.

Indeed, Adam and Jeanette survived during that most difficult period when they dealt with three children under the age of six and his mother's recovery from breast cancer surgery. For six months they managed babies and toddlers and doctors and hospitals. To this day they still don't know how they made it through. Thankfully, his mother was able to return to her independent life for many years to follow. He had witnessed Jeanette in a variety of states over the years, and this could be just one more version of her–as long as she was *present* with him. He could accept their physical separation as long as he had her smiles, words, or emojis. Today's Jeanette was distant. Was his wife slipping away? *No, you got her back.*

Her paw scratched his jeaned leg and interrupted his gloom. "Lucy," he said as he leaned down to pet his lab, "that was perfect timing. To quote Winston Churchill: 'Never, never, never give up.'" She immediately dropped and presented herself for belly rubs. He happily complied.

After Dr. Roman left, a stunned Jeanette stared unseeing at the Property Brothers while her phone continued to buzz with notifications. She couldn't bring herself to look or respond. *She was getting worse.* Eight days ago, she refused to believe she could even have this virus. Today, she could no longer hide from the truth. She was by nature an optimist, but COVID was a formidable foe. Unable to resist, she switched the TV to a major network currently reporting the number of people testing positive for the virus as well as the number dead on a crawler on the bottom of the screen. Without her glasses, the numbers were difficult to discern. She was about to change the channel when the unrecognizable reporter clearly stated that the American death toll as of yesterday exceeded 40,000. Jeanette mouthed 40,000 in amazement. Incredible! So many had died of the very coronavirus that also hijacked her body–and just in this country alone. The blurry chart on the screen gave the death toll across the world. *What hope do I have if all of them died?*

Jeanette began to hyperventilate and a coughing spasm followed with more blood. *What makes me think I can survive?* Panting from the exertion, Jeanette continued to watch the numbers scroll by. *COVID has reduced those people to a statistic!* Her phone buzzed again indicating her family–all healthy–wanted to connect. Anger welled up like a smoking volcano about to erupt. *Why me? How did I even get it?* She struggled against that victim mentality. Reasonably, she thought every one of the 40,000 people who perished may also have wondered the same thing. Jeanette was exhausted and under so much medication, rational thought was difficult to maintain. Buzz. *None of this is rational! COVID is crazy!*

Buzz. She looked at her phone and WhatsApp, text, and missing call notifications. Wrestling with emotional turmoil, she had nothing. In the end, Jeanette felt betrayed by her disease-riddled body and everyone else. *I'm all alone.* Buzz. The messages continued to mount. When lunch arrived, she didn't touch it. She turned off the TV and wallowed in self-pity instead. She was convinced no one uninfected by COVID could understand how she felt when Patti came in.

"Knock, knock. Excuse me, Mrs. Remington. Your husband just called the desk. He's worried because you're not answering your phone." Patti's PPE squished as she quickly crossed the room.

Her attention drawn to the PPE, Jeanette thought about the aliens flitting in and out of her room. *Even the doctors and nurses are protected and keep their distance.* The crushing isolation was maddening.

"I see you're awake. Do you mind if I check your phone?" Jeanette made no move as she did so. "Well, it looks charged, but let's plug it in." Taking a closer look, Patti remarked, "You look a bit uncomfortable. Since you've already had your physical therapy for today, would you prefer to be in bed?"

The two of them worked together to move Jeanette into the bed. Patti carried on minimal small talk requiring no response from Jeanette as she made her charge more comfortable with strategic pillows and blankets. Her task completed, Patti leaned toward Jeanette. Eying her patient, she asked, "Everything OK? Are you mad at your husband or something?"

Before Jeanette could answer, Patti's clipped radio beeped and "Code Ocean" was announced. Patti closed her eyes and took a deep, calming breath. "I have to go right now, but I'll be back."

When Jeanette didn't respond, Patti heaved an exasperated sigh. "Listen, Mrs. Remington. I told your husband I'd check on you, and he should call again. Please answer when he does, or I'll be in trouble!" Walking quickly out of the room, Patti added, "I'll be back as soon as I can with your meds."

It was a good thing for both of them that Jeanette answered when Adam FaceTimed again. For Jeanette, Adam's call had been a rope rescue off the cliff of desolation. *He's not physically here, but I can always count on Adam.* Energy expended from her outburst, Jeanette barely managed to respond to her family's texts and WhatsApp posts with emojis.

She was so proud of her children. They had grown into genuine people who found like-minded partners. Jeanette was confident that each couple would build their own oasis in this unpredictable world. She and Adam had done so; they would do so as well. Balm for her frayed nerves, their collective love cushioned her proverbial bed, and Jeanette was drifting off when Patti returned. The over-scheduled nurse exchanged little small talk with her patient as she competently administered her medication and updated the chart.

With the TV off and the door closed, the quiet was deafening. There was no visual or sound distraction from her illness. The oxygen made a slight hissing noise, but mostly Jeanette could hear only her own puffy breathing. Other than a sense of day or night, the odd-angled window provided no view. Listening intently, she felt a shift. Jeanette welcomed the quiet and calm into her troubled soul. So, she had COVID and was getting worse. Between the virus and her own upheaval, she had never felt so completely depleted. *How should I feel?* One thing she did know:

emotional outbursts would not help. It was time to face the music; Jeanette accepted the coronavirus.

Unbidden, a memory surfaced of Jeanette's mother. It was so vivid; Jeanette could feel her mother's warm, soft cheek on her lips as she kissed her hello. Palma was sitting in a wheelchair, leaning forward with her forearms crossed, wearing her favorite yellow and black blouse. She was completely dressed, down to her tied black orthopedic shoes. In fact, she looked like she was ready to discharge. It was a double room in a hospital rehabilitation center Palma had stayed in several times. Her mother had suffered a degenerative kidney disease for many years, succumbing when she was 82. During her years of failing health, Palma had been hospitalized and then sent to rehabilitation facilities too many times to count. Each time Palma slipped a little farther away.

During this visit, Jeanette was sitting on the tidily made bed helping her mother select the meals for the next week. Palma was an adorable little old lady with short white hair neatly brushed and soft brown eyes. She had an engaging smile which every care worker seemed to respond to. Twice a day she was engaged in physical therapy to regain her balance so she could navigate the stairs at home. Having already had lunch, they were waiting for the physical therapist to collect Palma for her afternoon session.

"Mom, Sunday sounds good! Which one: beef brisket or lemon chicken?" Jeanette asked, pen poised to circle the selection.

"They always do that," Palma complained. "Two good choices on one day!" Palma looked down at her hands to think. "Brisket," she declared looking up.

"Brisket," Jeanette confirmed circling the meal. "Monday is open-faced meatloaf sandwich or roast veal with gravy." Pen in the air, she anticipated her mother's answer.

Palma wrinkled her nose at the menu choice. "Neither."

Jeanette smiled. "I knew you would say that. Remember you can always substitute a sandwich. Or–"

"Jeanette," her mother interrupted. She reached forward, touching Jeanette's penned hand as they locked eyes. "This one meal doesn't matter. What matters is fighting every day to get better."

Surprised at her mother's change in tone, Jeanette tried to connect the dots in this conversation.

"I'll take a grilled cheese sandwich," Palma said pointing at the menu. "Now turn that paper in and bring me to physical therapy," Palma made a motion with her hand to hurry up. She raised her voice with urgency and announced, "I need to get better, so I can go home already!"

Faced with such determination, Jeanette could do nothing but obey.

Jeanette smiled weakly at the memory and admired her mother's fighting spirit once again. Palma had such a strong resolve to always improve; she refused to consider the alternative.

More moments with Palma swam in her mind. As more tears slipped into the pillowcase, Jeanette could feel her mother's warm, arthritic hand in hers. *I miss you so much, Mom!* Even all these years later, the sharp loss felt like a hole in her heart. When no more tears would come, Jeanette sobbed and coughed. Thinking of all the health issues her mom had endured, Jeanette realized acceptance did not mean resignation. *I want to go home.* Time and again, her mother had done everything in her power to recuperate and return to the life she loved. Jeanette could, too. *I want to go home.* She would fight COVID with all her might.

13

Tuesday, April 21, 2020 - Day #9

Since the stay-at-home order, they had the same routine. Both she and Jerry were working from their Chicago apartment. Beth had adopted a sofa table in the living room, and he was working from the desk in the bedroom. That way they could close the door and not disturb each other on work calls. After her early morning meeting online, she went into the small galley kitchen. Finding the Moccamaster carafe empty, she went about grinding more coffee beans as she rinsed the residue from the first pot. After refilling the water reservoir, she leaned against the counter and watched the water drip. Lost in the contemplation of how much their life had changed in recent months, she didn't realize Jerry was there until he kissed the back of her neck.

Eventually, she filled her favorite mug as Jerry filled his mug–both from their last vacation in Ireland. All their traveling plans, as well as their honeymoon plans, were curtailed by COVID. She peered at her handsome husband, noticing the tiredness evident around his eyes. "Anything new with your mom other than the WhatsApp?" she inquired, sipping tentatively at the hot brew. Jeanette had posted "Happy Tuesday," and everyone had responded with some encouragement.

Jerry released his pent-up breath. "No, but at least Mom has posted words instead of just emojis." He turned his full mug round and round on the counter. "Only two, mind you. But still, it's better than yesterday." Jerry retrieved the milk and added a splash to his coffee. "I texted Alex and Evie separately and we all agreed something was wrong; Mom hardly responded at all." Replacing the milk, he added, "But none of us wanted to ask in case it upset Dad." He turned back toward Beth.

Beth nodded and asked, "Why don't you FaceTime your mom today? It will make you feel better to see her." When Jerry didn't respond and continued to stare into his coffee she prompted, "Babe?"

Abruptly, Jerry turned away. "Maybe. I'm pretty busy. That client proposal I've been working on is due by 5," he responded. He took his coffee and returned to the bedroom closing the door behind him.

Beth stared at the door open-mouthed for a few minutes before pouring the rest of her coffee in the sink. She was walking on eggshells lately; Jerry was so edgy. Beth didn't want to say anything to upset him any more than he already was. *I'd be devastated if my mom were in the hospital with COVID!* She took a minute to text her own mother before returning to her makeshift office. There'd be plenty of time after 5 to FaceTime Jeanette.

In the bedroom, Jerry fell onto the bed and placed his face in his hands. Sheer terror washed over him. Yesterday, when his mom hadn't answered his texts or posted on WhatsApp, he feared the worst. Both he and Beth tried to avoid the news channels, but it still seeped in somehow. Death was everywhere in the country, especially in the New York metropolitan area where his parents lived. *What are the chances she can survive?* Corralling his run-away fear, he wiped his face and stood to pace around the bed.

Logically, he knew that even if he went to New Jersey weeks ago when his mother suggested it, she might still be sick. But he couldn't stop wondering if his being there would have made a difference. Not only did that thought haunt him, but he was always on a slow simmer about the changes this pandemic forced upon their lives. He tried to console himself with the knowledge that at least he was able to work from home. So many "non-essential" businesses had been shut down, including restaurants, retail stores, and public offices. Most of those employees either were getting paid less or not at all. One of Beth's friends managed a high-end store on Chicago's Magnificent Mile. She wasn't working, not getting paid, and not sure how she would be making her rent. Even though he and Beth, both consultants, could conduct meetings and continue their business online, he missed the separation of work and home. In the beginning, he found that both he and Beth put in too many work hours because the "office" was too accessible. To address this problem, they set timers. It was helping.

There were some benefits. He and Beth were enjoying more time together *sans* commuting as well as cooking delicious meals. Before the pandemic, they regularly had a packed freezer for efficiency. Long weekday work hours precluded cooking meals they preferred, so they usually spent Sunday cooking large meals that would be doled out for the week. Fortunately, there was a commissary on the first floor of their building which was usually well-stocked. Because only residents could shop there, they had continuous access to food, although not all products were available during this lockdown. Meanwhile, shortages were reported in many other areas in the city causing an uptick in violence. Unfortunately, the stress and fear of COVID and the economic repercussions were overwhelming for many. Everyone was hoping for the restrictions to be lifted and for life to return to normal. It was unclear to citizens of Chicago and across the country just when that would be possible.

True, the shutdown was stressful, but it was his mother battling the virus miles away that pushed him to the edge. He felt too disconnected, too removed. That's why he texted his brother and sister yesterday when Jeanette went no contact, worried that he would be the last to find out some crucial information. He consoled himself with the fact that his sister was also miles away and that no one could visit, not his brother or even his dad just in the next town. Also, there was the agreement.

Years ago, Dad broke his ankle and needed surgery to reset the injury. There were complications, and Dad wound up in the hospital for almost a week. Both Alex and Evie were still at home, but Jerry was away at college. He wanted to come home, which would have been difficult mid-semester. However, Mom and Dad called him together and convinced him to stay at school. Jerry had argued that he was far away and couldn't know for himself how serious the injury was. In response, it was his mom's idea to form the pact. They agreed that if anything serious happened at home while he was away, they would call and tell him immediately. He wouldn't come home at the end of the semester to find out some tragedy had happened a month earlier. They reasoned that it would be better for them to all deal with the issue at the same time. It would also free up his mind to focus totally on school, never having to worry what he was missing. In fact, his mom had made one of those calls when she totaled the family car. Thankfully, she walked away. She had also called to let him know when Evie had broken her arm during a high school soccer game. Jerry stopped pacing and texted his mother and father in a group text.

JERRY: Hey guys, I just wanted to remind you of our agreement from college. It still stands.

Both his mother and father replied with 👍

Almost immediately, Jeanette FaceTimed. He hesitated only a minute before accepting the call.

Jeanette waved. She was sitting in a chair and the camera was off-center; he saw half of her and the wall. As she fiddled with the phone on the table to adjust the picture, he took in her familiar wan face. "Working?" she asked.

"Yep, but I have time for you. How are you feeling, Mom?" Something unfurled deep in his chest. Beth was right; he did feel much better just seeing his mom's face. He didn't realize how scared he was.

She held out her hand to indicate so-so.

They shared a smile.

"No lie: this sucks," she announced.

He couldn't stop laughing from relief. This is exactly what he wanted, to know his mother would be honest. Jeanette's face registered her surprise at his reaction. She coughed, but he could see the smile around her mouth.

"That's what I hear!" he kidded. "Really, Mom, I'm worried I don't know what's going on there. I'm so far away!" Although he tried to keep the frustration out of his voice, he knew she heard it.

"Hard on you. Sorry." She pouted with sadness. She crossed her heart with her finger. "Promise you'll know."

They stayed on the call a bit longer. Jerry carried the conversation with small talk, mostly about what he and Beth were cooking and work. She yawned, and they wrapped it up. When Jeanette blew him a kiss and waved, he almost cried. *My mom is OK.* Jerry opened the door and peeked around the corner to be sure Beth was not on a work call before sharing the FaceTime conversation with her. He hugged and thanked Beth for knowing exactly what he needed. *Today, my mom is still here.* One day at a time. That's the only way to handle the unprecedented events that turned his world–nay, everyone on planet Earth's world– upside down. He returned to his desk and got to work on his slide deck.

She was still smiling from her conversation with Jerry when a knock sounded on the door. Dr. Roman purposefully strode into the room. Crinkling behind him in a single file were Patti and Annie pushing the computer cart. The white forms with their scrunching PPE halted across from Jeanette's chair. The silence that followed was filled with the click of Patti typing and rustling caused by Annie's finger wave. All three of them coming in together made Jeanette wary. *Uh oh!* Her smile became wooden.

"Hey, Jeanette," the doctor paused, "it's good to see you smiling." He pulled the cart closer so he could read from the screen. "Here are the symptoms we have so far this morning: fogginess, coughing seizures, heaviness in chest, shortness of breath, sore throat, headache, and coughing up bloody mucous. Any new symptoms to report?" the doctor asked as he closed the gap to assess Jeanette.

That's not enough? Jeanette shook her head no.

After his usual examination, he replaced the stethoscope around his neck. "Jeanette, as you know, you have ARDS, which is acute respiratory distress syndrome caused by COVID pneumonia. However, I have good news to report! Your latest X-ray and blood work indicate a slight improvement in your oxygen levels." He held up two fingers on his right hand to indicate an inch and waited patiently for the information to sink in.

Jeanette looked from Dr. Roman to a nodding Annie and Patti, who were giving two thumbs-up. Her eyes opened, and she sat forward a bit. Gesturing to herself she whispered, "Getting better?"

Dr. Roman's eyes squinted, and she knew he was also pleased. "That's what it means." He pointed to the computer, "This is very encouraging! Now, you are still battling COVID, Jeanette. But you're doing a great job. The next step is to wean you off the oxygen to see how your body responds. We'll do that, but after Annie conducts your therapy for today. In about two hours following, Patti will return and lower your oxygen level. We'll be continuing to closely monitor your progression." Another pause. "Any questions?"

Practically jumping off the chair, Jeanette asked, "When can I go home?"

All three aliens chuckled at that, and Dr. Roman placed his hand on her shoulder. He cautioned, "This is a good sign, but let's not get ahead of ourselves."

"Getting better!" she repeated with a sigh and cough as she fell back into the chair once again.

Annie stepped forward. "OK, Jeanette, it's time to put your money where your mouth is. Get going on your spirometer!" She commandeered the computer as Dr. Roman and Patti swished out of the room amid more chuckles and thumbs-up.

The past few days were a blur. Instead of sleeping upstairs in their bedroom, Adam was now sleeping in the family room. When he returned from dropping Jeanette off at the hospital, he sprayed Lysol on every surface upstairs and downstairs, including the family room, kitchen, and bathroom. Then he opened the windows to air it out so he and Lucy wouldn't gag. Lucy was doing a good job keeping him company, following him room to room all day long, and joining him overnight on the couch for sleepovers. The television had been playing constantly and was either tuned to Jeanette's favorite *HGTV* or the History Channel. Occasionally, he watched the local news, but only in small doses. Generally, he stayed in touch with the community through social media, which he also limited. Adam was still working from home to quarantine, but was feeling perfectly fine. *Where's the justice? It's not fair that Jeanette is so sick, and I don't even have a runny nose.* His fourteen days of recommended quarantine began the first day Jeanette showed symptoms, which was Monday. He still had about a week to go. Boring.

Besides keeping in touch with Jeanette and the children and operating the agency from home, Adam and Lucy took walks around the neighborhood. Adam had no intention of talking to anyone about anything; he kept the walks short and immediately crossed the street when he saw someone coming his way. So far, there was plenty in the frozen foods Jeanette had stocked as soon as she got wind the shutdown was coming. If needed, he could order from several local pizzerias or restaurants and pick up curbside. Nevertheless, he didn't have much of an appetite anyway. Adam was engrossed in reading and sending work emails when Dr. Roman's call from St. Peter's Hospital startled him. He never felt such warring emotions. On the one hand, he desperately sought news of Jeanette. On the other hand, the news might be bad. He moved outside to the sunshine on the deck with Lucy in tow to receive the call.

"Mr. Remington? This is Dr. Roman. I'm calling to give you an update on your wife." In the background, Adam could hear doctors being paged. He vaguely wondered if it were to Jeanette's room. "I actually have somewhat good news to report. Jeanette's blood oxygen levels have increased slightly."

Adam focused on the words "good" and "increased." "Blood oxygen levels?" he repeated.

"Yes. Jeanette is still in acute respiratory distress, and suffering from COVID pneumonia. However, there is a slight improvement in her oxygen levels according to the latest blood work. That indicates that her body is functioning more efficiently than it was to provide oxygen to her tissues," the doctor explained.

"Does this mean she's getting better?"

"I am cautiously optimistic. We are still learning and studying the variety of symptoms presented with this novel coronavirus. She is by no means out of the woods yet, but it is a positive sign."

Adam had been walking the length of the deck with Lucy observing expectantly. Adam halted, closed his eyes and welcomed the sun warming his skin. "Thank you, doctor, that's great news! What can we expect next?"

"Adam, for now, we're continuing all the same treatments and monitoring her condition closely with X-rays and bloodwork. Time will tell. I'll let you know when there are any changes. Meanwhile, how are you? Any symptoms?"

"Nope, not a one."

After they ended the call, Adam stood for a few minutes soaking up the sun on the deck. He noticed again the transformation of renewal spreading across the yard. The cycles of life were so obvious here; could he count on his faith for Jeanette? *I'll take this "positive sign."* Adam chuckled thinking doctors must be taught evasive language in medical school. "I guess he can't tell me what he doesn't know, Lucy," he told the pup as he reached down to pet her head. "Still, he does know Mom is showing improvement! Mom's getting better! Let's celebrate this win!"

They both reentered the kitchen and the comforting familiarity of the space struck Adam. How much time over the years had they spent sitting at the kitchen table? First, her parents' table or his parents' table, then their own table. Then their own table with one, two, and then three children. The everyday moments spent here in the kitchen at the table as a family had evolved into now.

Sitting in his usual chair, Adam posted on WhatsApp to get the good news out to his family as fast as possible.

ADAM: Jeanette, kudos! Your blood oxygen levels increased! You're getting better!

Almost immediately, the congratulations posted.

EVIE: WOO-HOO!

JERRY: Way to go!

ALEX: Awesome!

BETH: Yay!

SUE: Wonderful news!

KEVIN: Fantastic!

Adam watched as Jeanette loved each post.

JEANETTE: Getting better! Love you all

He had just put the phone down on the table when the call from Alex came in.

"Hey, Dad! This is a conference call with Jerry and Evie. We're all on the line," he explained.

"Oh. Almost all my favorite people in one place!" Adam jested.

Evie and Alex chuckled.

Ignoring the small talk, Jerry got directly to the point. "Dad, is Mom really getting better?"

"Everyone, the doctor said these exact words: 'cautiously optimistic.' It's fantastic!" he enthused.

"Dad, really?" Evie hesitated. "What else did he say?"

"Dr. Roman used other words like 'good' and 'increased.' She has a way to go before coming home, but it is a positive development!"

"What a relief!" Alex announced.

"Dad, you're sure?" Jerry persisted.

"Cross my heart!" his excitement couldn't be contained. "Guys, your mom is improving!"

Expressions of elated relief filled the line. They bantered a while more before Adam concluded, "Guys, I know you're all worried. Let's stay positive! You've done an excellent job texting and calling your mom. Let's keep it up until she comes home!" Amid agreements, they hung up. Adam looked around again at his kitchen as Lucy shifted her weight on his foot. Erupting with emotion and bursting with pride, he clutched the phone to his heart. "Our family *is* amazing! Jeanette, we've done an amazing job!"

Lucy responded to Adam's enthusiasm by slowly standing and smiling at him. Adam rewarded her with petting and affection.

Reflecting on his marriage, it didn't bother Adam to admit that throughout the years he hadn't always liked his wife, although he always loved her. They were both human, after all. At the times when he didn't agree with her, or she infuriated him (which she did expertly), he always recognized and appreciated her importance to their family. In fact, there was never a doubt how much Jeanette loved her family. She showed her love in a myriad of ways every day by being so involved in all of their lives. When the children were young, Adam would come home mentally exhausted from long days at the office to find the kids' bedtime routines in progress. Jeanette would still be making lunches or cleaning up from a day of busy activities. She kept a tight schedule and took great pride in her children having all the tools they needed to do well, whether in school or sports. They all attended to their jobs during the week and were rewarded with weekend family time. *Where did all those years go?*

Later, when Jeanette FaceTimed, he knew she was spent.

"Hey," he greeted as he noted that she was in bed and not the chair.

"Hey," she confirmed. "Worked hard breathing today," she smiled and puffed air. He could tell she was proud of herself.

"Good. Keep it up! How do you feel?" he inquired.

"Wiped," she confirmed as she closed her eyes.

"Jeanette, you're on the right track. You're getting better," he encouraged.

"Hmmm," was all she could muster.

"Have you eaten yet?"

"Nah."

"Make sure you keep your strength up. You have to eat to get better. And you have to get better to come home," he reminded.

She opened her eyes and smiled. "Want to come home."

"Well, you keep up the healing, and you'll do just that."

She gave him a thumbs-up.

"Hey, in case you didn't know, we have amazing children," he confided.

Now she smiled and put her hand on her heart. "I know."

They lingered a bit before expressing their love. When the dinner tray arrived, he convinced her to disconnect and eat with what little energy she had left.

All at once Adam was exhausted. Exhausted from the constant fear of losing his wife. Exhausted from being the rock for his family. He rummaged through the refrigerator, found more leftover pizza, and ate it cold standing up. He took Lucy out and checked the locks. Then they settled on the couch for their sleepover. Tonight, Adam would follow his own advice and take the win. For the first time since Jeanette began to cough, he slept.

14

Wednesday, April 22, 2020 - Day #10

Enough. He was going out of his mind. Calling the hospital, Zooming with the children, walking around the neighborhood with Lucy–it was all so bizarre! This pandemic turned the entire world upside down and inside out. Just a month ago, life was normal, and his Jeanette was completely healthy ...

"Stop! Just stop!" Adam yelled at himself. The dozing Lucy sat upright. He had to stop this line of thought. It was useless and made him feel useless. He made the decision, went upstairs and got changed, donned a mask, and went into his office.

No COVID symptoms had manifested, and he was sure they wouldn't. Lucky him. When he got to the office, he told his staff that he was cleared by the doctor to return. Still, out of respect for them, he would stay masked in his office and remain at least ten feet away. Thankfully, he had his own restroom adjoining his office, so there really wasn't a concern. He was texting constantly with the children, and he was still in touch with the hospital. It was such a great relief to be somewhere else and hear his staff talking on the phone. Still, the knot in his stomach remained. *Will COVID kill Jeanette?* Try as he might, he couldn't get past that thought racing around his mind. *No, she was improving!* He closed his eyes and inhaled when he felt his phone buzz. Adam was somewhat relieved when he glanced down and confirmed that it was a WhatsApp notification and not the doctor calling. In his current negative spin, if he received actual bad news about Jeanette's condition, he would completely lose it.

Remington Family WhatsApp:

JERRY: Hey, everyone! I was thinking of that time we went to Disney. We were pretty young, and it was blazing hot in Orlando.

Adam loved Jerry's post and said aloud, "Bless that boy for bringing up good times!"

ALEX: Of course! It was great! I still have my Goofy hat!

ADAM: Speaking of hats, I remember a certain young man who insisted on wearing his Daniel Boone fur hat even though it was about 100 degrees! You were all about 7, 5 and 3.

JERRY: HAHA the Boone hat! Mom, you tried to talk me out of it ... but I had to have it! I remember you made me drink more water because I was sweating so much!

Jeanette loved Jerry's post and added to the discussion.

JEANETTE: Adorable!

BETH: I want to see that hat!

ALEX: We all had to drink and "reapply" the sunscreen lol.

Sue tagged Adam's post with a laughing emoji.

SUE: So that's where it comes from! You tell me to drink and reapply when we go to the beach.

Evie tagged Sue's post with a laughing emoji.

EVIE: I vaguely remember seeing a picture of all of us and I had the Minnie hat.

ADAM: That was our first real vacation. We loved it!

EVIE: I do remember having breakfast with Mickey!

JERRY: Lol everyone has breakfast with Mickey in Disney.

ADAM: We went to a character buffet. We did have breakfast with Mickey.

ALEX: Did they have better cartoons there?

ADAM: ?

ALEX: Mom, I remember being in the hotel room watching TV with you.

EVIE: I remember seeing Snow White ...

JERRY: That hotel was cool!

ADAM: We splurged and stayed in the Grand Floridian. What a great time!

ALEX: Did we stay in the same room?

ADAM: Yep. It was great!

EVIE: I remember fireworks!

ADAM: 👍

JERRY: Yep, fireworks!

ALEX: Yeah, fireworks. But cartoons?

JERRY: Hmmm. Not sure.

JEANETTE: Alex, you were sick.

Adam added a thumbs-up to Jeanette's post and added his comment.

ADAM: It was really hot, and we figured you had a bit of heatstroke. You and Mom went back to the hotel to rest.

Jeanette added a thumbs-up to Adam's post.

ADAM: We went on the teacups. Remember, Jerry and Evie?

JERRY: Teacups! Yes! And Space Mountain!

EVIE: I remember! That was soooo fun! And I had chocolate ice cream all over my dress!

KEVIN: You had chocolate ice cream on your shirt yesterday!

Adam and Jeanette laughed at Kevin's post.

Alex gave Jerry's post a thumbs-up.

JERRY: I don't remember Alex being sick. I do remember, Mom, when we tracked down Jafar for his autograph. From *Aladdin*. Do we still have that autograph book?

Jeanette added a thumbs-up to Jerry's post at the same time as Adam's posted.

ADAM: Probably.

EVIE: I remember getting Snow White's autograph!

Jeanette loved Evie's post.

ALEX: You used to love Snow White!

KEVIN: She still does!

EVIE: 🖤 Yeah, she kissed the autograph book and left her lipstick on the page. I loved that!

Jeanette loved Evie's post before responding.

JEANETTE: Me, too!

ALEX: Mom, I remember having a good time watching those cartoons.

Jeanette and Adam loved Alex's post.

ADAM: That was a great vacation!

Jeanette, Jerry, Alex, and Evie all loved Alex's post. A few minutes passed before the posting continued.

JERRY: Mom, how do you feel?

JEANETTE: Better!

After a minute, one by one emojis appeared.

JERRY: ❣ We love you, Mom!

ALEX: 🙏 We're praying for you, Mom!

EVIE: 🤍 You're getting better, Mom!

ADAM: 🤍

Jeanette loved all their posts. Warmed by her family's love, she smiled as she thought about that vacation. They made so many wonderful memories, and she had to credit Adam; it had been his idea. *My children have been blessed to have Adam for a father.*

Alex loved this backyard. It belonged to them–Sue and him. They had scrimped and saved the down payment for this bungalow in a small town with good schools. Currently on a lunch break, he stood in the bright spring sunshine and planned the landscaping and gardening he wanted to install before the baby was born. His baby. His son.

Sue stood at the kitchen slider screen and called, "Sweetheart! Sandwiches are ready!"

"Great!" he replied as he jogged toward the house.

Inside, he kissed his wife as they stood side by side at the kitchen island eating peanut butter and jelly. This had been their lunch for the past several weeks during the lockdown.

"Delish! I just can't get enough PB&J!" Beth had been craving these sandwiches, along with potato chips, since the end of the first trimester. "Are you sure you don't mind eating this again?"

"Nope!" Alex meant it. PB&J was fun and filling. It made him feel like a kid.

"Anything new about your mom?" Beth asked between bites.

"Just what you saw on WhatsApp."

"It's kind of weird to see your mom use so many emojis. She's usually so long-winded." Beth was horrified at how critical that sounded. "I mean–"

Alex chuckled. "I know exactly what you mean, and I thought the same thing."

She smiled back as they continued to eat.

"I have a meeting soon, but after work I'm going to even out some soil and outline the area for the garden. I think we should plant seeds because we don't know if or what plants will be available next month."

"Agreed. It's a good thing Home Depot is considered essential." She refilled her water from the refrigerator and helped herself to some chips.

"Could you think about what kind of vegetables you want?"

"Sure. I'm pretty excited; we've never had a garden before!" she exclaimed.

"Well, Mom always grows a salsa garden, but I'd like to expand it. That's why I want to go tonight, before all the seeds are gone," Adam pondered. "And since Home Depot is limiting the number of people allowed in the store, going later will probably be better. Less people. I stashed some of those masks my dad gave us in the car, so I won't get caught without one."

"Good idea. Less people are good for all of us. About the garden ... definitely tomatoes and peppers. Hey, how about cucumbers? I've always wanted to make pickles. Although I'm not sure how much time I'll have for that after the baby is born," she amended.

"Well, do some googling and make a list of possibilities. I'll surprise you," he smiled.

They fell into a companionable silence as they finished lunch and picked at chips.

"Sue, I've been thinking ..." Adam didn't look up from his paper dish. "If Mom doesn't get to plant a garden this year, we can share ours." He began to turn the empty plate around in circles. "I remember when we were little, Mom would let us each pick seeds to plant in the garden. One year I planted carrots." Alex was lost in the past.

When he grew quiet, Sue prompted, "Tell me."

"I didn't know how long to wait, and the tops were tall, so I picked them." He met her eyes and smiled. "The carrots were about this long," he chuckled and indicated about an inch with his forefinger and thumb. "Another summer I chose watermelon seeds."

"Why watermelon?" she asked.

He laughed out loud and said, "That's what my mom wanted to know!" They both laughed and he continued, "I figured if I was going to plant something, it should be something big!" They shared another chuckle. "Well, the plants took over the garden, but no watermelons. Mom was annoyed that the vines climbed all over her tomatoes," he confided.

When he quieted again, Sue put her arm around him. "You have so many great memories with your mom. I want to make garden memories with our son, too."

I do have really great memories. Thanks, Mom! Alex reached down and placed his hand on her baby bump. "We will, Sue, we will." Looking into her deep chocolate eyes, Adam could tell Sue was about to say something encouraging about his mom. So, he cut her off. "Oh, the meeting ..."

He knew Sue meant well, but he just didn't want to go there. He'd decided as he lay awake night after night with his wife uncomfortably tossing her growing belly around the bed that he would accept life as it came. Becoming a father was a major life change, and he welcomed it wholeheartedly. Alex saw this as an opportunity to evolve into who he really wanted to be. He was thriving in a job he liked and grateful to be working remotely, especially now. He knew this precious time in their new home with his pregnant wife was a gift. The pandemic shutdown meant more time to prepare for their son and for the two of them to be a couple before becoming parents. He needn't worry about the bills; they had planned for Sue to leave her job when the baby came anyway. And as far as he was concerned, the childbirth details weren't an issue; the baby would be born regardless of masks and COVID tests.

The only problem in his life right now was that his mother was in the hospital fighting COVID. The whole family had to accept–whether they wanted to or not–the impotency forced upon them. His worry for her would not change the outcome, any more than worry about his baby would change his birth. He would be as positive about both situations as possible. He refused to allow this virus to mar all that he had accomplished. That would be giving in. Rather, he chose to relish all the positive she had instilled in him and strive to pass that on to his growing family. Still, he wished his mom were safe at home.

When Alex returned to the office, he quickly tapped a text to Jeanette.

ALEX: Mom, going to plant a garden.

Jeanette loved Alex's text.

JEANETTE: Now?

ALEX: Yeah, getting seeds later.

JEANETTE: 👍 Baby?

ALEX: Good. Sue and the baby are good.

Jeanette loved Alex's text.

JEANETTE: You?

ALEX: Ok. Wish you were home.

JEANETTE: Me, too

JEANETTE: Soon

Alex loved Jeanette's text.

JEANETTE: Love you, love you, love you xo

Alex smiled at the words typed instead of heart icons; that was so his mom. She was still here.

ALEX: Love you, too!

JEANETTE: Take care of family 👶 Getting better.

Please, God, help me heal. I want to meet my grandson.

Thursday, April 23, 2020 - Day #11

She welcomed the dark. So tired. Jeanette was utterly and completely exhausted, both in body and spirit. She felt cocooned in the chair and relished her aloneness. Where once it was isolating, now the sheer silence of this hospital room was welcome. The interruptions in this place were constant: food, medication, therapy, X-rays, blood tests. It was always something. Even now, she observed the white beings through the window scurry outside her closed door. She hoped they would keep on going. Jeanette had submitted to any and all intrusions, so they could make her better. If only she could get a handle on herself. How many days had it been since COVID took over her body? The physical toll was undeniable; she felt weak and feeble. Jeanette had never felt so sick in her life. The mental toll was also undeniable; she couldn't even think straight. Sometimes thoughts would just stop ... midway. Nothing she had ever experienced prepared her for this. Never before had she felt so utterly powerless over her own body. Not even when she was pregnant. Then, she had initiated and welcomed that change. Not this. Not COVID.

She felt her constant companion in her hand once again: her phone. It was currently plugged into the wall outlet, as usual when she was sitting in the chair. This had been her lifeline, her connection to her family. Just as being here in the hospital was necessary for her physical body to fight this crazy COVID, her phone was necessary for her emotional body. Opening her phone, she brought up her photo library. Jeanette began to swipe through her pictures. Some were ridiculously unimportant, like homework assignments or shopping lists. Among those daily nuisances were images of her heart: Adam, Lucy, Jerry, Alex, Evie. Images of her life before this. As if she conjured him, Adam's call came through.

She sighed, closed her eyes, and whispered, "Adam."

"Hey. What's up?" he asked.

Jeanette didn't answer.

"Jeanette? What's going on there?" he repeated.

"Nothing. Just breathing."

"That's a good thing," he joked.

"Where are you?"

"Home. Lucy says hi. She misses you. So do I."

Jeanette clutched the phone tighter as her agitation increased. Her puffs quickened.

"Adam, I want to go home. Come and get me. I want to go home ..."

Adam closed his eyes against her words. "Jeanette, honey ..."

"Scared ... I don't want here."

The strange cadence of her words frightened him. For several long moments, he couldn't speak. "Aww, Jeanette, listen–"

"I want to go home ... I want home ... I want home ..." she repeated. Between her whispering, sobbing, and puffing she was almost incomprehensible.

Yet, Adam understood her perfectly. "I promise, Jeanette, you *will* come home." Speaking quickly and louder, "Jeanette, honey, I will bring you home. I promise, once you're better, our life will return to normal–here at home." His voice grew louder as hers dwindled away. "Jeanette? Jeanette?" he listened for her response. He heard her struggling for air.

Patti squeaked and swished into the room with her cart. "Now, now, Mrs. Remington ..." She quickly came forward, evaluated her patient, and took control. "OK, Mrs. Remington, tell whoever it is you have to go," she said as she took the phone from the overwrought woman. While Jeanette continued to battle for control, Patti announced loud enough to be heard by the person on the other end, "Mrs. Remington is indisposed right now. Please call back in about 30 minutes. Thank you."

Patti pressed the red phone on the screen and tucked the device between Jeanette's thigh and the pillow. "Looks like you need a minute," she murmured gently patting her shoulder. "Try to breathe ... that's it ... just breathe." Patti continued her ministrations while Jeanette weakly complied. "We all need a moment sometimes, Mrs. Remington. Now, tell me what's wrong. Are you in pain?"

Jeanette shook her head no. "Home," is all she said.

"Oh, of course. You want to go home." Patti poured more water from the pitcher into the cup and pushed the straw toward her mouth. "Here, take a sip of water," she instructed. Again, Jeanette complied. Patti recognized the all too familiar COVID meltdown and knew exactly how to handle it. "I get it. As much as we're enjoying your company here, Mrs. Remington, we want you to go home, too!" She chuckled at her own joke. Patti learned long ago to keep the tone light-hearted and positive. "You're doing a great job! We need you to stay with us. Try to relax and just breathe!"

Running on autopilot, Patti soothed and settled Jeanette down. Sadly, this floor had taught the nurse common coronavirus symptoms and deterioration. She patiently updated the file on the computer while alternating calming words for her charge.

Leaving the room, Pat sighed deeply and leaned against the door. She had talked many afflicted with this virus down from the ledge in the last several months. She stood outside for a moment eyeing Jeanette through the small window in the door. It was satisfying seeing Jeanette much calmer and quieter than when she entered. It was Patti's job to offer care and comfort and healing; she'd say or do anything to save someone from these outrageous circumstances. COVID was a stone-cold killer. Was she looking at the next victim? Only time would tell. Patti's radio went off, forestalling her own emotional breakdown for the car ride home.

Jeanette needed him. That's all he could think as he grabbed his keys from the counter and got into his car. Opening the garage door, he peeled out of the driveway, not even seeing those neighborhood walkers who jumped up on the sidewalk to get out of his way. He headed toward the hospital in the darkness. His Jeanette was in pain, lonely, and scared.

"I'm coming, Jeanette," he said aloud. He was, for once, appreciative for the lack of cars on the road. Since the lockdown, there was an eerie emptiness where traffic jams had previously existed. "I'm coming, honey," he repeated.

The bare lanes on the local state highway brought to mind the online article that measured the lack of human vibrations on planet Earth due to the lockdowns around the world. This pandemic affected not only each and every human, but nature as well. What power and influence! Before long, Adam turned into the hospital's parking lot and drove toward the emergency room entrance he used when he was last here – when he dropped off Jeanette. He pulled into a parking space and turned off the car. For the next half hour, he watched in silence as people arrived at the emergency room in varying conditions. Some were walking, some walking with assistance, some pushed along in wheelchairs, and one delivered on a gurney by EMTs. All were masked; some were gloved. He checked his phone one more time. He had hoped that Jeanette would call back, but 30 minutes had long passed and she had not. He decided to give it a go, donned a mask, locked his car, and entered the ER.

The noise reached Adam as he breached the outer doors: coughing, talking, intercom announcements, urgent calls. The room was packed with masked people standing, sitting, leaning in chairs, and lying on gurneys around the room. He inwardly winced, steeled himself, and went toward a harried nurse covered in PPE behind the desk.

Suddenly, a masked security guard stepped in front of him. The muscled older gentleman had his hands on his hips in a way that suggested he was ready for action. "May I help you?" he stated authoritatively.

"Yes," he spoke slowly. "My wife was admitted, and I'm looking for information."

"Sir, was she admitted today?" the older gentlemen asked gently.

Encouraged, Adam replied, "No. She's been here several days. I'd like to visit her …"

At this, the guard immediately straightened and tensed. "Sorry, sir. You can use the phone on the wall to page her doctor, if you'd like. But no one is allowed beyond these doors unless admitted. You can see the order posted there by the governor," he said as he pointed to a document on a floor sign. "Do you yourself need medical attention?"

He stood several moments, deciding what to do. Deflated, Adam shook his head. "No, I just need my wife back."

"Sir, I'm sure the doctors are doing the best they can. Would you like to page her doctor? Dial 0 and ask the operator to do that. If he's in the hospital, hold on until he picks up." As he was giving these directives, the officer effectively gestured and walked Adam over to the wall phone.

The guard was drawn to assist a woman calling out in distress. Adam stood frozen among the chaos considering whether he could find the COVID floor and Jeanette. His heart rate was rising. When EMTs came noisily flying into the already packed room with a gurney carrying an unconscious, overweight elderly woman with an oxygen mask covering most of her face, Adam fled. He removed and discarded the worn mask in the outside garbage bin as he walked as quickly as possible to his car. There he fumbled with the fob to unlock the door and practically jumped inside. Immediately he dug the hand sanitizer out of the glove compartment and liberally applied it to his hands. Sheepishly, he also dabbed it like cologne on his exposed face and neck. *I can't afford to get COVID!*

Sitting in his car, his heartbeat eventually returned to normal. His reaction surprised him. Until now, he was not really concerned about contracting the virus. He had had no compunction about being with, touching, or even kissing Jeanette. Obviously, however, things were different now. *If Jeanette is gone, I have to be here for the children.* Yet another way his life had changed. Yet more pressure.

Jeanette answered on the third ring.

"Hey. Feel better?" he asked.

"Yeah. Sorry."

"Hey, no worries. Guess where I am?"

"Dunno."

"Outside the hospital. As close as I can get to you. I'm in the parking lot."

She sighed deeply and coughed. "Why?"

"Well, I can't go in. They won't let me. But I wanted to try."

"Crazy." Her voice carried her smile.

"That's me. Crazy for you," he admitted. "Jeanette, I love you. It's killing me to know you are here–but you are *not* alone. I'm here, too."

"Thanks," she whispered. "Stay."

"Sure. Whatever you want. How about I play my car radio and we listen to a few songs together?"

"Hmmm."

Adam tuned his Sirius to her favorite channel. Billy Joel was singing "Just the Way You Are."

When the song ended, he lowered the volume in awe. "Our wedding song. That's a message, Jeanette."

"It's always been you." Her voice was stronger than before.

He knew what she meant and relished it for a moment. "Did you request that song?" he laughed.

"Maybe," she teased.

He closed his eyes in relief and smiled. "Well done, honey!"

"You're welcome."

They chatted a bit more, and he was heartened by her light and teasing tone. It was a definite improvement over the distraught wife he had encountered only an hour ago.

"Sleepy … love you," she whispered. "Come back tomorrow."

As he drove home emotionally empty, he decided that his impromptu trip to the hospital was randomly the best decision he made in several days. It felt right to be there. In fact, he would call Jeanette from the hospital parking lot tomorrow. Maybe he would call his wife from the parking lot every day until she came home.

15

Friday, April 24, 2020 - Day #12

Her rapid, short puffs and lack of response alarmed Patti. Every morning before this, her patient was either awake or stirred instantly when Patti entered the room. Patti took a long minute to observe the laboring Jeanette lying in bed on her side propped with pillows before creating a disturbance to wake her. She noted the pulse oximeter was not on Jeanette's finger, and reattached it. Patti didn't like Jeanette's pallor.

She intentionally kept her tone light. "Mrs. Remington, good morning sleepy head!" Patti caroled loudly as she opened the blinds. Her PPE swished and crinkled as she moved about the room, bringing her cart closer to the bed. "Rise and shine! How are you this fine morning?"

Patti continued her banal comments as Jeanette roused slowly and blinked against the light. Her breaths continued in fast, shallow wisps. Her mouth was bone dry, and she struggled to come out of the fog inside her head.

Examining the oximeter, Patti frowned behind her mask. Immediately, Patti reached behind Jeanette on the bed and increased the flow of oxygen on the wall. "Let's sit you up, Mrs. Remington. I want to check your cannula and take your vitals."

Patti was doing all the work; Jeanette was like a sack of potatoes and still hadn't verbally responded. She expertly readjusted and elevated her patient comfortably by repositioning both the bed and the woman. Patti realigned a tangled IV, recorded a very low blood pressure and noted a rapid heart rate.

In that opportune moment, a short alien knocked. All white and squeaky with a long grey-streaked ponytail escaping her head cover, she nodded to both women as she alighted into the room. She walked to the other side of the bed and deposited the breakfast tray, at the same time moving the bedside table within Jeanette's reach. Another nod and she was gone.

Patti's tone signaled all business. "Mrs. Remington, do you know where you are?"

Jeanette nodded.

"Where?" Patti persisted.

"Hospital," Jeanette whispered licking her dry lips.

Patti opened the orange juice, stuck in a straw and instructed, "Sip." After a few starts and stops and more cajoling by Patti, Jeanette finally downed several ounces. "Can you hold this juice, Mrs. Remington?" Patti asked.

Jeanette nodded and awkwardly held the small plastic container with two hands.

Patti went to the computer and input the data. "Doesn't that taste good, Mrs. Remington? Keep drinking; you look parched." She went around the bed, checking the oxygen level and oximeter again. "Better," Patti confirmed.

Slowly, Jeanette was gaining presence. Carefully she placed the juice on the tray and lifted the dome over the plate. Scrambled eggs (no doubt powdered), turkey bacon, and an individually wrapped slice of wheat bread.

"Go on and eat while it's hot, Mrs. Remington," Patti encouraged.

Opening the small condiments, Jeanette sprinkled pepper on the eggs. Forking a lump into her mouth, she hesitated.

"What is it?" Patti asked.

Jeanette put down the fork and took a small bite of the bacon. "Uh, no flavor."

"Have you been eating, Mrs. Remington?"

"Some." She held up the bacon strip. "No taste." Jeanette shrugged and nibbled another morsel.

"Do you remember what you ate last night for dinner?" Patti queried.

Jeanette nodded side to side as she chewed.

"Mrs. Remington, lack of taste is another symptom. We're not sure how long it will last," Patti informed while typing more notes into the computer. "Did you taste the orange juice?"

Jeanette picked up the container, took a hesitant sip, and shook her head from side to side.

"Hmmm. Can you smell the eggs and bacon?" Patti prompted.

Jeanette wrinkled her brow while she sniffed and considered. "Not sure."

"We find that smell and taste usually go together. On the positive side, you're looking much better than when I came in. Your oxygen level was low but has improved. You do need to eat to keep up your strength. The IV is delivering just enough fluids to be able to medicate you. You must still drink, Mrs. Remington."

Obediently, Jeanette reached for the small water bottle and struggled to remove the cap. Patti reached over, opened the water, and handed it to Jeanette. She sipped gingerly. Removing the wrapper, she then gnawed at the tasteless bread. Observing her charge chewing incredibly slowly, Patti inquired about Jeanette's bowel movements and urine output as she updated her file. One more check on the oximeter, another round of vitals and more notes followed.

"Now that you've eaten a bit, here are your meds." Patti handed Jeanette the water to wash down the pills. "Keep up the good work on that breakfast, Mrs. Remington," Patti ordered. "Want to move to the chair now or when Annie comes in a bit?"

Jeanette motioned for later.

"Fine, Mrs. Remington. To quote Arnold, 'I'll be back!'" she laughed and finger waved as she and the cart squeaked and clattered loudly out of the room.

Jeanette pushed the tray away and leaned back. Food felt strange in her cotton mouth and stuck in her irritated throat. Her phone buzzed, and she reached across the food tray to retrieve it. She winced and grimaced at the pressure in her chest. Lying back, she rearranged herself to find a more comfortable position. Her phone insistently buzzed again, so she gritted her teeth and puffed until she had it in her hand. She waited for the discomfort in her chest to dissipate before opening her phone.

Jeanette had missed several texts and notifications. Reading Adam's text account of his sleepover with Lucy brought a smile. She responded with smile and heart emojis. On the WhatsApp, Jerry and Alex were in a bake-off. They shared pictures of Sue's and Beth's home-baked breads. The French and focaccia loaves certainly looked delicious—way more appetizing than the cellophane-wrapped sawdust still sitting on her tray.

She posted "Jealous" and sent out a picture of her bread. Her post was instantly met with thumbs-down and laughing emojis.

Their bake-off reminded her of last summer's pasta war. Both Jerry and Alex enjoyed cooking with their ladies, and they decided to make fresh pasta. Although Jeanette had never done that herself, they both assured her it was not complicated. As her sons experimented with recipes, they elevated their efforts. For months, the couples posted pictures of their various pasta dishes with reviews. The culmination was a variety of ravioli.

The global pandemic and more time at home had reinspired their love of baking. She smiled, thinking how proud she was that both her sons cooked, grilled, and baked. Jeanette saw their baking as an outlet for their creativity. It was a fun and productive way to spend time at home. Evie enjoyed fresh bread as much as her brothers, but preferred outdoor activities to in-home entertainment.

Knocking, Dr. Roman noisily advanced into the room with Patti and the cart in tow. The previous silence amplified their noisiness. "Hey, Jeanette. How are you today?" He first checked her oximeter and then began to listen to her lungs as she puffed quickly.

She held out her hand and jiggled to indicate so-so.

He was listening intently to her front and back. "Any new symptoms?" he inquired.

"Can't smell or taste," she whispered between puffs. She placed her hand on her chest, grimaced and said, "Chest feels ..."

"Heavy? Do you feel pressure here?" Dr. Roman asked laying his gloved hand on top of her own.

She confirmed with a nod.

"Jeanette, the lack of smell and taste is a common symptom. It's unclear how long that will last. Meanwhile, I'm waiting for your blood work results from this morning. Your oximeter reading has fallen, and we've increased your oxygen to where it was a few days ago." He was reading from the computer screen. "Your breathing is a bit more shallow and much faster, which could be a result of your chest heaviness."

Jeanette continued to stare blankly at Dr. Roman. The small sliver of exposed face revealed nothing. His tone was detached and dull, completely opposite from the positive vibe of the last few days. She looked at Patti, who said nothing. Jeanette was reminded of the *Star Wars* Legos Jerry and Alex used to play with–the masked white storm troopers.

"Although you've been getting X-rays every other day, and you had one yesterday which showed no change, I've just ordered an additional X-ray today, Jeanette," he said while typing.

Jeanette closed her eyes and tried to relax. *Not good news.*

"Is there any reason you're not in the chair?" he inquired.

She shook her head no.

"OK, Patti's going to help you move there now. I want to you continue your respiratory therapy with Annie today. I've also ordered an additional breathing treatment; it may help open you up."

Patti quickly moved in front of Dr. Roman and negotiated Jeanette into the chair. She grunted and groaned a bit, but Patti made her as comfortable as possible. *Are the storm troopers the good guys?*

Once outside the room, both Dr. Roman and Patti looked through the window at Jeanette holding her phone with an uncomfortable look on her face.

"Patti, I'm afraid COVID is winning," he whispered.

More aliens descended upon Jeanette, ostensibly to fulfill Dr. Roman's orders. Annie came and went in a flurry of red hair and glasses. Jeanette did the best she could, and Annie also seemed subdued.

Jeanette kept up with the texts and WhatsApp posts throughout the day with emojis. When Adam FaceTimed from the parking lot, she gestured or gave short answers. If he thought she was different, he didn't say. He had propped the phone on his dashboard and continued a steady stream of small talk, as if he knew this conversation may be the last. She actually fell asleep on him, and woke up with a start, disoriented. He was still there, staring at her, and spoke soothing words.

"Love you," she whispered.

"Love you, too. Go ahead, go to sleep. I'll just sit here in case you need me again," Adam responded.

"Creepy," she said shaking her head no. She couldn't keep her eyes open.

"Jeanette, I've been watching you sleep for years," he reminded her.

"Still creepy." Making a sweeping motion with her hand, she replied, "Go."

Adam didn't answer.

"Tired." She opened her eyes, blew him a kiss, and waved goodbye. She reached for the phone, and before he could protest, she was gone.

It was such a relief when the dinner tray arrived. Not that Jeanette was hungry; in fact, without the ability to taste and smell, she had no appetite. The reason Jeanette was relieved was because the day was over. She didn't have to struggle through the spirometer with Annie, or smile at Patti's jokes. She could crawl back into bed without comment from anyone and didn't have to pretend she was okay in the chair. She didn't have to keep up a brave face for Adam. She didn't have to continually respond to texts and posts from her children. Talking, listening, reading, posting, smiling: it was all a struggle. Now Jeanette could just be.

She was most definitely *not* okay. In the miasma of COVID she now inhabited, Jeanette felt her body slipping away. No, it wasn't slipping away; it was being eaten away. Like a tapeworm, COVID was consuming her life force from the inside out. It was so strange to think these thoughts without having emotion. Well, there must be nothing left. She had cried and panicked for nearly ten days straight. She had progressed from overwrought and overwhelmed to exhausted and vapid. COVID was depleting her life, body and soul. *I love my children and my husband. I don't want to leave them. But I'm tired.*

Jeanette's phone was blowing up. She looked over at the table and could see the notifications flying by on the screen, but couldn't focus on the words. Instead, Jeanette was drawn once again into the hazy fog inside her head. She was taking quick, shallow breaths and wishing for a hot shower. She was cold from the inside out, exacerbated by the flowing oxygen, with no way to warm her bones or her flesh.

More and more her thoughts were disjointed. Wanting a hot shower made her somehow remember bath time. Jeanette could picture Jerry, Alex, and Evie as three small children as if it were happening right before her eyes. Adam was traveling for business, as usual for about twenty years ago, and the bath routine unfolded with the usual fanfare. Jerry and Alex would bathe together, playing with their boats and action figures. Jerry particularly liked any Batman, and there were many. Two were allocated just for bath time. Alex loved anything that moved. So, his boats would carry Batman to save the day, or ferry away one of the X-Men to safety. Her boys had such vivid imaginations. Jeanette loved to sit on the floor and listen to them spin a narrative while Evie colored in her Barbie or Powerpuff Girls coloring books. After drying the boys and helping with their pajamas, it was Evie's turn in the tub while the boys played with Legos. Evie's favorite bath toys were the yellow ducks of varying sizes. She loved pretending it was a family of ducks swimming along in her bathwater. When all the children were dry and ready for bed, they went to the kitchen for a bedtime snack. Jeanette had moved the Little Tykes table into the kitchen long ago, when Evie discovered how to climb out of her high chair. So, the children usually ate all meals at their picnic table when Adam was traveling. When he was home, they all gathered together as a family at the kitchen table. All had milk, and Jerry had his favorite Fig Newtons while Alex and Evie had apples or Teddy Grahams cookies.

During the snack, the three children would answer Jeanette's questions. What did each like best about the day? What did each want to tell Daddy about when he came home? They were generally well-behaved and happy, until they weren't. Then it was past bedtime, and that moment could come at any minute. The one thing that could be counted on was for the children to be predictable, sometimes in an unpredictable way. Jeanette could picture the second when it hit the fan, and usually it was Evie. She could picture the whining that would turn almost immediately to a very cranky and irritable baby girl. The good news was that Evie would immediately want to go to sleep. A kiss goodnight from Mommy, and she was off to dreamland.

The routine with the boys, however, was a bit more involved. First, they would go to Jerry's room, and Alex would choose which book she read to the both of them. Alex sat on her lap as she snuggled Jerry in his bed. Then Jeanette and Alex would leave while Jerry chose one more book. While he rifled through his books to decide which she would read, Jeanette would lay down with Alex, which is what he wanted, in his bed. Either he wanted her to count to one hundred, or he wanted to hear a song. She complied until he was asleep. Then Jeanette went to Jerry's room again to read one more book. As the oldest, Jerry had earned the privilege to stay awake the longest. She read the book he requested, and if he was not ready to go to sleep, he could stay up and "read" one more book by himself. Usually when she checked on Jerry five minutes later, he was asleep.

Thinking of these details reminded Jeanette of how immersed she was in the daily routine she established. As a stay-at-home mom, she was the primary caregiver during the day and night when Adam was traveling. After caring for three extremely active children all day, Jeanette relished her downtime. Whatever time it was, there were always a few chores still to do: clothes to wash or fold, dishes to load, sneakers to clean, etc. Then she'd make a cup of decaf tea and sit on the couch to unwind.

In those days, when the children were so young, every moment of Jeanette's life revolved around them. Each day she managed the logistics, and the days became weeks which turned into years. How many times did she make dinner, change the sheets or go food shopping? How many peanut butter and jelly sandwiches did she serve? How many homework assignments did she explain? How many practices did she drive to, team snacks did she organize, cleats did she clean, or soccer and baseball games did she watch? One by one the children grew older, learned to drive, and went to college. What an adjustment!

Now, Jeanette's children were successfully adulting. Once she ran the minutia of their everyday lives; now she knew almost nothing of the trivial moments that filled their days. Jerry, Alex, and Evie no longer needed her in the role of daily provider and problem solver. The distance between having been that caregiver and being a fringe on their life blankets had given her a completely different perspective; her focus changed from seeing the trees (Jerry, Alex, and Evie) to seeing the beautiful, bountiful forest. When she thought of her family, they were all together. Sure, they were all individuals with distinctive stories. Yet even in different states, they were all together in her mind. She thought of her children as a triumvirate, their partners as part of the Remington tribe. No doubt her best times were when they were all together. And when only two of her offspring were gathered, Jeanette was usually keenly aware of the one that was missing.

The last time they were all together, before the COVID craziness, was Christmas. Although everyone loved being together to continue their

Christmas Eve and Christmas Day traditions, holidays were generally split among the significant others' families, juggling Thanksgiving and Christmas. This past Christmas was especially memorable because everyone came home. The season started when Jeanette and Adam selected their Christmas tree from their favorite lot. After giving the tree a few days to settle, they shared a date night where they ordered in dinner and decorated the tree using all the ornaments they had collected over the years. They had souvenirs from every vacation, like Disney, as well as mementos from the children's activities and interests. Guitars, soccer balls, and baseballs merrily joined Santas and snowmen on the boughs. Lights and decorations warmed the house. Both Jeanette and Adam eagerly anticipated having the entire family together.

Jerry and Beth arrived December 22 from Illinois, Evie and Kevin the following morning from Florida. Alex and a slightly pregnant Beth joined for pizza and baking. First, the sugar cookie dough was formed and placed in the refrigerator. Then the couples took turns mixing and baking their favorite cookies, and the kitchen was hopping. The standing mixer whirled nonstop. They all caught up with each other's lives as they talked, laughed, drank wine, and baked. The evening ended with everyone decorating the sugar cookies together. Every couple once again contributed something to the Christmas Eve and Christmas Day meals. For four days the clan gathered, laughed, cooked, and ate. Just thinking about it made Jeanette smile. She was utterly drained once they all left; nevertheless, it was all worth it.

The house was alive and warm with everyone home. Lucy loved the attention and was on the constant lookout for stray morsels. Google's Alexa was playing Christmas music in the kitchen, and favorite movies were playing on a loop in the family room: *A Christmas Story* and *National Lampoon's Christmas Vacation*. The couples rotated through the kitchen, baking and eating and taking breaks to watch whatever movie was playing. At times all the siblings were together, or all the ladies were together, or it was just the men. It was wonderful that all of the partners, while markedly different, fit right in. Jeanette and Adam shared winks and secret smiles that they would relive for weeks later.

Jeanette pictured the sugar cookie decorating fun: bodies around the kitchen island creating edible works of art. Each had their favorite shape to make and decorate: Evie cats, Jerry dogs, Alex Christmas trees. The partners expanded the shapes to include seasonal staples such as stars and stockings, as well as whimsical pineapples. It would also provide future smiles when Jeanette cleaned that green, yellow, and red decorating sugar from nooks and crannies all over the kitchen well into January. By the time the dishwasher was humming on its third cycle of the day, everyone collapsed into the family room. Eventually Alex and Sue returned to their home, and couple by couple, the group retired. Early Christmas morning, before anyone else was awake, Jeanette woke to care for Lucy and begin the Christmas Day turkey. After mass, Alex and Sue would return. Then they would start another round of opening gifts, cooking, frivolity, and festive fun. Inevitably, at the end of the day, Jeanette regretted the lack of pictures. Although she took a few, the crew complained loudly at the intrusion, so she tucked her phone away sheepishly.

This was how it was now. As they had grown and changed, her role in their lives had also grown and changed. Sometimes she missed the little people they used to be; sometimes she was awestruck that her little people evolved into *these* amazing adults. She was more than just a little proud of her clan. And as for the work of raising children, she was content to have it behind her. Yes, it would be wonderful to have those loving hugs and adoring smiles aimed at her again. But she was younger then, and they were her sole focus. She, too, had evolved. She was just beginning to figure out who she was, and she and Adam were planning to travel. And weren't they on their way? Two sons married to wonderful ladies–she couldn't have chosen better herself–and her daughter engaged to a wonderful man? It was up to them, along with their partners, to build the future they wanted for their respective families.

What are the other patients here battling COVID thinking about? She supposed they also thought about their children, if they had any. Jeanette could relax; she did the best job she could. It's not like they were still babies; they were all grown, educated, with life partners. They were on their way. If she weren't there to help them, if it were her time to leave, it would be OK. They were on their way. Besides, they'd still have Adam; he would parent for the both of them. She relied on her tried-and-true method for falling asleep, which was praying. Focusing on the words to The Our Father helped distract Jeanette and keep her from panicking. She ended her prayer with, "And lead us not into temptation, but deliver us from evil. And take care of my children. Amen."

Jeanette's phone went unanswered.

16

Saturday, April 25, 2020 - Day #13

Jeanette was swimming in clouds. No, floating. Had they fallen on her, or was she in the sky? Either way, she was light, and it was warm. She must have been in the middle of a cloud because she couldn't see anything ahead of her. Yet, she didn't feel restricted. For days she felt heavy and somehow restrained, but now she felt free. Then someone touched her, and she jolted.

"It's OK, Mrs. Remington. It's me, Nurse Patti."

Jeanette heard the voice come from seemingly far away. She opened her eyes, which took a great amount of effort, and looked at a white cloud hovering on her left side. The cloud was moving, had eyes, and was talking to her. *Cool.*

"You're doing fine, Mrs. Remington. Can you hear me?" Patti was asking.

"I'm taking your vitals."

Wow! Clouds can talk! Jeanette felt somewhat numb, and wished she could just drift away. Stay on the white, puffy clouds and float away. It reminded her of a beautiful sunny, summer day. Like a day at the Jersey shore. The kids used to love to go to the beach when they were little. They'd play for hours in the sand, digging and building. She used to pack a cooler with drinks and sandwiches. They ate upon arrival, before getting too sandy. They especially loved getting ice cream cones from the boardwalk on the way to the car. What a treat!

Jeanette heard a buzz from far away, but didn't register it. She remembered the quick Sunday trips to the shore in late October and November when the beach was mostly empty. They brought Lucy who wasn't allowed on the beach during the summer, and the kids chased the dog and the seagulls. She and Adam would sit in the sand and watch Jerry, Alex, and Evie be crazy. Special memories carved out of ordinary days.

That reminded Jeanette of her mother, Palma, who also loved the beach. That was her happy place. She occasionally went to the beach with the Remington clan when she was able. No matter the water temperature, Palma would always "dip her toes" before she left. One thing about Palma: She really knew how to enjoy the moment. Before her illness, she embraced adventure and took every opportunity to travel. She took great pictures, carefully shopped, and selected just the right mementos. Jeanette wished she was a bit more like Palma in that regard. For some reason, Jeanette was always saving for a rainy day. But the children were grown and independent. She and Adam could travel now and enjoy themselves. Why didn't they travel more? Oh yeah, crazy COVID. Sheer panic struck as she realized exactly where she was and why. In a flash, she went from floating with a cloud to struggling for breath. And that coughing! Couldn't someone help that person stop coughing?

"Mrs. Remington! Jeanette!" Patti's cold, gloved hand clutched Jeanette's clammy fingers. "Listen to my voice!" Patti insisted.

Jeanette tried to focused on the nurse's face as her own cold body closed in around her. Tighter and tighter. Squeezed–she was being squeezed like a lemon.

"That's it, shallow breaths. No big gulps! Short, shallow breaths like this," Patti instructed by imitating the technique.

Her chest was in a lemon juicer being pressed to pulp. Jeanette visualized stringy tissue where her heart and lungs once were. Her head was in a vice clamp like the one in Adam's garage workshop. Her skull, she imagined, was being pinched off at her neck from the rest of her body and her brains were oozing out of her ears. She closed her eyes against the pain.

I choose the clouds!

Patti, pushing the computer cart outside the room, anticipated the news she received when intercepted by the solemn Dr. Roman a few minutes later. Unfortunately, she'd seen far too many patients go down this road.

"I've ordered an arterial blood gas," he confirmed. They shared an understanding nod. "Annie will be in shortly to take it. I'll wait for the results before notifying Mr. Remington."

Patti understood that Mrs. Remington had taken a turn for the worse. She was losing the battle against COVID, like so many others. The next step would be a move to ICU. "Chances are good he'll call here before you call him. Her phone was blowing up. Meanwhile, I'll check with ICU on availability," she offered.

Patti was right. When she returned to the nurse's station, Mr. Remington was waiting on hold. Sighing, she knew it would be better not to mislead him about his wife's health. Yet, without the diagnosis from the ABG, nothing was certain except that she remained very ill.

"This is Patti," she muttered hoping that he had given up the hold.

"Finally!" came the exasperated reply. "Patti, this is Jeanette Remington's husband. My wife is not answering her phone. In fact, she didn't respond to any texts or messages since 8pm last night." His voice conveyed both his urgency and concern.

"Hi, Mr. Remington," she responded without inflection. "Mrs. Remington is currently indisposed for tests Dr. Roman ordered." She left it there. It wasn't really a lie; it just wasn't the full truth.

"Um ... ok ... what kind of tests?" he inquired hesitantly.

"Well, Dr. Roman would prefer to explain the tests and results himself. I'm sure he will call you as soon as the information is available to him."

"Ok ... but what about my wife? Can I speak with her after the tests?" he persisted.

"Mr. Remington, I'm sorry, but we're shorthanded here, as you know. She's waiting in a queue by the lab, and her phone is in her room. I'll make sure she knows you're anxious to speak with her." Patti had recited this hospital-provided excuse more times than she wanted to admit. Policy dictated that while the nurses could confirm known conditions, only doctors could inform family members about changes in disease progression or regression and treatment. Patti said a silent prayer that Mrs. Remington, the pleasant woman always talking about her family, wouldn't be the next victim.

Totally frustrated, Adam hung up. It wouldn't be right to harass the nurse. He'd be calling back in an hour anyway.

Adam was not a patient man. He had called twice, only to leave messages with other nurses. He had a strong feeling that both Patti and Dr. Roman were evading his calls, and he was looping on why. It couldn't be good. Was Jeanette failing? Or maybe it was just what Patti said. Either way, within one hour he would be getting into his car and driving to the hospital. It might be unreasonable, but so what? Who, during this outrageous pandemic, was being reasonable?

Adam was petting Lucy when his phone buzzed with the call he both desired and dreaded.

"This is Adam."

"Mr. Remington, this is Dr. Roman. I know you called several times, but this is the first opportunity I've had to call back." He paused, but Adam didn't respond. "I'm sorry; your wife's condition has deteriorated. I was waiting for a test result before calling. According to an arterial blood gas draw, your wife is unable to maintain adequate oxygenation, even with the current medical protocol."

"In English, doctor," Adam demanded.

"Your wife's lungs are so compromised by COVID pneumonia that she doesn't have enough oxygen for her organs, including her brain. The inflammation in her body has reached life-threatening levels. It's time for more intervention."

"Inter ... Intervention?"

"Mr. Remington, we're moving your wife to intensive care. In the ICU she'll receive 100% oxygen, and all her organ functioning will be monitored around the clock. We'll be able to provide specialized attention."

His mind spinning, Adam asked, "What exactly does this mean?"

He paused, then Dr. Roman's voice wore his exhaustion. "It means your wife is gravely ill, Mr. Remington. COVID is winning."

"Can I come in?"

"You know you can't. Not now, anyway," Dr. Roman added.

"But maybe later? When?"

"Mr. Remington, that's putting the cart before the horse. Let's get Jeanette into ICU and fully evaluate her current condition. Then we can determine next steps."

"Next steps … like what?" Adam was horrified what that might be, yet he needed to know.

"Mr. Remington, Adam, if Jeanette's condition continues to deteriorate, it may be necessary to put her on a respirator to keep her alive," Dr. Roman confirmed.

Neither spoke for several long minutes while those words were absorbed.

"Doctor," he breathed the words more than asked them, "what are her chances? For survival?"

I hate that question! "Listen, Adam, this virus is all so new–"

Adam cut him off. "Please. We both know you've seen enough COVID. What do you think? Just tell me."

Dr. Roman blew out a breath and debated. Adam deserved the truth. "Remember, she's not on a respirator. Not yet. Once on a respirator, my experience is that patients have a 50/50 chance."

It was Adam's turn to exhale. *Oh, my Jeanette! What are you thinking?* "Doctor, how does Jeanette feel?"

"She's in discomfort and very lethargic. That will improve slightly when she gets to ICU and receives 100 percent oxygen."

"Doctor, my mind is reeling. I'm sure there is something I should ask, but …" Adam wiped at his face. "Well, can I speak with her?"

"Yes, but she'll have on an oxygen mask. Also, when she initially arrives in ICU, which will be within the next hour or so, she'll be evaluated by the specialists."

"Which means …"

"They won't allow her to use her phone at all." As difficult as this conversation was for him to say, he knew that it was much more difficult for Adam to hear. Out of respect, he tried to keep the impatience out of his voice. "As I said, in the next 24 hours she'll be monitored closely."

"Well then, I want to talk with my wife before you move her anywhere," Adam demanded.

"Of course," Dr. Roman readily agreed. "I'll ask Patti to go into Jeanette's room and assist her in placing a call to you. Give us some time, though, Adam. We're really swamped, as you can imagine."

"Doctor, I *need* to hear my wife's voice."

"I understand, Mr. Remington." Having delivered his news, the doctor began to speak faster. "Remember that you'll be able to call anytime for information. However, the specialist won't call you until they have something new to tell you."

Patti squished into the room in advance of the orderly. She listened to Jeanette's labored breathing for a few beats. "Mrs. Remington, can you hear me?"

Jeanette opened her eyes.

"Mrs. Remington, we're moving you to a new room. Before you go, your husband wants to talk to you. He's been calling you. Isn't that sweet?" As she spoke, she lifted the phone still clutched in Jeanette's hand. "How about we call him back? Can you do that? Or do you need me to help you?" Patti was leaning over the bed and holding up the phone to Jeanette's face.

Jeanette struggled to escape the fogginess in her head and focus on the phone. Out of sheer repetition, she clicked on FaceTime and called Adam. Patti held the phone for her.

"Hey, beautiful! Where have you been?" he said holding up the phone so both he and Lucy were in the picture. "Lucy says hi!"

Jeanette smiled weakly and managed a small wave. It was an effort just to stay awake.

"Ah, you look tired." Adam was looking closely at his wife, and he could see and hear her struggle. "Jeanette, I love you. You know that, right?" Adam inquired gently.

With her eyes closed, Jeanette smiled and nodded. She blew him a kiss.

"I hear you're moving rooms," he said trying to gauge her understanding.

She didn't agree or disagree, but opened her eyes and looked at Patti for confirmation. After Patti nodded, Jeanette closed her eyes again and shrugged ever so slightly.

"I might not be able to talk to you or see you for a while. But I want you to know that I'm there with you. Remember, I'm coming to the parking lot later so I can say goodnight." *I have to stay positive.* He sniffed and tried to sound as upbeat as possible. "In case you don't get to text back tonight, do you want me to tell the kids anything?"

Blinking slowly, Jeanette opened her eyes, and they looked at each other across the miles for long minutes. Adam waited expectantly for her response. "Love," she whispered and closed her eyes again.

Patti had tried to remain silent, but Mrs. Remington really needed to get to ICU. Her health was obviously failing, and her transport was waiting.

Keeping the phone aimed at Mrs. Remington, Patti announced, "Mr. Remington, Mrs. Remington's transport is here, ready to take her to ICU. She has to hang up now."

"I'll stay on the phone. It'll be fun to go with you, Jeanette!" Adam suggested with false good humor.

"I'm sorry," Patti interjected, "that's against hospital policy." To Jeanette, Patti said, "It's time to move you. Please say goodbye to your husband, Mrs. Remington."

Adam's heart broke when his wife sluggishly opened her eyes, looked at him, and whispered two words he would never forget: "Love. Bye."

Speaking quickly as the finger entered the picture, Adam yelled, "Jennie! I love you, Jeanette! I–" His wife was gone.

Patti placed the phone carefully in Jeanette's hand again. Then she reached into the cabinet, removed the bag of clothing Jeanette had worn upon admittance, and placed the bag on the end of the bed by her feet.

"OK, Mrs. Remington, it's time to go upstairs. Take good care ... I may not see you again for a while," Patti was saying to her lethargic patient. She heard herself and recognized the sadness in her voice. How many more patients would move from the COVID floor to ICU? How many more mothers and fathers?

She couldn't form any words to say to Patti. Jeanette did not open her eyes to see the extremely tall, PPE-clad man place the hood over her head again and attach both her IV and oxygen to the bed she was on. When he wheeled her out of her dead-silent room, Jeanette felt relieved at the motion. *I'm moving out!* She smiled, raised her hand, and gave a slight finger wave to Patti, who was presumably standing behind the bed as Jeanette was pushed through the doorway of her protected cell. The squeaky wheels of the bed interrupted the spark of noise in the hallway as doctors and nurses ceased their conversations. Jeanette squinted to see several white-encased aliens, who all parted to the sides watching her as she rolled by. She felt like she was in an episode of *Ancient Aliens* and felt compelled to wave. The absurdity of that made her smile. There was the sound of an automatic door opening and the ding of an elevator. When the orderly negotiated her bed forward to back her into the elevator, she could see the aliens gathered, watching her still. They had resumed their discussion in much lower tones. All of a sudden, Jeanette remembered to be afraid. As the doors to the elevator closed, a tall alien facing away from her pressed a button and the car lurched upward. Jeanette focused on remembering why she was so afraid. Then she heard a pitifully weak woman's muffled voice saying, "I want to go home! Please, take me home!"

The car hesitantly bumped along slowly, as if it didn't want to go. Again, she heard the fragile voice say, "Home! Take me home!" The elevator dinged again and the tall, PPE-clad form exited, turned, and pulled the gurney out of the car. Who had been speaking?

17

Bright, dark, bright, dark. As she was wheeled down the corridor by the alien man walking backward, the overhead fluorescent lights formed a mesmerizing pattern to punctuate the squeaky wheels. The hallway seemed empty of people, although there were gurneys lined up along the left wall. There were more closed doors and white dry-erase boards with names. She couldn't see into the rooms.

When they made a turn in the corridor, another short alien with a spray bottle was busily cleaning. As Jeanette was pulled closer, she observed the gloved hands put down the bottle, wipe the thin mattress with a bright blue cloth, and then flip it. In response to Jeanette's approaching gurney, the figure looked toward the noise, turned, and seemed to melt into the wall. As they came upon the half-cleaned item, Jeanette could see the white figure outlined against the closed door watching her wheel by. *Adam, where are you?*

Eventually, Jeanette could see the doors clearly marked Intensive Care Unit as the tall white alien swiped the card at the end of a lanyard around his neck. The doors swished open á la *Star Trek*. Despite the Xanax, she was having an out-and-out meltdown as she was wheeled into her new home. Immediately, more aliens came forward as Jeanette squeezed her eyes shut and let go. *Adam, I love you! Take care of them all!*

Nurse Amy Lettey worked quickly and efficiently to assess her new patient. Jeanette Remington was clearly losing her fight with COVID, but she wasn't gone yet. In the past months, Amy had cared for many patients who succumbed to the virus, though a scant few had made it back to the COVID recovery floor. While she felt each loss keenly, her gut told her there would be countless more. She had never seen anything as insidious as this virus. Amy knew they were in for the long haul, yet she had faith in the system she served. She had to; the alternative was just too horrific to contemplate.

A registered nurse for more than twenty years, Amy moved to ICU five years ago. After a particularly nasty divorce, she completed the advanced training necessary and accepted a position here in St. Peters for a new start. Amy found ICU very challenging, but also very rewarding. She worked well with Dr. Marino, an excellent and compassionate critical care physician. Prior to COVID's arrival, the ladies had often enjoyed a lunch or coffee together while chatting about their shared love for travel. Unfortunately, they hadn't had the luxury of such discussions recently. Heavy workloads with insufficient staff precluded long breaks, and of course, social distancing requirements forbade such close contact. Still, Amy spent more time with Dr. Marino than any other human these days, other than the patients.

Dr. Marino, seated at the rolling stool by the computer desk, tapped her signature purple pen on the keyboard. Even though most notes were digital, she still kept her pen handy on the lanyard with her key card around her neck just in case. She frowned and read the accumulated file as Amy was connecting all of the monitoring devices. They each worked in companionable silence among the swish of PPE, squeak of rubber shoes, blips, sounds, and gentle whistling of equipment. When Dr.

Marino was satisfied that she knew her patient's history, she moved forward to examine Jeanette.

"Mrs. Remington, can you hear me?" the doctor asked as she listened to Jeanette's quick, short breaths.

Jeanette fought the haze to return to the present. Squinting, Jeanette gazed into clear blue eyes behind goggles and a face shield anchored by a blue head covering and blue mask. Reminded of a cloudless sky, Jeanette wanted to again float away. The stout, round alien was assessing her very closely.

"Good. I'm Dr. Marino, and Amy is your nurse. You're in the ICU, Mrs. Remington. We've increased your oxygen and we're waiting for a few more test results. How do you feel?"

For real? Strangled coughs and breaths spoke volumes.

"Ah, relax. You're in the right place, Mrs. Remington. We'll be monitoring your condition very closely here in intensive care," the doctor assured. "I understand you're married, Mrs. Remington." She paused and waited for a response.

Jeanette nodded.

"Mrs. Remington, you are not well. Some decisions may need to be made about your care. Are you capable of making those decisions? Or would you like us to speak with your husband?"

Jeanette blinked and whispered haltingly, "Husband not here."

"Yes. I know." Dr. Marino was all business. She stared into Jeanette's eyes for a few beats and seemed to relent. "I can see that you are very tired, Mrs. Remington. Again, some decisions will need to be made about your care."

Automaton Jeanette nodded and watched Dr. Marino sit and type. *Decisions? Do I have choices? Was COVID a choice?*

"Amy, let me know the minute the results are in. Meanwhile, continue full oxygen and prepare for the next steps." Sighing deeply, Dr. Marino entered more notes and then logged off the computer. She went once more to the bedside.

"Mrs. Remington, I'm going to check on my other patients. If you need anything–anything at all–let Amy know." She patted Jeanette's shoulder. "I'll be back soon; we'll talk more then."

Jeanette watched as Dr. Marino whistled, swished, and squeaked from the room. When the door automatically slid closed, Jeanette wondered what it would be like to be one of the aliens instead of one of the humans.

Her world included two realities: being in a hospital bed with COVID and floating among the clouds. When Jeanette was in the hospital bed in her isolated room, one of the very gentle nurses would talk to her, reassure her, move her, and tend to her. Always they explained exactly what they were doing and why. Jeanette was also poked and prodded by other disembodied voices muffled by masks, unknown and unfamiliar to her. She bore all manner of indignity hoping it would be over quickly. It was difficult enough to simply breathe; protesting or asking questions led to more discomfort. Furthermore, it was oddly soothing to let go and put her life in the hands of these strangers, who were at this moment her only physical contact.

Floating was easy, calming. On the edges of her consciousness, Jeanette felt the discomfort of her body like an itch she couldn't scratch. Jeanette welcomed the fogginess in her brain. Otherwise, COVID was just overwhelming, frightening, horrifying. When floating, Jeanette almost felt free.

In this state, Jeanette was transported through time. She was both here and in the past. It was as if she were watching her life play out on a big screen. She saw snippets of scenes of Jerry, Alex, and Evie in various stages and situations. Their faces and bodies revealing their emotions. Sports games, friendly gatherings, birthday parties: images of days gone by. Sometimes Jeanette would challenge herself to remember more of the scene or put it in context. For example, she had pictured Evie playing in several different soccer uniforms. It took effort, but Jeanette remembered all the school and travel teams Evie had played on. The same was true for Jerry's baseball teams and Alex's soccer teams. These mind games were helping Jeanette both pass the time and stay conscious. It reminded her of the television show *This Is Your Life!* As time was rewinding, Jeanette's thoughts drifted toward her own mother.

Palma was a strong, independent woman. A widow at 38, she raised two children with little income, a ton of grit, and incredible family support. At times in their relationship, like most mothers and daughters, they disagreed. When Jeanette told her mother she wanted to be a school teacher, Palma disagreed. At the time, few teaching jobs were available, and Palma thought Jeanette would have more of a future in a corporate environment. Citing Jeanette's skill with numbers, Palma wanted her to be an accountant. It was a tense four years until Jeanette landed her first job, and her mother's fears were proven unfounded. Following, Jeanette mildly resented Palma for not supporting her career choice. The one topic they always agreed on was Adam: both Palma and Jeanette fell in love at first sight. While they shared a close bond, Jeanette was ultra-sensitive to Palma's criticism. When Jeanette became a mother herself, everything shifted. Over the years, they seemed to share an understanding that had been previously lacking.

In hindsight, Jeanette could see that it was her own insecurity that caused her to be so prickly. Whenever Jeanette was unsure, she'd assume Palma was criticizing and react negatively. As Jeanette matured and became more confident in herself, her mother didn't affect her the same way. Instead of criticism, Jeanette saw the love, support, and concern in Palma's words and actions. Like when Palma used to stay with Jeanette and Adam to babysit or help out around the house. Like when Palma played checkers or Skip-Bo or any other game the kids wanted to play.

Like when Palma attended every school play, concert, and playoff game she could. Like when Palma came with doughnuts to every birthday, graduation, communion, or confirmation party. Like when they were renovating the kitchen, and Palma came to help Jeanette manage the chaos. Like when they were dropping a child off at college, and Palma came to stay with the younger children. Whenever Jeanette needed her mother, Palma was there. That was the way Palma showed her love. Palma's grandchildren were her greatest joy; she was a tangible presence in their lives. Her support made a real difference–both to Jeanette, Adam, and the children.

When a friend's mother died, she told Jeanette, "Everyone feels like an orphan when her mother passes." Jeanette had nodded, but not understood. Her own mother's gradual decline was devastating. Looking back, Jeanette could see the progression of the disease. At the time, however, she convinced herself that Palma had good days and bad days. When Palma passed two years ago last month, it was not wholly unexpected, yet it was a surprise; Jeanette didn't see it coming. She regretted that she was not with her mother at that last hour. The absolute loss was incredible. As a result, Jeanette felt untethered. She was still in mourning.

"Mrs. Remington, can you hear me? It's me, Nurse Amy." Lowering her voice, she leaned into her patient, "Aww, don't cry; I'm going to take good care of you," the petite blonde said as she dabbed at the tears leaking from Jeanette. "You're here in ICU. You're very sick, Mrs. Remington, but you are not alone."

After ending the call with Jeanette, Adam sat stunned. His worst nightmare was coming true. He had an inkling that Jeanette was in trouble when she hadn't answered calls, texts, or WhatsApp since last night. Still, he talked himself into believing she had just fallen asleep, as she seemed to be doing more and more lately. But after his conversation with Dr. Roman, and Jeanette's lackluster response on the phone, there could be no doubt. COVID was winning.

Jeanette was in the fight of her life, and he felt useless. Long after the update from the doctor, Adam sat looking at his phone. Minutes ticked away until Lucy nudged him back to the moment. Then he looked dazedly around the kitchen. He was missing Jeanette, and he might never get her back. In this kitchen, this common and safe space, Adam's life may have changed forever. Lucy whined at the door to go out, finally gaining his full attention. Saying nothing, he walked over, opened the door, and closed it behind her. Lucy turned and stared at him through the slider.

Adam leaned against the closest counter. He had to inform the kids; he absolutely dreaded it. All this time he was encouraging them to believe their mother could make it. *Was he wrong? Was this the beginning of the end?*

As if on cue, Evie posted a picture of a beautiful Florida beach on the Remington Family WhatsApp.

EVIE:

Jerry loved Evie's picture.

Adam began to type, but deleted and switched to the WhatsApp account they had set up without Jeanette.

ADAM: Pretty beach. I just got off the phone with the doctor. I have news. Let's Zoom in 15 minutes.

How will I tell them this?

ALEX: Dad, something new? Is Mom OK?

Adam typed, deleted, and retyped before pressing send.

ADAM: Mom still fighting.

JERRY: ?

ADAM: Zoom in 15, please.

I can't type these words!

EVIE: 👍

Jerry and Adam added their approval to Evie's post.

Adam realized Lucy was still standing outside the door watching him. He walked to the door, opened it, and when she stepped backward, joined her on the deck. "You need me to take you down?" he asked the pup. In answer, she turned and went down the steps, stopping midway to be sure he was following. He did so woodenly.

Anger swelled yet again at the unfairness of this situation. He breathed deeply, pulling in the scent of the earth as he followed Lucy onto the grass. Immediately, his anger dissolved into despair. *Jeanette has been moved to ICU. The next step is a respirator! How will I tell the children? Dear God, give me the words.*

He'd procrastinated long enough. It was time to circle the wagons. This virus was challenging Jeanette–and all of them–to keep going. Adam walked Lucy around the yard for business, and then took the fastest shower in history. He wasn't sure exactly what he would tell them, but he hoped inspiration would strike. He needed to stay positive, yet he didn't want to give false hope. She was definitely getting worse. He needed to warn them; it wouldn't be fair for the children to be blind-sided. Adam sat himself in his usual kitchen chair, opened his laptop, and launched the meeting. Watching them join one by one, he could picture them each as toddlers. He remembered them as rambunctious children, when their height indicated their age. He and Jeanette had marveled at their commonalities and differences many a Friday night over dinner or on the deck. Indeed, their children had always been, and still were, their favorite topic.

Adam noted they all looked worn, and he took a minute to evaluate each one's state of mind. Generally, Jerry and Alex hid their discomfort well; neither wore their hearts on their sleeves like Evie. However, it was obvious right away that they were all very worried about their mother; very few words were spoken as they waited for the most recent update. Although he couldn't remember exactly what he said, Adam would never forget the stricken looks and tears as he shared Dr. Roman's news with his family. And while he was telling them all to stay positive, Jeanette was moving to ICU. Whatever her new reality was, he had to face his. Right now, he alone was responsible for keeping his family together. No matter his own doubts and fears, he had to remain upbeat and reassuring for their children.

Again, it was his emotional Evie that reacted immediately, "ICU? We just texted with Mom yesterday! What happened? Dad, is she worse? Is that what ICU means?" Kevin seemed to be holding what was left of Adam's daughter together in the box on the screen.

"It means that your mother needs more care. And they will be giving it to her in ICU."

"But," Jerry interjected, "*what* more care, Dad?"

"Well, more oxygen. Full oxygen. It's also the level of attention. She'll be monitored more closely by a critical care team 24/7. They're doing more testing, so I haven't spoken with anyone in ICU yet. I really don't know specifics ..." he trailed off. Given this reception, now was not the time to drop the possibility-of-a-respirator-as-a-next-step bomb.

Adam asked leaning forward, "Dad, what can we do?"

I wish I knew! Several moments of silence followed while Adam tried to think of something that wasn't dismissive or trivial. He shook his head from side to side as he took in his children on the screen. Lucy's barking by the front window interrupted the call. "I'll be right back," Adam said as he got up from the kitchen table to see what all the fuss was about.

Lucy was looking out the window at people walking by the front of the house, but turned immediately when Adam came into the room. Her tail automatically began to wag and she bounded toward him. Adam crouched and took a minute to hug his dog and leaned back to let her lick his face. "Ah, good idea, Lucy."

As Adam walked into the kitchen, he could hear them talking amongst themselves on the Zoom call. He paused in the doorway and caught snippets of their conversation, including concern for their mother as well as affirmations about the baby, working from home, and each other. When Lucy sidled up and leaned into him, Adam reached down to touch her, too. Yes, they were concerned, but being together made them stronger. He stayed out of the camera view and listened to them encouraging each other for a few more minutes until they seemed to run out of things to say. Inspiration struck.

"I'm back," Adam said moving into the screen. "I have an idea. Send your mother your love!" Adam said enthusiastically. "Send it now and send it often. Keep sending her your love and strength until she has enough of her own."

Jerry and Alex were nodding as they picked up their phones right away while Evie asked a few more questions. They were all sad and quiet as the meeting ended. They each poured their emotion, their love and their support for their mother into their texts. At Evie's suggestion, that also included voice-recorded texts and short videos. They were desperate to keep Jeanette; it was time to make sure she knew how desperate they were!

Remington Family WhatsApp:

JERRY: Hi Mom! I'm thinking of you and sending you healing love. 🤍 🤍 Get better soon, alright? Beth and I are OK here, don't worry. I'd love to talk to you. Call me! xoxo

ALEX: Sue and I want you to know the baby is doing fine and looking forward to meeting you! 👶 We love you, mom! Xoxo

EVIE: (VOICE MESSAGE): Hi! It's me! Mom, I miss talking to you. I hope you feel better. I ... ah ... Mom, I really love you. I miss you, too! [sniff] Take as long as you need ... but please get better! [sniff] Kevin says hi. Talk soon. Bye.

ADAM: Our children are the best! They love you, Jeanette, almost as much as I do. Come back to us! 🤍 🥺

Jeanette's phone lying beside her on the bed buzzed repeatedly, but she didn't notice.

18

Group text between Evie, Alex, and Jerry:

EVIE: Hey, I'm going home.

ALEX: ?

JERRY: You mean New Jersey?

EVIE: Yep

JERRY: When?

EVIE: ASAP

ALEX: How?

EVIE: Not sure, driving probably. Will rent a car.

JERRY: Good.

EVIE: 🤍

ALEX: Agreed. I'll check on Dad, but can't stay long. Can't expose Sue and the baby.

JERRY: Yep. It'll be good for all of us to have boots on the ground. Just in case Dad is sugarcoating. When you get there, let us know how bad it really is.

EVIE: Exactly! I don't know if we're getting the whole story ...

ALEX: Let us know when you make your plans.

Jerry added a thumbs-up to Alex's post.

EVIE: Will do! 🤍

The doorbell rang, and Lucy valiantly impersonated barking. Adam didn't move. Since the Zoom call with the kids, he had been sitting still in the silent family room holding his phone. A muted episode of *Beachfront Bargain Hunt* was showing a young family finding a vacation home in Ocean City, Maryland. Adam was using the episode to reminisce about the time he and Jeanette had gone there with the boys before Evie was born. He was watching the episode and remembering two toddlers stumbling in the sand. Adam smiled thinking of Jeanette waving the sunscreen saying, "Reapply!" Meanwhile, in the present, he hadn't even noticed it was dusk. He was lost in his memories and his fears. What if he got a call from the hospital? What if he had to tell the kids that their mother was on a respirator? He was trying to zone out and hoping he would have 24 hours to adjust to Jeanette's latest condition.

He hadn't ordered delivery, so who would be at his door? The Fed-Ex, UPS, and Amazon drivers still delivered during the pandemic, thankfully. However, they practically threw their deliveries from five feet away so as not to be exposed to any homeowners. None of the neighbors really knew him; Jeanette was the chatty one. He remained seated listlessly willing the interruption to go away.

"Dad? Are you home?" Alex called loudly as he stepped into the house.

Adam jumped up and went toward the front door. He was surprised to see his masked son crouched in the entry hallway petting Lucy, whose tail was going a mile a minute. At his dad's confused look, Alex said sheepishly, "I have my key, remember? I hope it's OK; I let myself in ..."

Adam teared up with the relief of seeing his son in person. "Absolutely! You have *absolutely* no idea what a sight for sore eyes you are!" As they warmly embraced and thumped each other on the back, both men held on for a few extra beats. Lucy jumped up between them, making them both laugh as they stepped apart.

Adam hooked a finger toward the back of the house. "Hey! I'm no longer quarantining, but I know you're being super careful with the baby on the way. C'mon, let's talk on the deck so you can take that God-awful mask off, and I can see your face."

"Perfect," Alex agreed as Lucy danced like a puppy between them. "Saving a few bucks on the electric bill, Dad?" Alex asked chuckling.

"Huh?"

"Uh, didn't you notice it's getting dark?" Alex said pointing to the yard outside the kitchen sliders.

Adam shook his head and continued to the deck. He put on the deck lights as they stepped outside. It was a bit cool, but they both had sweat-shirts on, so they moved to the railings and leaned back. As soon as they were at least six feet apart, Alex removed his mask. Lucy remained leaned into one of her favorite humans, and Alex enthusiastically petted the lab. That was when Adam noticed his son's usual smile was missing.

It had been at least three weeks or so since he had last seen Alex; Adam was aware immediately of the stubble and lines showing on his young, usually clean-shaven face. Despite the pleasant temperature, a chill caused Adam to cross his arms. He watched his son with Lucy, and he waited until she was somewhat satisfied and settled herself against Alex, so he could stand upright. "How's Sue and the baby?"

"Oh, good. They're good," Alex nodded and evaluated his father as closely as Adam had done a few minutes prior. "You look tired, Dad. Even more in person than you did on Zoom."

Adam didn't have anything to say to that observation, so he added one of his own. "And you also look a little worn. How's work?"

Nodding, Alex said, "Same," and put his hands in his pockets.

As they stood staring a bit awkwardly at each other, Adam was reminded of how alike they were in communication style. Both men definitely believed that less was more. Funny that they both married women who disagreed. Since Alex had come here to see him; he must have an agenda. Adam sat down in a nearby iron chair and waited.

"Dad, I'm worried," he confided as he lifted his shoulders in a tall shrug. "How is Mom *really*? What's going to happen to her?" Alex's soft words were almost lost to Adam. "What does moving to ICU *really* mean?"

Adam blew out a breath he hadn't realized he was holding. When would he breathe normally again? "Alex ..." he uncrossed his arms and spread his hands on the table. "Alex, I ... I wish I knew. I mean, I haven't physically seen your mother for days ..."

Lucy took that moment to get to her feet and excitedly run down the stairs off the deck to chase a squirrel. In the illuminated yard, Adam and Alex both took a minute to watch the elderly lab jump on hind legs when she reached the fence. They couldn't help but chuckle in appreciation and good humor when the squirrel squawked at Lucy from the safety of its perch six feet high before running away into the neighbor's yard.

Some of the tension left the deck. "Sit," Adam instructed. After Alex complied, he continued. "Alex, you cannot begin to imagine how sorry I am that your mother has COVID. That our family has to go through this," he waved his two hands in front as if the trouble was sitting right there on the table. Another heavy sigh. Haltingly, he continued. "But we *are* going through this. And we're not done yet. I–" he touched his chest, then motioned to include the both of them, "*we*–don't know what's going to happen." Then, to lighten the moment, he added, "Unless you have a crystal ball ..." He was rewarded with a small smile on his son's face. "Your mom is fighting, and we have to appreciate that just like us, she's doing all she can do."

Alex began rocking on the deck chair. "Dad, I don't know what to think. I'm excited and thrilled about the baby, and we're wrapped up in our own world. COVID actually does us a favor because I can work from home, and Sue can also stay home. We're enjoying our little slice of heaven ... and then Mom gets sick." He stopped rocking and sat forward gesturing like a thespian. "She's Mom, so she'll be OK; but now she's in the ICU." Alex choked out, "How can I be happy about anything with Mom in ICU?"

Adam stared hard at his son. It was only sheer will that kept him from jumping across the old table and pulling his son into his arms. Another sigh, and with deliberate slowness, he intuitively told his son what he needed to hear. "You have a wonderful life event happening. Alex, your son is growing, and you have every right–" Adam lowered his voice and pointed directly at his son to emphasize the next words, "no matter *what* COVID craziness happens in this world–*every* right to enjoy *every* minute. Especially and including meeting him when he arrives." He paused as Alex's tears rolled down his face and waited for his son to absorb his words. "Nothing is more precious than life." Adam's voice choked on emotion, knowing the truth of his words. "*Nothing!*"

They both swiped at their faces and retreated to their own thoughts while Lucy sniffed around the perimeter of the yard.

He cleared his throat and looked back at his father. "About Mom–" Alex began.

Adam returned his attention to Alex. "Your mom would be the first one to tell you, and all of us for that matter, to stay positive. Yes, she has COVID. Yes, she is very sick. But as of right now–for this moment–she is being cared for in ICU. She's still here; she's with us." He clutched at his own chest. Unconsciously, Adam was standing. He took a step closer toward his son.

"And if that changes?" Alex whispered looking up. All of a sudden, he appeared to be ten years old again, not the grown, married, successful man expecting his first child. After a few beats, Adam turned away from the raw emotion in his son's eyes, and the image of the past.

Nothing will ever be the same again. He continued looking at Lucy wandering slowly back to the deck and felt exhausted. In a small, quiet voice he replied, "Alex, let's cross that bridge if and when we come to it. I'm praying we won't have to." He looked back at his son. More confidently he added, "I'm not giving up on your mother. As long as she's still alive, there is hope she'll get better."

They continued to chat a bit more until a relieved Alex rose. "I'd better get home. Sue thinks I'm putting gas in the car," he admitted sheepishly.

Adam rolled his eyes and said, "Geez!" as they shared another short but robust hug. The three of them moved toward the kitchen slider door.

"I'll tell her I was here when I get home," Alex admitted over his shoulder.

They walked through the house to the front door. "I hope so!"

"Oh, Dad, head's up. Evie has been texting Jerry and me about coming home."

"Here?" Adam was caught totally off-guard.

"Yep."

They walked through the house and Adam stood on the threshold of the front door while Alex stood at the bottom of the steps. Lucy stood inside the doorway with no intention of leaving the safety of her home.

"Because of me?" Adam asked. The last thing he wanted was for his children to think they had to take care of him.

"Nope. Because of her. She feels too far away and disconnected. She's completely stressed out," Alex shared.

Adam nodded. Of course, she was. Weren't they all? "Hmm. That might not be the worst thing." A thought occurred to him, "What about Jerry? Is he considering coming home?"

"Well, even though Jerry and Beth are both working from home, they have a lot going on. I think they're considering staying at Beth's parents in Indiana for a short while just to get out of the city. They can get back from there quickly if needed." They both paused to watch a stray car drive by. "You know they're making New York and New Jersey sound like ground zero on the news." He paused and pressed the fob to unlock his car sitting at the curb. "But Jerry and I both think it'll be good to have Evie home here."

Adam nodded and waved as Alex, with more pep in his step than when he arrived, jogged to his car and drove away. Stepping into the house and closing the door, Adam said aloud, "Jeanette, our son is a good man." He pictured the return smile she routinely gave when he complimented any of their children.

As he entered the dark family room, he turned on a few lamps, raised the volume slightly, and realized he was a bit hungry. He looked down at the lab that had dogged his every step. "Lucy, how about pizza ... again?"

Having made up her mind, Evie continued to pack. She would get a rental car at Miami airport. Once she was ready, she would take an Uber to the airport, pick up the car, and drive to New Jersey. If she needed to sleep, she could do so in the car. No problem. At this point she had all the time in the world. Or did she?

Kevin finished his last call of the day and went in search of Evie. Hearing the rustling in the next room, he entered the bedroom and absorbed the scene. He knew what was happening. He leaned against the doorjamb and calmly asked, "Hey, what's going on in here?"

She looked up briefly and once again he saw the strain on her face. "Packing. What does it look like I'm doing?" His Evie could get a bit touchy when upset.

"I see that. Where ya goin'?" As if he didn't know.

"Where'd ya think? New Jersey!" Her voice grew shrill. "My mom with COVID has just been moved to ICU! I ... C ... U! And where am I? Stuck here, in Miami!"

He walked to her and took her hands. When she would have brushed him aside, he gripped them tighter. "Evie. Stop. You can't go to New Jersey right now."

She stared him squarely in the eyes, pulled her hands away, and declared in a low, menacing tone, "Try and stop me!" She returned her attention to her packing.

Kevin released a pent-up sigh. "Please, Evie, let's be reasonable."

The high pitch of her voice confirmed his tragic word choice. "Reasonable?" She tossed clothing in the luggage on the bed. "You want *me* to be *reasonable*? Is it *reasonable* that we're in the middle of a global pandemic? Is it *reasonable* that my mother has COVID? Is it *reasonable* that she's in the ICU–*ALONE*?!" Besides her voice, her wild, gesticulating hands demonstrated her unstable mindset.

Kevin had never seen Evie so unbalanced. One minute she was crying and the next she was fuming. He knew he would be terrified if his mother were in the hospital with COVID. It was amazing how quickly all their lives had changed. The nonsensical turn of events struck him—and apparently everyone else–hard. Prior to her mother's hospitalization, Kevin and Evie had both enjoyed the Sunshine State and working from home. They were happy they were "safer at home" in such a beautiful location. Now, the bubble had been forever popped. As the youngest of three, Evie needed her family. This threat to her bedrock was difficult for her; it would be difficult for anyone.

Kevin stepped forward and took her fingers and kissed them one at a time. Evie watched without comment. Then he gently tugged her hands until she was sitting on the bed beside him. "Evie, I know you're upset. You're going crazy here while all this is unfolding miles away. I know you want to be closer, but please listen. You really need to give this a few more days."

She began to get up, but he held on tight.

"No, hear me out. I love you, and I know how much you're hurting. What, exactly, is your plan?" He could see the desperation on her face changing slightly to determination. She squeezed his hands, pulled away and continued her mission.

"Well, flying is out; many flights are cancelled. Besides, I'm not sitting in an enclosed aircraft with who knows how many infected people," she waved as she dismissed that idea. Evie leaned across the bed and continued speaking as she folded items she had deposited there. "And, of course, driving will be easier for Harry. He doesn't care for flying, and you know it."

Gaining momentum, Evie grew effusive. "And I can take more stuff. Who knows how long I'll be there? I'll rent a car at the airport. I'll drive to New Jersey. That way I can limit my exposure. In case I do get to see my mother in the hospital, I can't worry about infecting her again."

The havoc wreaked by COVID was evident in her appearance. Her hair was pulled back in a messy ponytail, her face was ruddy, and her shiny eyes red-rimmed and bloodshot. Yet another obvious sign of the impact of this virus. "Kevin, I can go alone. I won't put you in danger. You can stay here."

Once again, he took her hands in his, effectively stopping her packing efforts and forcing her to meet his gaze. "You are going *nowhere* without me! I would *never* let you go alone, and you know it. All I ask is that we call your dad and tell him what you're planning." He was pleased that she no longer looked crazed, and even sported a smug look, although she was fully committed to her idea.

She rose, moved from the closet and threw more clothes into the open luggage on the bed. Offhandedly, she replied, "Well, I guess you could come with me; we can share the drive. We're both working from home, which means we can work anywhere. We'll set up shop at my parents' house in Jersey. You know my boss knows about my mother, and I emailed that I may have to move. She agreed that wouldn't be a problem; she even approved PTO."

Evie gained momentum. "Who knows how Dad is really holding up? He probably needs emotional support. And if the rules change at the hospital and visitations are allowed, I'll be right there. Even if I can't visit, I can help when Mom comes home." Evie stopped for a moment, and looked directly into Kevin's eyes. She was challenging him to contradict her assertion that her mother would be getting better.

"Evie ..." Kevin began, then stopped. No way he was going to be the voice of doom. She looked away and continued packing. Kevin relented. What would it hurt to go to New Jersey? Florida had fewer restrictions overall, but between three adults they should be able to figure things out. And he knew his determined Evie. Once she had an idea in her head, it was a sure thing. "Have you talked to your dad about this? Does he know that you're planning to go home?"

Evie paused in her packing. "Not yet."

"Don't you think you should check with him before you–we–go?"

Evie was looking past Kevin, calmer now, but her mind was fixated on her packing.

"Ok. Let's say that we do *drive* safely from here to there. Then what? How long can we stay?"

"As long as needed! Look, Kevin, I have to do something! I can't just sit here so far away while my parents are living this nightmare! I feel so isolated ..." And they were back to Evie's breaking point once again. He pushed away the luggage, and they sat on the edge of the bed.

"Kevin–I have to go," she repeated, her defiance replaced with despair. She looked around the room as if the answers could be found there. "I don't know how sick my mom really is. I don't know how long I'll be there. I don't know anything ..." she whined as she pressed her palms to her eyes. Evie's hands fell away as she released a tremulous breath. She murmured, "Kevin, I *need* to go home."

This raw emotion affected him more than her wildness.

"Yes, oh yes, Evie, I see that," he crooned pulling her close. She nodded, began to sob again, and laid her head on his shoulder. He hugged her tightly, rocked her gently, and murmured quieting words. She cried until her tears were spent.

Finally, she pulled away, swiped at her nose with the back of her hand, heaved a great sigh, and drew her phone from her back pocket. "OK, let's call Dad."

Kevin was extremely grateful that Adam had been able to convince Evie that they should get a good night's rest, reserve the car and Uber tonight, and begin their journey to New Jersey in the morning. When her dad confirmed he was no longer quarantining, but insisted that he himself did not need Evie's help, Evie tearfully confessed needing to be home. Understanding his daughter, Adam repeated the party line that their childhood home was always open to all three of them. "You are *always* welcome; you know that! There's plenty of room for all of you, even Harry," Adam offered. "Kevin, I know it's a straight run on I-95 from there to here, but I'm not sure you should let Evie drive ..." Adam had quipped. Adam's levity worked wonders on Evie, and after the call she and Kevin had cuddled on the bed.

He felt her breathing even out, indicating Evie was sleeping. Kevin knew it was from sheer exhaustion; she had been unable to sleep well since her father's first call. He dared not move himself for fear of disturbing whatever rest she could manage. Now that the decision was made, it was only a matter of time. Foreseeing this eventuality, Kevin had asked a cousin living in nearby Pembroke Pines to look in on the apartment until they were able to return. Kevin knew once Evie set foot in New Jersey, she would be there for the duration. How long would this predicament last, and how would it end? Whatever the case, he would be there to help her face this COVID crisis. He prayed once again for his future mother-in-law to recover as he, too, succumbed to a troubled sleep ahead of tomorrow's tiring trek.

"Beth, what do you think?" he asked as she met him at the kitchen island for dinner.

Jerry and Beth had been discussing their current lockdown situation; it seemed untenable. Their hostage situation had gotten worse. Their work schedules had taken over, and what made Chicago a livable and charming city had yielded to COVID. Chicago's lockdown directives precluded them from going out to the public parks during the day. Many of their friends had left the city. Adding even more pressure, Beth had recently inherited Aunt Sarah, who still lived alone in Bucktown. Beth's older cousin had to go to Texas to help her husband's mother. As a result, Beth was the only relative in Chicago that could look in on her elderly aunt.

"Well, it could work," she answered taking a bite of the pot roast. "I talked to my mom again about the situation with Aunt Sarah today. Mom suggested that Aunt Sarah go to Indiana and stay with them for a bit. You know how stubborn Aunt Sarah is, but she says she's considering it." Beth eagerly took a few more bites of their delicious meal before continuing the story. "If we go to Indiana, then we can pick up Aunt Sarah on the way and make sure she's settled in with everything she needs, just in case it turns into a longer visit."

"OK. Do you want to stay at your parents' house in Indiana with them and Aunt Sarah?" Jerry asked scooping more of the pot roast juice onto his rice.

"Well, yeah, I think so," Beth considered. "I mean, there's plenty of room. We can both work from anywhere right now. And if they do open my office on a rotating basis like they're saying they will soon, we're only a few hours away, so we can get back quickly," she confirmed.

He nodded and swallowed. "I can't see any way that your office will open anytime soon," he offered in between bites. He got up to refill his water glass at the refrigerator. "I'm not even sure why they would say that. I mean consider the elevators. Due to social distancing, maybe four people can ride at a time. It would take an hour just to get workers to their floor. Then there are so many other restrictions around the bathrooms and cafeteria." When she lifted her glass, he placed his on the table and refilled hers at the refrigerator as well.

"Thanks," Beth murmured as she took a sip. "I'm not sure either. Between Aunt Sarah and the threat of returning to the building, I feel trapped here," she admitted. "At least if we go home to Indiana, we can sit outside in the yard and take walks around the neighborhood." She longed for the comfort of the quiet suburban town where she grew up. "Honestly, I'd really love the break."

"Trapped is a perfect description," he concurred. He didn't need to mention the ongoing violence in the city that kept them in at night.

"OK, so we're agreed," he pointed at her with his fork. "Tonight, let's pack a week's worth of clothes. Tomorrow, you'll corral Aunt Sarah, and I'll do some shopping. I don't want to arrive empty-handed. We'll pack it all up and drive to your parents. You're sure they won't mind us all there?"

She put down her utensil and leaned toward her husband. "Jerry, if we don't go there soon, they may come and get us!" Beth exclaimed.

He chuckled, "Fair enough." After a few more bites Jerry added hesitantly, "Babe, what about going to New Jersey? Have you given any more thought to that?" They had talked the last several evenings into the wee morning hours about both their family situations. Beth was an only child, and very close to her parents. Technically, Jerry had two siblings who could help his parents, one who was already in the same state. While that did alleviate both his obligation and worry to some degree, Jerry was getting more and more anxious about his distance.

"Yeah, I have. Let's see how it goes in Indiana. I think if the Aunt Sarah issue is solved, and if my office issue is settled, we should go."

"What about your parents?"

"Sure, I'm worried about them. But they're OK, and your mom isn't. Also, if we go to New Jersey, we can drive back here or to Indiana if we needed to, couldn't we?"

"Of course! It's only thirteen or eleven hours. In either case, we'd be back in a day," Jerry confirmed.

She raised her glass to his and they clinked. "Jerry, we have a plan! Maybe your mom will get better before we can even drive there," she added hopefully.

Jerry took a long minute to continue chewing his food and seemed to have difficulty swallowing. "To Mom's speedy recovery," he whispered and held out his glass for another clink.

"Here, here," Beth smiled as she clinked with her husband. She kept her grin fixed and her eyes on her husband she brought her glass to her lips. She continued to watch him as he sipped, lowered his gaze, and abruptly stood up with his plate. He turned away, pushed his uneaten food into the sink's disposal, and loaded his dishes into the dishwasher. As he began to clean up, she took a few more small bites and said a silent prayer for her mother-in-law. Although they had gotten somewhat used to the seemingly never-ending tension caused by COVID, it would be nice to see her husband smile again. Yes, a real smile would be nice.

Sunday, April 26, 2020 - Day #14

Remington Family WhatsApp:

EVIE: Leaving the Sunshine State for the Garden State! Be home soon!

JERRY: Driving?

EVIE: Yep. Kevin and I will take turns, despite what Dad says lol

JERRY: Us, too. Leaving Illinois for Indiana later today!

Adam added 😂 to Evie's post.

ADAM: Drive safe all of you!

Evie and Alex added 👍 to Jerry's post.

ALEX: Keep Harry in the carrier!

ADAM: Hand sanitizer after every stop!

Evie added 👍 to her dad's post.

JERRY: Using double!

ADAM: Keep us updated! Be careful! 🤍

Evie, Alex, and Jerry added 🤍 to Adam's post.

Dr. Marino had observed her patient for 24 hours and all the test results were in. She could wait no longer; it was time. "Amy," she said softly.

Amy, checking the IV on the other side of the bed, turned toward her colleague.

"Let's go," Dr. Marino said as she swished over to the bed. When the doctor and the nurse were on either side of the patient, the doctor placed her hand on Jeanette's shoulder to gently shake her COVID-wracked body.

"Mrs. Remington? Can you hear me? It's Dr. Marino. I need to speak with you," Dr. Marino was saying loudly. "Can you hear me?"

Jeanette first felt the shaking, then realized someone was calling her name. She struggled to think clearly through the clouds in her head. It was like waking up from a dream, except the dream was more real than reality. She was taking quick, shallow breaths. She grunted.

"Yes, Mrs. Remington. Open your eyes, please. I'm your doctor, Dr. Marino."

Jeanette squinted and realized she was cold. She began to shiver.

"Oh, Mrs. Remington, I'll get you another blanket," Nurse Amy said as she squished away to the corner of the room. "There, how's that?" Amy asked when she placed another blanket atop Jeanette.

Jeanette closed her eyes and nodded her appreciation.

"Mrs. Remington, you're wearing an oxygen mask. You must speak up so we can hear you."

"K."

Dr. Marino and Amy exchanged another glance. "Mrs. Remington, I have something very important to discuss with you. Your tests show COVID has caused inflammation in your body. In fact, you're in respiratory failure, and now all of your organs are in danger of failing. Mrs. Remington, your body is at a crucial point which I believe you can feel." Dr. Marino paused and used her penlight to look into Jeanette's eyes.

Jeanette blinked, turned her head aside, and nodded.

"Can you say 'yes,' Mrs. Remington?" Dr. Marino asked.

"Yes."

"Your body can't continue much longer. Mrs. Remington, I'm sorry, your chances of surviving on your own are slim. Your kidneys and heart are on the verge of failure."

"My children ..."

"Yes, Mrs. Remington, I know you have children. Three, right? As well as a husband?"

"Yes."

"Mrs. Remington, please listen." Dr. Marino spoke loudly and slowly. "We've done all we can. Medically, we can continue to give your body the support it needs to fight the coronavirus. To do that, we must help your lungs by putting you on a ventilator."

Jeanette squeezed her eyes shut and expelled the little breath she was capable of holding.

"Do you understand me, Mrs. Remington? If you don't or if you prefer, I can ask your husband to make the decision."

"Decision?" Jeanette repeated.

"Yes, Mrs. Remington." Dr. Marino met Amy's eyes across the bed, then returned her attention to Jeanette, whose hand felt ice cold in her own gloved claw. "Jeanette, in order to put you on the ventilator, we have to sedate you; we have to put a tube down your throat. We need your permission to do that. We will do everything possible to keep you alive, but we need your permission. Can we intubate you, Mrs. Remington?"

"Alive," Jeanette whispered.

"You want us to keep you alive, Mrs. Remington?" the doctor asked.

"Yes." The response was weak, but irrefutable.

"Good! Mrs. Remington, we will do everything possible, but we cannot guarantee that you will survive. Once we sedate you, you may not come back." The doctor paused and spoke slowly and deliberately. "Do you understand, Mrs. Remington?"

"Yes." *Adam, where are you? Take good care of the kids!*

"Amy, I'm noting on the records that Mrs. Remington gave permission for intubation on 4/26/20 at 09:09."

"Yes, doctor."

"Adam," Jeanette squeaked.

"Amy, can you call the husband?" Dr. Marino asked.

Amy went to the ICU room phone on the small stand and lifted the receiver. She dialed the number as Dr. Marino read from the record displayed on the computer screen. The doctor leaned over her patient and used her gloved fingers to smooth Jeanette's hair from her forehead.

Amy held the phone receiver aloft so everyone in the room could hear and be heard.

Adam answered within the first ring. "This is Adam."

"Hello, Mr. Remington. This is Dr. Marino here in ICU. Your wife and I are calling you together with an update. Mr. Remington, Jeanette has consented to be placed on a ventilator. She understands that medically, this is all that we can do now to help her body heal from the COVID-19 virus. She has agreed to be sedated and intubated, even though she may not recover."

He was standing, once again, at the kitchen island with Lucy at his feet. The call he had dreaded was here. It was happening. He couldn't speak. He closed his eyes and laid his head on the cold granite.

"Mr. Remington, are you there?" Dr. Marino asked. "Mr. Remington?"

"Adam," Jeanette whispered.

"Jeanette," he moaned.

Dr. Marino met Amy's eyes over Jeanette. "Hello, Mr. Remington. I'm Dr. Marino. I'd like to give you a few minutes with your wife. Before that, however, I want to outline your wife's current condition. COVID pneumonia has compromised her lungs and placed undue stress on her kidneys, liver, and heart. She's in full respiratory failure. We will sedate and intubate her, and place her on a ventilator to control her entire body's metabolism to allow her body a chance to heal. During this time, we will be monitoring all her organs 24/7 for signs of failure, and taking daily chest X-rays and blood draws looking for signs of improvement."

Adam swallowed and tried to assimilate all that information. "How long can she be on a ventilator?" Adam croaked.

"Jeanette will stay on the ventilator until we see signs of improvement. Our longest patient so far has been on a respirator for 61 days."

That number sounded ridiculously high to Adam. What would he be doing for 61 days while Jeanette was on a respirator? He chose to focus on the positive. He had heard on the news that ventilators were in high demand, and that some hospitals were experiencing a shortage. He was glad Jeanette would be receiving the treatment she needed. "What would be a sign of improvement?"

"Higher blood oxygen levels, clearer chest X-rays, improved lung function. Jeanette will be monitored for any improvement at all."

When Adam didn't ask another question, she continued. "During this time, we will be alternating her position to allow for better oxygen profusion. We'll place her in a reverse transdelenberg position, which is feet up and head down, for at least six hours each day. This position helps the lungs expand." She paused and looked at Jeanette.

"Ok, Mr. Remington, Nurse Amy and myself will be with your wife almost every day. We rotate infrequently here, going nine days on and nine days off. Before we switch, we'll make sure you are aware and introduce you to our colleagues who will continue to take good care of Jeanette."

Dr. Marino was relieved that it seemed Mr. Remington would not be contradicting his wife's instructions. It was damned stressful when the family member did that.

"Do you have any questions, Mr. Remington?" she asked.

"Yes, how will I talk to my wife while she's on a respirator?"

"You won't be able to speak with her until she is taken off the respirator," the doctor confirmed. "Something else, Mr. Remington. While your wife is sedated, you are the person on record. We will be contacting you to make any decisions that are needed about her care. Are you OK with that?"

Decisions. He choked out, "Whatever Jeanette needs." *Don't think about it now.* "When can I visit?"

"Mr. Remington, no physical visits are allowed. However, our ICU policy is that we arrange a certain time every day for you to join a Zoom call. We have an iPad situated on a cart which we place in the room focused on your wife. Then you, and anyone you give access to the link, can join."

"As long as she is in the room and isn't needed for testing, you can visit for 15 minutes. Of course, she'll be sedated and unconscious. She won't be responsive; it's like she's in a deep sleep."

"Jeanette, do you hear that? Is all that OK with you?" Adam asked his wife.

She nodded and tried to raise her arm toward the phone.

"Mrs. Remington has indicated yes. Perhaps you'd like to see your husband before you are sedated, Mrs. Remington?"

Jeanette nodded yes.

"Mr. Remington, your wife's phone is still with her. Once she's sedated, hospital policy demands we turn it off and place it with her other possessions until she can use it again. If you call or FaceTime her now, Nurse Amy and I will make sure she answers you. That is if you want a few minutes ..."

"Absolutely. I'll hang up and call her right now."

Almost immediately, Jeanette's cell rang on the bed. Amy helped Jeanette answer the phone.

Dr. Marino said loudly, "Hello again, Mr. Remington. You can have a few minutes with your wife." Dr. Marino nodded to Amy, who first waved at Adam and then adjusted a blanket on Jeanette's chest and leaned the phone so her patient and her husband could have privacy. She placed Jeanette's hand over the phone to hold it in place.

Looking at Adam with the kitchen behind him, a wave of homesickness overcame Jeanette. Her tears flowed unchecked as she clutched at the phone on her chest. If only she could be home in her own kitchen with Adam. If only ...

"Oh, baby ..." Adam wept. "I love you, Jeanette."

"The children ..." she whispered.

"What?"

"Jerry, Alex ..."

"Yes, Jerry, Alex, and Evie love you, too, honey. They're all thinking of you."

She squeezed her eyes and struggled to breathe and talk.

"Love them ..."

"Yes, I know you love them. They know you love them, honey."

She nodded and considered giving up. *Just one more try.*

"You ... have ..." Adam leaned closer to the phone when he realized she was trying to tell him more. She was difficult to understand with the mask on her face. She ground out, "to ... love ... them ... for ..." and she touched her throat, "me."

He nodded slowly and squeezed his face to keep in the tears. "Jeanette, I will. But *I* need you. We *all* need you here. Come back to us."

Now that he had understood her message, she relaxed against the pillow and loosened her grip on the phone. "Love you," she whispered.

As they spent more minutes struggling to stay connected over the airwaves, Jeanette didn't notice the others who had come into the room. When Dr. Marino spoke loudly, Jeanette looked up to see several more aliens of varying heights aside several carts of equipment between the door and the bed. *Is that a microwave?*

"Mr. Remington," Dr. Marino called without moving the phone away from Jeanette. "We're ready to begin the procedure now to sedate and intubate your wife. She needs the ventilator, so she can heal. Please, it's time to say goodbye."

"Never goodbye, Jeanette ... see you soon. I'm waiting."

I'm so sorry, Adam, to make you cry. Jeanette showed Adam a peace sign with her fingers, and then touched those same two fingers to her mask to blow him a kiss. When Jeanette turned her open palm in a goodbye wave, Amy pressed the red end button on the phone, and everyone moved forward toward Jeanette.

Dr. Marino leaned into Jeanette, grasped her hand again, and said, "Like your family, we will not give up on you. But you need to do your job, too. Keep fighting, Mrs. Remington. Fight this virus with everything you've got! You have so many people who love you waiting for you." When Jeanette began to sob and cough and struggle to breathe, Dr. Marino looked up at the nurse standing near the IV and said, "Amy, administer the sedative now."

19

As the aliens were moving and working around her, she tried to focused within. Breathing was difficult, and so was thinking. What should she be thinking? Everything was so tangled in her mind. Exactly what was happening? She thought of Adam, Jerry, Alex, and Evie. *Did I say good-bye?* She panicked. Breathing even faster, Jeanette grasped the bed rail and fumbled to pull herself up.

"Whoa, Mrs. Remington, what's going on? What's the matter?" Dr. Marino asked and took her patient's hand in hers. In the meantime, she looked up at Amy. "Hold," she whispered. Amy tipped the syringe upright.

Jeanette tried to focus on the purple pen dangling between her and the doctor. What did the doctor say? That she had to do her part? What was that? The thought of never seeing Adam or the children again was horrifying. *But everything hurts! And breathing is so hard!* She wanted to let go and return to floating.

Panting now, Jeanette eked out a broken and barely comprehensible, "What do I do?"

Speaking slowly and clearly as if to a child, Dr. Marino explained, "Do? Mrs. Remington, you heal. We'll help. You just heal. Can you do that?"

She breathed even faster. "Don't know!" Jeanette wailed. She was reaching out frantically at the railings.

Just then there was an alarm on the doctor's radio clipped to her shoulder. "Code Ocean."

The doctor spoke into the radio, turned and said a few words to the assembled group. "Mrs. Remington, please, relax and try to breathe. We have an emergency in another room right now; we must help another patient. In the meantime, Amy will stay with you. We'll be back as soon as possible."

"Yes, I'll stay," Amy said reaching across Jeanette to the bed table. "By the way, Mrs. Remington, your phone has been blowing up! So many new messages and texts. Why don't we read all these messages your family has been sending? I know it will help you relax. Would that be OK?" Despite Jeanette's frazzled state, Amy began to speak.

At first, Jeanette couldn't make sense of the words, but when she realized Amy was reading a text Jerry had sent, she stopped all motion to listen intently. One by one, Amy read notes of love and encouragement from Adam, Jerry, Alex, and Evie. When she appeared to have finished, but the crew had not yet returned, Amy read the older WhatsApp and text messages. Jeanette closed her eyes and pictured her children saying these words. *I wish I could be with them.* Knowing they were doing OK produced a ghost of a smile curving her lips.

When Dr. Marino returned, she found a much-subdued Jeanette struggling to breathe. She nodded at Amy across the listless woman in the bed and grasped her hand once again. "Well, we're back. It's time, Mrs. Remington, to get to work. You *can* do this. You *can* heal. You have your family sending you love and pulling for you, besides all of us. Look at *all* of us here to help you," the doctor said as she motioned toward the bodies amassing around the bed. Amy nodded back when the sedative was delivered into the IV.

Jeanette closed her eyes as the aliens returned and closed rank around the bed. *Adam, where are you?* She whimpered like a wounded animal.

"OK, Mrs. Remington, it's all going to be OK. Just relax and try to breathe. That's it," Amy crooned as the doctor turned toward the surgical table, opened a drawer, and began to assemble the equipment needed.

Swiftly, the doctor was giving orders and the other aliens were responding. There was movement all around the bed as everyone focused on their task.

"That's it, Mrs. Remington, just breathe. You're going to be OK," Amy repeated. Jeanette looked in the direction of the voice, but it took incredible effort to keep her eyelids open. Everyone was talking and moving in slow motion. She was beginning to float away when she felt it. There was a warm hand on her right cheek. The ungloved skin-to-skin contact brought a gasp and tears as Jeanette leaned into it and wondered how long it had been since Adam touched her. How long had she gone with only completely clad aliens for company?

Then she heard it. It was only a whisper. She had to focus.

"Shh, Netty, it's time to let go," her mother said.

Mom? Oh, how wonderful to hear that voice again! No one had called her Netty in years! Relief flooded her COVID-wracked body.

"I'm here. I'm always here with you. Oh, don't cry, Netty," Palma spoke soothingly as Jeanette's tears rolled once again unheeded. "Everything's OK," Palma was saying as she stroked Jeanette's forehead. "I love you."

How she missed her mother's voice! The soul-deep ache lodged since her mother's death unfolded.

"Honey, you must listen to me. Netty, honey, listen," her mother whispered. "I have a message for you." Palma stopped stroking Jeanette's forehead and placed her hands on either side of Jeanette's face. "Remember I am always, *always* here with you," Palma repeated. "You are never alone."

I'm afraid! It hurts, Mom! I don't want to leave!

"Netty, I know how you feel. You're going to be OK; you've done so much hard work. Hold on; just stay and heal."

Although she heard the voice, Jeanette was having trouble seeing her face. *Mom?*

"You did a fine job with your family. They're fine, Netty. They're all doing so well! I'm so proud of all of you," her mother whispered as she stroked her cheek.

How much she missed her mother's touch! While the tears continued, Jeanette breathed shallowly and focused on the feel of her mother's fingers. Any hurt, she knew, could be eased by a mother's touch. Jeanette couldn't drag her eyes open now. She could only sob.

I miss you, Mom!

"Shh ... relax, Netty. I can stay a short while. Remember: A mother's love can *never* be erased by time or circumstance. That's our gift to the world." Palma touched Jeanette's chest. "I'm here. In your heart. With you. *Always.*"

I feel you!

"Netty, the kids are grown now. They still need you, but in a different way. It's time for you to get closer."

Just like us.

"Yes. Just like us."

Oh, Mom. I miss you so much!

"I know. But I'm always here with you," her mother repeated.

Jeanette placed her hand over her mother's hand on her chest. *Mom, I'm so scared!*

"Relax, Netty, and have faith. All is as it should be."

I love you, Mom!

"Oh, I love you, Netty."

Lulled by her mother's words and loving touch, Jeanette felt liberated. She was no longer struggling for breath. She was not alone. The pain was gone. She let go.

After successful intubation, the ICU team shifted Jeanette into the reverse transdelenberg position for better lung profusion. She was now lying on her stomach with her feet elevated. Jeanette's head was turned to the side to accommodate the huge mask and tubes that comprised the ventilator. Every organ's function was monitored using multiple connections and leads, including those attached to her exposed upper back for her lungs. They had checked that all the equipment was working properly to keep her body alive. Then they left Amy to care for Jeanette.

Her patient was crying again. Amy dabbed at the tears running along the mask and pooling on the pillowcase and uttered a deep sigh.

"Please, Mrs. Remington, hang in there," Amy urged. She rearranged pillows and retrieved a fresh blanket from the warmer, covered Jeanette to make her more comfortable, then stepped away from the bed. The constant rhythm of the beeping monitors and pumping oxygen lulled Amy into a welcome trance. She watched the dials as every pulse assisted Mrs. Remington's life. The Remington's emotional scene and tension throughout the procedure had exhausted Amy. When her own phone in her pocket buzzed, she welcomed the distraction. She smiled as she read her mother's text.

MOM: Just left a few meals in your fridge for when you get home, including your favorite chicken parm. Take care of my baby! xoxo 🩶

AMY: I will, I promise! Thanks for the meals! Love you 😘

Amy and her mother had not been together in an enclosed room for two months, meeting only outside wearing masks since COVID cases filled the ICU. The last visit, Mom not only brought her famous fudge, but a lawn sign that read "Hero Nurse Lives Here." It was one of the community gestures turning up around town to demonstrate support for the medical workers who showed up during the pandemic. So many were worried about contracting COVID that they simply abandoned their jobs. Although the recognition was warming, it was also a bit uncomfortable. Amy was committed, but these were crazy times. She would rather remain anonymous among her neighbors, just in case she, too, decided the risk was far too great. If she did not fear for herself, Amy most certainly would not expose her mother to this virus. She knew her mother was worried Amy would contract COVID, but she understood Amy's dedication. Her mom was very proud of her "hero."

Amy looked back at Jeanette. She turned off Jeanette's phone and added it to her bag of clothing. Amy's days here at the hospital were filled with mostly COVID cases. As per hospital protocol, she monitored her charge from at least six feet, and limited close contact to no more than 15 minutes in an hour. There was enough experience now that Amy could recognize the stages of the virus's progression. At this point in Mrs. Remington's situation, the goal was to keep the patient alive long enough for COVID to give up. Looking at the woman in the bed, Amy could be grateful that her own mother was home safe and well. She logged onto the computer and updated the chart before checking on her next patient. That was all she could really do. It was up to Mrs. Remington now.

20

After the hospital ended the call with Jeanette, Adam fell to the kitchen floor. Lucy leaned in as Adam held on to the lab and buried his face in her yellow fur. He was still prostrate when Evie posted on the WhatsApp.

EVIE:

JERRY: Making good time!

EVIE: So far so good! No traffic lol

Alex gave a 👍 to Evie's post.

ALEX: Drive carefully!

Oh, Jennie. How could you leave me? How could you leave me to tell them? They were just as vulnerable as he was. Didn't she see that? He pictured the lethargic, coughing shell of a woman that could barely lift her fingers to blow him a kiss. COVID had stolen his Jeanette away from him. Adam roared, and squeezed his eyes against the dull throbbing in his head. Lucy retreated and cowered. "Lulu ..." he reached out to her. Skittish, the lab continued to back away from him, which only enraged him more. He saw spots!

"What's your problem?" he yelled.

Lucy turned tail and ran out of the kitchen into the safety of her kennel in the office.

The pounding in his head got louder, and he thought he might explode. Afraid of *him*? His lab was afraid of *him*? There was a stone-cold killer moving freely about the country, and the dog was afraid of him? Abruptly, Adam jumped up from the floor and stormed out the kitchen slider onto the deck. He slammed the screen door, causing it to fly off the track. He ran down the deck steps and around the perimeter of the yard. Once, twice ... he stopped counting after ten, but was still running. By the time he dragged his exhausted, sweaty, burning, winded body up the deck steps, the red haze was a pink fog. He could begin to think again. Lucy was inside the house, no doubt still hiding from his outburst. He fell into an iron chair, closed his eyes, and focused only on breathing. By sheer will, he wrangled his emotions under control. *I cannot let COVID win!*

Sometime later, he realized a few things. First, it was amazing that it took him this long to explode. Barely eating, barely sleeping, watching Jeanette slip away. Exactly how had he managed to keep himself somewhat together until now? Two, he was recovering his composure. He had just learned his wife was on a ventilator because she couldn't breathe for herself. Upsetting, yes, but it beat the alternative. Without the ventilator, she would be dead. If she had to be a hot mess for a few weeks, so be it. He must remain positive and hopeful, for himself and his children. If needed, there would be plenty of time to mourn. Third, the sun was shining, and it was a glorious day. He let the warmth calm his soul, and for a few precious minutes he let go. Just let his mind be blank. He was aware of the gift of life as he took deep, cleansing breaths unavailable to Jeanette.

Lucy scratched at the dangling screen door, pushing it even more off the track. The noise brought Adam back to the present, and reminded him of his responsibilities. Until Jeanette was back in this house, he was all Lucy and his children had. COVID had complicated all of their lives. His overwrought daughter just left behind her job and life in Florida, embarked upon a 24-hour road trip with her fiancé, so she could be closer to home and her sick mother. His older son was also traveling, helping his wife support her family all while worrying for his mother. His younger son was protecting his pregnant wife, preparing for his firstborn while possibly preparing for the loss of his mother. Although they all had separate lives, they were one family unit. How could they all *not* be affected by these circumstances? He was definitely not OK, but so far, he was managing his business during a lockdown and his wife's COVID affliction. So, he went a little crazy. Who could blame him? Certainly not Lucy, who nuzzled and licked his hands.

Much calmer now, Adam decided he needed to place a group call. Evie was driving with Kevin, and Jerry was possibly driving, so Zoom was out. But they had agreed on full disclosure at all times, and it would only become more difficult to discuss. This was their new normal, and all he could do was embrace that. This news was likely to further unbalance his children's worlds, and although he was reluctant to do that, he knew honesty was always the best policy.

He placed the call to Alex first, then conferenced in Jerry and finally Evie. After determining that his sons were both at their home workstations and instructing Evie to pull over (Kevin was driving), he told them that Jeanette had been placed on a ventilator. The update was greeted with silence. He credited his children; apparently the news was not wholly unexpected. They must have all googled "ICU" and "COVID treatment" and "respiratory failure" like he did. Adam heard the heavy sighs and quivering voices indicating that they were upset and emotional, but not surprised. They asked many questions.

"How long do they expect Mom to be on the ventilator?"

"Not sure. Could be days or months. However long it takes for her body to heal."

"Can she talk?"

"No, she's been sedated. She's basically sleeping until she gets better."

"How will they know she's better?"

"When the tests show improvement."

"What are her chances?"

"Well, as long as she's with us, her chances are great!"

"What could go wrong?"

"Her organs could shut down, from either COVID or the medication. That's why she's being monitored so carefully."

"So, what should we expect now?"

"We expect to hear from the hospital every day about her condition."

"Can we visit?"

"No visitors allowed. But we will be able to Zoom for 15 minutes every day."

"What can we do?"

"Pray and send your love."

"Do you need anything, Dad?"

"Just for your mother to get better."

After a stilted silence, the conversation pivoted as Evie and Kevin described the extremely light traffic on the roads. With a stay-at-home order in most of the country, they expected little congestion to continue all the way north on Interstate 95. They were limiting their exposure as much as possible by stopping only for gas, and they had packed drinks and light snacks from their apartment. They were only planning to drive through McDonald's (Evie's favorite) or Burger King (Kevin's favorite). If needed, they would be sleeping in the car, but as of right now they were hoping to drive straight through. They discussed their current ETA in New Jersey, as well as their music playlist.

Jerry updated everyone on Beth's family situation. They were planning on being at Beth's parent's house in Indiana by evening with Aunt Sarah in tow. They hoped to stay in Indiana for a week. Meanwhile, they were waiting for Beth's job to make a decision about returning to the office with a staggered work schedule. But at this point, they expected to return to Chicago.

When Alex gave the latest update on the baby, everyone was stunned. He had moved from his office into the living room to share the call with Sue, who was currently resting with her feet up. She had apparently experienced some light spotting overnight. After an emergency ultrasound first thing this morning at the doctor's office to ensure that the baby was fine, the doctor determined that Sue was "overdoing" it. While not on bedrest, Sue was expected to stay off her feet as much as possible. As a result, Alex was going to step up around the house, in addition to working from home and running all the errands. Everyone expressed concern, and Alex said he didn't want anyone to worry. He joked about "Queen Sue" lounging and directing him from the sofa. Sue chimed in from the couch, telling everyone she may never get up again.

The call ended with everyone's half-hearted chuckles, and wishing Sue well. Adam told everyone that he would be providing information about the first Zoom call, which wouldn't be until 48 hours. He forgave himself this lie; he wanted to keep Jeanette all for himself the first time. He couldn't imagine what he would see, and wanted to prepare them for what it would be like. He figured that if his conscience got the best of him, he could always tell them at the last minute. Everyone told Jerry and Evie to drive carefully, and they were all released to their separate worlds once again.

After the conversation with the children, Adam fixed the screen door. It took a bit of time to bend the lightweight frame back into shape. He took Lucy for a short walk around the neighborhood. On this beautiful spring day, the street traffic consisted of children riding bikes, since there were almost no cars. In fact, when Adam and Lucy drove to the parking lot of the hospital, it seemed downright silly to stop at red lights when there was no opposing traffic. It took about half the time it would normally to get to St. Peter's, although there was more traffic as he approached the hospital. Once he parked in the lot, he put the windows down a bit as Lucy moved up between the console to sit in the passenger seat. He came here to feel close to his wife.

He began to talk to Jeanette, then decided to keep a record so that he could share it with her when she came home. He unlocked his phone, pointed the camera at the Emergency Room door, and started to record a video. "Hi, Jeanette. Lucy and I are here in the parking lot, so you're not alone." He described what each Remington was doing. He ended his video by turning the camera toward himself and Lucy, blowing her a kiss, and saying, "See you soon. I love you." He sent the video to his email, so it would be dated. He and Lucy lingered in the parking lot watching the activity in and out of the busy Emergency Room entrance. Instead of thinking of the day he dropped Jeanette off here, Adam imagined what it would be like when he was picking up Jeanette to bring her home.

Now that he was unable to really communicate with her, there was less pressure to keep a brave face. He wouldn't have to put on a smile and pretend everything wasn't falling apart. At least with the children, there were other topics to distract the conversation: their work, their plans, their in-law families. But the last several times he spoke with (or to) Jeanette, it became increasingly difficult to actually communicate. Her decline apparent, he was totally on the hook to maintain the interchange. It was both exhausting and depressing. The respirator relieved him of that duty. After "I love you," anything said to someone who may be dying of COVID sounded trite or loaded. However, now that Evie was on her way, things would be changing. Adam would no longer be alone. Right now, he was unsure if they would add to his burden or alleviate some of it.

Driving from the hospital, Adam traveled a bit out of his way to a nearby strip mall in the next town. This vast parking lot for this popular shopping area was oddly attended. Most of the smaller stores were closed, but the anchor stores, Walgreens and Acme Supermarket, were definitely open. The majority of the traffic was going into and out of those businesses. Masked patrons were single filing into and out of the stores. Adam continued to the middle of the mall and pulled into a spot near two other parked cars. He harrumphed at the irony. The Xtreme Fitness location was closed due to the lockdown, but High Times Liquors was open. People were going to be unfit and drunk when this pandemic ended. Finding this to be more proof of the absurdity of the entire situation, he thought his first toast would be to the governor for deeming liquor stores essential to remain open. Adam turned off the car, donned a mask, went inside, maintained six feet of separation, and bought a bottle of Glenlivet while Lucy waited patiently in the back seat.

Once home, Adam fed Lucy, settled on one of Jeanette's protein shakes for an easy meal, poured a generous amount of amber liquid, then sat on the deck in the setting sun. Lucy enjoyed a walk around the perimeter of the yard and took care of her business before rejoining

Adam on the deck. Adam enjoyed the quiet in advance of Evie and Kevin's arrival. There was nothing new on TV to watch since the baseball season was cancelled due to COVID, and he had no desire to view a previously recorded game. HGTV was on, as usual, in the family room for background noise. Time was passing, even with their activities limited as it was due to the COVID lockdown. He and Lucy eventually left the chilly deck, went into the family room, and checked in on the family WhatsApp.

ADAM: How goes the trek?

EVIE: Still making good time! We're tired, though, and will stop to sleep a few hours. Plan to be there in the morning.

ADAM: Smart. Don't drive tired!

JERRY: We're in Indiana. Got here early. All good.

ALEX: Glad to hear you're both well! All good with Sue and Baby Rem. See you soon, Evie and Kevin!

Adam, Evie and Jerry responded to Alex's post with 👍.

ADAM: Stay safe! We love you guys.

Everyone responded with 🤍.

He didn't have to explain that "we" was he and Jeanette. He smiled to himself thinking he couldn't remember being singular, and no matter what happened he would never think of himself as single. *It's up to you now, Jeanette.* Assured that Evie would arrive tomorrow, Adam raised one more toast to Jeanette and drank until he was oblivious. He and Lucy shared yet another sleepover on the sofa.

21

An exhausted Evie and Kevin finally arrived in New Jersey at 7:30 am. Adam was waiting on the driveway when they pulled in. When Evie saw her father, she launched herself out of the car before Kevin had even come to a full stop. She cried and sobbed, like she did when she was five, and her daddy hugged her tightly without speaking until it was over. When she pulled away to take Harry who was meowing in the carrier from Kevin, Adam and Kevin shared a handshake that evolved into a sideways man-hug.

Evie reached into the back seat and triumphantly held up the signature yellow arched bag for Adam's approval. "Breakfast, anyone?"

"Oh, yes! You know I love McDonald's! Let's go in and eat before it gets cold. We'll get the luggage later."

The young couple eagerly went into the house, and were immediately greeted by a happy Lucy, who was thrilled to have both their company and Harry to play with again.

"Oh, they are still so cute together!" Evie exclaimed watching Lucy's wagging tail as she sniffed Harry. The cat reciprocated by licking Lucy's ear.

Adam, watching the ruckus and listening to the exchange, realized he was just as thrilled as Lucy to have his daughter home. Adam made them all coffee as Kevin and Evie ran upstairs to "disinfect." They came down about ten minutes later having showered quickly and changed clothes, which Evie immediately threw in the washer with Adam's permission.

Finally, they settled into the Egg McMuffins and lamented the missing hash browns due to the limited COVID menu at McDonald's.

As they caught up, Kevin and Evie shared details about the tiring drive and lack of people on the road. "It was like something out of an apocalypse movie," Kevin reported.

"I never used a bathroom so fast in my life," Evie announced.

Looking at their faces, Adam gleaned the discomfort they felt while driving on I-95. "Well, it's great to see you here, safe and sound."

Evie looked up and exchanged a small smile with her father.

Adam shared the latest about everyone else. He had texted with Jerry last night and Alex this morning and there was nothing new to report about their situations.

Evie was about to take a bite, when she rested the muffin on the wrapper and asked, "What about Mom? Anything new from the hospital, Dad? How is she?"

"No news is good news, as they say. Nope, nothing new. I'll call as soon as I get to the office this morning. Are you two OK to settle in here by yourselves?"

Amid bites, they confirmed that they planned on setting up their work-stations and taking a nap. Then they asked about the agency.

"Things are slow, but holding firm. One agent is home quarantining this week, and won't be back for a bit. Julia's somewhat freaked out by this whole shutdown, and has two school-aged children at home. I think she's weighing the pros and cons of a paycheck. It wouldn't surprise me if she doesn't come back."

They all chewed on that, and the conversation turned to other situations. Evie was particularly concerned about the restaurants that couldn't provide the required restrictions and were forced to close down. Of course, she was talking about Florida, but the same mandate had been enacted in New Jersey. "How will those people make money? How will they pay their bills?" She shared how regular patrons were contributing to the GoFundMe pages popping up on social media.

Having no answers, and eager to get out so he could see Jeanette by himself this morning, Adam shook his head and said, "None of us have any idea where all this is heading." He was sorry their conversation had taken such a negative turn, but how could it not, given the current state of affairs? "Evie, let's focus on the positive. We're all here, together. Your mom is holding her own, your brothers and their wives are safe, and Baby Rem is getting bigger every day."

She nodded and smiled, they exchanged more hugs, and he left. When Adam left the house, ostensibly to open the office, he went directly to the hospital. Sitting in the Emergency Room parking lot, he used his phone's Zoom app to log into the hospital's link at 9:00 am. The call was accepted, and on the screen, Adam could see a white blur as the iPad was turned toward a bed.

"Good morning. Nurse Amy here. Mrs. Remington is the same as yesterday. She's holding her own. Let me know if you have any questions." Then the picture came into focus as Amy moved away from the tablet so that Adam could see Jeanette.

Adam swallowed and did not look away from his wife's still form, not for a second. It was definitely his Jeanette, wearing a huge clear mask strapped to her face which was completely slack. The blue hair covering was still in place. From the angle at the foot of the bed, he could see the rise and fall of her chest and one arm limp at her side. He could hear the pulsing of the oxygen pushed into and out of her body by the ventilator. *Oh my God! That's Jeanette! Oh, my Jennie. My poor Jennie!* No matter how painful it was to see her nearly lifeless, no matter how frightening the sounds of the equipment that were keeping his wife alive, he did not look away. Tears flowed unchecked down his face while his mind went numb.

Minutes into his precious fifteen minutes, he wondered if he should be speaking to her. *Would you be able to hear me? Do you know I'm here with you?*

He cleared his throat several times before saying, "Hey ... Jeanette ... It's me, your favorite husband."

No response.

"I, uh, I ..." he stammered. His inane words sounded ridiculous to his ears. What could he possibly say to make a difference? *Jeanette, are you still there?*

While he was grasping for words, a blue finger edged into the corner of the picture. He nearly jumped at the unexpected movement.

"Mr. Remington, Amy here again ... I promise I'm not eavesdropping. I stuck my head in to check your wife's vitals, and I heard you. If I may make a suggestion? I know it feels awkward to talk to your wife because she's unable to show that she can hear you. But my experience with previous patients is that they can hear you in this unconscious state. I suggest you talk to your wife as much as you can. We all do that here."

"Uh, OK. Amy ... I was wondering ... how will she eat?"

"Oh, we're providing nutrition intravenously. Don't worry about that, Mr. Remington."

"OK." Adam expelled the air he was holding in his lungs. "OK." He collected his thoughts. "Jeanette, guess what? Evie and Kevin are home. Yeah, that's right, they came home this morning."

Surprisingly, once he began talking, Adam couldn't stop. He shared updates about the children, and what they were doing. He knew Jeanette would want to know. So, he told her all the details of Evie and Kevin's trip, about Jerry and Beth in Indiana, and about Baby Rem causing a few issues for his mom and dad. After exhausting all the topics dealing with the children, he voiced his ideas about his agency. Adam informed Jeanette that he was thinking of opening the office by himself only for reduced hours, and putting his staff on hiatus until the lock-down was lifted. He explained Julia's issues and how that was affecting the whole office. In fact, the other agents were also a bit stressed, and the shutdown meant the work wasn't exactly flowing. Many other agents had closed, and he could, too. So, opening even four hours a day would be a real service to his customers.

When Amy appeared in the periphery and pointed with a gloved blue finger to an imaginary watch along her white-clad wrist, he was shocked. Now that he started, he still had so much more to say!

"Time already?" he asked.

"Yep."

"Jeanette, I'll be back tomorrow with the kids. You keep getting better. We love you and miss you so much!"

At Remington Central, Harry and Lucy got along famously, and it only took a few hours for Evie and Kevin to ready her childhood bedroom and set up their makeshift workspaces. While Kevin worked in their bedroom overseeing Harry's scratching post, Evie insisted on sharing Lucy and her mother's office. Reverently, she stacked all of Jeanette's notebooks and textbooks along with her school computer as if it were a shrine. Being home was such a balm for her! As the youngest, she had yet to set up a permanent home for herself, having moved among several apartments since she graduated college. Now that she and Kevin were engaged, although this crazy global pandemic precluded any kind of wedding planning, they would begin to think about setting down roots of their own. In the meantime, as far as she was concerned, this was home base. Tired as they were, they both logged on and went to work.

That evening, Alex and Sue came over for a very short while to celebrate their homecoming. The five of them stayed outside on the deck so that they didn't have to don the requisite masks and maintained six feet of separation following their brief hugs. Sue refused to stay at home, no matter how much Alex had entreated. She had been idle all day, and also wanted and needed the comfort of the Remington clan. As an accommodation for Alex and the baby, Sue wore a mask and sat down immediately on the deck's uncomfortable iron chair. Her husband quickly brought another chair closer, so she could elevate her legs once again. Although the group was thrilled to be together, they were well aware of the missing members: Jeanette, Jerry, and Beth. The stay-at-home orders and public distancing created a desperate need for connection; the fact that Jeanette was fighting against the reason for the distancing only made their need greater.

On a whim, Adam decided to FaceTime Jerry so he and Beth could join. Everyone was happy that they were available, moving from Beth's parent's kitchen into Beth's old bedroom to join the group. While the New Jersey contingent was seemingly well (aside from Jeanette), unfortunately, Beth's Aunt Sarah began showing symptoms of COVID this morning.

"That's terrible! How is she?" asked Adam.

"Well, she feels lousy. Beth's mom immediately took her to a drive-up testing site, and Aunt Sarah tested positive."

"What are her symptoms?" Alex asked.

"So far, she has a headache, fever, and coughing. She's isolated in her bedroom and my mom is taking care of her. The rest of us are staying clear," Beth explained.

"Uh, were you exposed?" Evie worried.

"Yep." He brushed his hand through his hair, a tell-tale sign of his disturbance. "Dad, we were thinking of driving out to New Jersey. Now that's out of the question, at least for the next ten days."

Adam was surprised. "Oh. I didn't realize you two had plans ..."

"We didn't. We were only thinking about it," Jerry replied looking over at Beth.

"Well, how are you feeling, Jerry?" Alex asked.

"No symptoms. None of us have any symptoms. But it's early yet. Aunt Sarah just tested positive today. It can take, they say, up to ten days." Again, Jerry and Beth exchanged looks.

Adam wanted to tell Jerry not to worry, that he was also exposed and didn't contract the virus, but felt too guilty. Jeanette was now on a ventilator, and here he was with his family ... In his home.

"Wait ... If you're all quarantining there, how about food? Are you able to get delivery there in Indiana?" Kevin asked.

"Yeah. Luckily, Beth's mom had been having her groceries delivered since January, so they already had an online account and were regularly scheduled. We've talked about how hard it is to add an account to get groceries delivered right now."

Everyone nodded as they considered that since the stay-at-home order was enacted in all the Remington locales (New Jersey, Illinois, Florida, and now Indiana), many people tried to start their grocery shopping online. Businesses were overwhelmed, didn't have the staff to deliver all the food, and many were shut down or weren't receiving shipments. Only those patrons who had existing accounts before the pandemic were able to consistently get delivery. Everyone else must follow the masking and social distancing rules to go in person to stores with limited stock. While toilet paper was the first casualty of the shutdowns, with eerily empty shelves or signs limiting purchases, there were rolling shortages of products in all areas.

"At least we don't have to mask up, wait in line outside the Meijer, and walk super slowly around people with carts chock full to maintain six feet of distance. Or wait at the check out for the cashiers to wipe down all the surfaces between orders." Jerry rolled his eyes. "What an ordeal!"

Again, everyone agreed. The conversation lagged while everyone digested the new COVID threat states away. Adam wondered how he would feel if Jerry fell ill. He knew how Jeanette had felt about Jerry being so far away. He resisted the urge to tell Jerry to jump in the car immediately and come home. He was needed there with Beth's family. But he acknowledged to himself that he wanted all his children safe at home, his home. This thought had not occurred to him before now ...

"Well, Jerry, keep us posted about everyone there, including Aunt Sarah. Beth, tell your parents we said hi and to take care."

"Will do," Beth replied.

"Dad, when we're cleared, would it be OK for us to come there? We're thinking we could drive and stay a bit. I mean, we want to be there when Mom comes home."

At the mention of Jeanette, everyone lapsed into silence.

Choked with emotion, Adam could only nod. *Your mom would love that!* He smiled and nodded again.

"Anything new about Mom?" Jerry asked.

Adam nodded no, then realized Jerry was waiting for an answer. "Nothing new. Same."

Buoyed by their family connection, yet still sober, they ended the call. Now two more Remingtons were in direct line of COVID fire. Everyone retreated to his or her own world with their partner.

Alex and Sue talked little on the way home; Sue held Alex's hand. They had agreed to end every night with positive Baby Remington talk. After Sue went to bed, Alex decided to send his mom a text outlining their current plans and thoughts about the baby. Tonight, he focused on the baby's room, and how they were planning to decorate it. They had already chosen a space theme, and he detailed their progress. He took pictures of the baby's room as it was, and sent them with the long text. He ended his text with: "Mom, I can't wait to share all these details and moments with you. Baby Rem can't wait to meet you. We all love you, Mom. Come back to us. 🤍 🤍" Alex lingered in the room, touching all the baby things they were receiving from Amazon. Boxes and piles of newborn outfits that Sue was going to wash in advance. Finally, he checked all the doors and locks as he did each night to keep his growing family safe. Ironic, he thought, since COVID was the biggest threat to his happiness right now; locks would not keep *it* at bay. He stood at the door a few more minutes, then turned to join his wife in bed. Sleep did not come quickly.

Jerry and Beth felt down and isolated in their bedroom. Beth was watching her favorite show on the Cooking Channel, called *Girl Meets Farm*. Neither spoke, lost among their own thoughts about possibly being infected with COVID. They were in the car with Aunt Sarah yesterday for almost four hours. Was that long enough to contract the virus? They both felt fine, but also had a tickle in their throats. Was it imaginary? Neither were hypochondriacs, but really, COVID was killing people by the thousands. They had Jeanette as an example of how fast the virus attacked. Jerry stared blankly at the episode until an emotionally wan Beth fell asleep.

I need my mom. Quietly so as not to wake his troubled wife, he went into the adjoining bathroom. There, Jerry recorded a voice memo to Jeanette. He told her their situation, shared his worries for himself, Beth, and her family. He asked Jeanette's advice. What should he do? What would it feel like to have COVID? When he had exhausted his anxiety, he saw that the recording was more than 22 minutes long. He did feel better having poured his soul out. And he knew that Jeanette would have some precious grains of advice. If only she could talk to him. He ended the recording with, "See, I still need you, Mom. Get better. We all need you. Love you and hope to see you soon. Bye, Mom." He thought about it for a moment, then rerecorded the ending. "See, I still need you, Mom. Get better cause we all need you. Love you. See you soon. Bye, Mom." Jerry sent the voice memo to his mom, left the bathroom, and joined his wife in bed. Sleep did not come quickly.

Adam drove to the hospital as usual and recorded his video and message to Jeanette. He emailed it from the parking lot. When he returned to the house, he took Lucy out one more time, and closed up. With Evie and Kevin in the house, he should go to sleep upstairs. Lucy looked confused that they were not having their sleepover on the couch, but went willingly to her kennel in the office. Adam saw how Evie had organized Jeanette's things, and went to the pile on the credenza. He lovingly touched her books, notebooks and laptop, and wondered at how important she thought all this work was. Her teaching. During a pandemic. Laughable.

Not only was his wife in ICU right now, but his son was exposed and could also have COVID. What could he do? He was shaking his head, and felt powerless. Moving to the sideboard in the dining room, he poured and drank a solid four fingers of whiskey. He'd need it to lay down in Jeanette's bed for the first time since she went to the hospital. He stopped on the stairs to the second floor, returned to the dining room, poured and drank another two fingers. Adam really wanted to sleep. Tomorrow was another day; his children would be joining the Zoom call in the morning with their unconscious mother. He stood in the doorway and eyed the bed for several long minutes before laying down atop the covers fully clothed. Sleep did not come quickly.

Evie listened to her father coming up the stairs, and wondered how lonely he must be right now. She considered getting up to say good-night, but changed her mind. She and Kevin were both lying in bed reading, hoping to exhaust their eyes if nothing else. When Kevin got up to use the bathroom, Evie pulled out her phone. Without explanation, her father had left the house earlier. Of course, she was curious, but she wanted to give him space. They were in for a long haul here at Remington Central, and she knew she'd have plenty of time in the future to ask him questions. While he was out, she scouted her parent's shared walk-in closet. Evie touched her mother's hanging sweaters and her favorite flannel shirts piled on the shelves. She lovingly fingered the gowns her mother had worn at her brothers' weddings and remembered the great times. Being in her mother's closet made her feel closer to Jeanette, just like being in the office with all of Jeanette's work things. *Mom has to come back; she loves her work! And she looked so beautiful in these clothes!* Impulsively, Evie had hung up one of the gowns and taken a picture. Texting quickly now, she sent the picture to Jeanette along with a text of Evie's reminiscences. Evie wrote about Alex's wedding, and the excitement they all shared. They had a wonderful Remington gathering; the entire weekend had been magical! Evie ended her text with a reminder of the future. "By the way, Mom, don't forget I still have to get married! We need to go dress shopping! 👰 💒 You've never been the mother of the bride! We have so much more to do together, Mom! We all love you! Come home! Xoxoxo." Evie finished just as Kevin returned to bed. She put her phone aside, and snuggled her fiancé. Even though they were overtired from their long drive, sleep did not come quickly.

22

They were all silent until Adam spoke. Evie and Kevin were at the kitchen table with Adam. Jerry and Beth were in her old bedroom in Indiana. Alex and Sue were also at their kitchen table. He had prepared them as much as possible for the sight of their mother on a ventilator. One advantage was that with four callers on the screen, Jeanette looked smaller and farther away. Definitely a bit less scary. Or so Adam hoped ...

"Jeanette, we're all here today with you." He didn't want to emphasize that he had Zoomed yesterday, and hoped that Nurse Amy wouldn't mention it. "So, let's do this in age order. Jerry and Beth are currently in Indiana. Jerry, why don't you tell your mother how you got there and what's going on?"

"Ah, s-u-r-e," Jerry looked at Beth, but she just stared back at him.

A few minutes passed, and Adam said, "In the interest of time, I'll speak a bit. I'm afraid the 15 minutes will go fast! So, Jeanette, how are you? Nurse Amy and the doctors say you're holding your own. Good job!"

That seemed to break the tension, and Jerry spoke up. "Ah, Mom, it's great to see you! I hope you can hear me. Beth and I are in Indiana with her folks. Remember Aunt Sarah? She has COVID, too. Her case is not half as serious as yours, though." When he realized what he said, Jerry looked up. Was it OK to talk about how sick Jeanette was?

Adam jumped in to fill the void. "Alex, why don't you and Sue give your mom an update on Baby Rem?"

"Of course! Mom, Baby Rem may be a bit fussy. He gave us a little scare, but all is well. Right, Sue?"

"Yep! Baby Rem's kicking as we speak!" she smiled.

Evie jumped in. "Hey, Mom! I'm here! I mean Kevin and I drove here to New Jersey. Ugh! What a long drive! The roads were creepily empty, but we made it OK. Looking forward to having tea with you when you come home!"

"Yes, Jeanette, and besides the kids, Lucy and I miss you, too!" Adam asserted.

The conversation continued, to Adam's delight, somewhat upbeat. *I guess it's better for them to see her than to wonder how she's doing in ICU.* Each taking turns, and with their signature banter, there were no more lags as the 15 minutes ended. He could tell Jerry and Alex were ready to sign off, but Evie wanted to keep going. Nurse Amy ended the call, everyone shared get well wishes for Jeanette, and Evie sighed deeply.

"What do you think?" Adam asked his daughter.

"Good. She looks good. She's healing, I can tell." Evie's radiant smile lit up the room. In that moment, Evie reminded Adam of her mother.

Minutes turned into hours turned into days of the "new normal" of Remington Limbo.

Every morning at 9:00 am the Remington clan signed on to a Zoom call arranged by the nurse Amy or Rachel and talked to an unresponsive Jeanette. Generally, the nurse made a short statement like, "Mrs. Remington is the same," or, "Mrs. Remington is holding her own," before turning the iPad toward her for their visit. The same gloved finger would indicate that time was up, and they ended the call.

Jerry and Beth quarantined and worried about developing COVID. Jerry continued his nightly voice memos to his mother asking her advice for everything from work issues to family issues to what to wear the next day. Anything to keep talking to Jeanette.

Alex and Sue prepared for Baby Rem's arrival. Every night Alex sent his mom a text with the progress made that day, and pictures as their house transformed into a nursery. All keeping Jeanette in the loop.

Evie and Kevin had no issues working from New Jersey. Every day when her father went to his office for four hours, Evie wandered the house looking for traces of Jeanette. Every night she sent her a picture of something Jeanette loved: her favorite tea cup, her favorite blanket, her favorite slippers, her husband, her Lucy. All reminding Jeanette to return to the life she loved.

Adam let his office staff go and operated the office himself for only four hours a day. He spent more and more time in the parking lot each evening between closing the office and returning to Remington Central for dinner. Evie never questioned him; she seemed to know he needed time alone. The whiskey helped him sleep. When he went to bed, he still lay atop the covers.

23

He was so proud of his children. He was barely keeping it together, but they were supportive of him and each other. That was the silver lining in this situation. He was sitting in the hospital parking lot and had just begun recording his daily video to Jeanette reminding her of their fantastic children and partners when the phone call interrupted.

When he received the call from the hospital, he swallowed down the vomit, closed his eyes, and stilled. This was the first time anyone had called him outside of their morning Zooms, and he feared the worst. The call almost went to voicemail, but he accepted.

"Hello."

"Mr. Remington? This is Dr. Marino."

Adam's heart was a racing locomotive heading over the cliff. He clutched his chest. He hadn't talked to Dr. Marino since Jeanette was placed on the ventilator. *Oh My God! This is it!*

"Mr. Remington, I have encouraging news! This morning we noted a mild improvement in your wife's breathing, and today's chest X-ray also shows the inflammation in her lungs has decreased slightly. Oxygen levels and organ function indicators in her blood have also slightly improved. I'm cautiously optimistic."

Adam shook his head to clear his fear and follow along. "Optimistic? That's good, right?"

Dr. Marino chuckled. "Yes, these are all good signs. Remember that the respirator was only a temporary measure. Our goal was to help her breathe to give her body time to heal; it was never a long-term solution." She paused and waited for Adam to respond.

"OK..."

"These positive indicators tell us it's time. If she continues like this tomorrow, the next step is to wake her up, and see if she can maintain this improvement on her own, without the respirator. Do I have your permission to move your wife to the next step?"

"Wake her up? What exactly do you mean?"

"Right now, your wife is sedated. We'll bring her out of sedation, take her off the respirator, and monitor her condition. If she can hold her own for 24 hours–that is maintain her own blood oxygen level – without the respirator, we'll move her out of ICU to a COVID recovery floor."

"Wait ... recovery?" Sitting up in his seat in the car, Adam asked, "Are you saying that Jeanette no longer has COVID?"

"Well, she still has COVID, but the pneumonia is clearing up. Mr. Remington, your wife has a long haul ahead of her, but the first step is removal of the respirator. Do I have your permission?"

"What if she can't breathe without it?" he asked.

"If she can't maintain her own breathing with the assistance of oxygen, we'll have to sedate her, intubate her, and hook her up to the ventilator again until more signs of positive progress. While that's not the ideal situation, it has happened in the past."

"You're saying this is 'positive progress'?"

"Absolutely! Again, we won't know until we try. So, we'll monitor all test results until tomorrow morning to be sure. We'll know at your morning call if all indicators are a go. How does that sound?"

"Doctor ... forgive me ... are you saying that tomorrow my wife will be awake?"

"Yes, Mr. Remington, I hope so." Quietly she added, "I can't guarantee anything, Mr. Remington. We're doing the best we can here. We'd all love a win, and your wife's chances are looking very good!"

Air escaped his lungs. "So exactly what will you be doing tomorrow?"

Dr. Marino took that as a yes. "If all continues as is, we'll bring your wife out of sedation, remove the breathing tube, and disconnect the respirator. I assure you we will be monitoring her closely. If she holds her own oxygen levels for 24 hours without the respirator, we'll move her out of ICU to a COVID recovery floor."

Adam stammered, "Out of ICU? Jeanette's going to wake up? And come out of ICU?"

"Well, we hope so. She's not out of the woods yet, Mr. Remington, but all signs are very positive. We won't know for certain until after we wake her up."

"Oh My God! I have to call my children immediately!"

"Uh, let's not get ahead of ourselves, Mr. Remington. I strongly suggest that you don't set an expectation with your children for tomorrow morning. Again, she has to continue this positive progress before we can proceed."

Her back-pedaling confused Adam. Didn't the doctor just say Jeanette was getting better? "I don't understand. Is she better, or not?" he yelled.

"I'm sure this sounds contradictory to you, Mr. Remington. I just wanted to make you aware that your wife is showing positive signs of recovery. If it continues overnight, we'll attempt to remove the ventilator tomorrow. We'll know during your call."

"Let's say you take her off, and she does well. When can I pick her up and bring her home?"

"It all depends on your wife. If she continues on the road to improvement, she'll stay here for at least another week before we discharge her to a COVID rehab facility. The good news, Mr. Remington, is that you'll be able to visit her there, with precautions."

No words.

"Mr. Remington?"

Oh, to be with his Jennie once again! "That's great news!" Adam sputtered. "Thank you, doctor!"

"Remember, we have a bit to get through still. It will be days yet, Mr. Remington. Even though Jeanette has fought valiantly through this virus so far, I must caution you. Remember that Jeanette could suffer a setback at any time–"

"Nope," Adam interrupted. "Nope, my wife is coming home. Soon. Thank you, doctor!"

"I sincerely hope so, Mr. Remington."

They exchanged a few more details before the doctor confirmed, "Join the Zoom call as usual at 9:00 am, unless she takes an unexpected turn. In that case, I'll call you immediately. Do you have any questions?"

"Uh, doctor, I'm reeling with this good news!"

"Mr. Remington, your wife is still fighting the remnants of a grueling COVID infection. We still have a way to go."

"Thank you," Adam whispered and hung up.

Overwhelmed, Adam sat still. Suddenly, he let out a whoop of joy so loud that people standing by the doors of the emergency room turned toward his car. He laughed aloud at their curious expressions.

"We're going to make it!" he shouted slamming his fist on the steering wheel. Whispering now, Adam continued. "Jeanette, you're going to make it!" He threw his head back against the headrest and began rocking slightly. "I was so afraid, Jeanette, that I was hoping for too much. But, no, you're doing it! You're actually doing it!"

Adam fumbled for his phone and began a new recording. "Jeanette, you're doing better. Tomorrow you're coming off the ventilator! Oh my God, Jeanette! You've had me so worried! But I know you're coming home! The doctor just called and said ..."

When he ended his video with his signature lines, he knew that his children needed this good news. He opened the Remington family WhatsApp and realized it had gone dormant along with Jeanette. He knew that he and the children were sending her texts, voice memos, pictures, and emails. It was time to resurrect the group communication.

ADAM: Jeanette, keep up the good work! The doctor just called to say you're getting better. We love you and we miss you XOXO. Get out of ICU and come home already! 🏠 🥴

EVIE: Woohoo! Way to go, Mom! 🥳

JERRY: OMG! 🦾

ALEX: We love you, Mom! 🫶

Beth, Kevin, and Sue loved Adam, Evie, Jerry, and Adam's posts.

Not for the first time since this ordeal began, Adam marveled at the strength generated by the love of his family. *We raised a tough family, Jeanette!*

24

On the 9:00 Zoom call, the Remingtons were upset.

"I'm sorry to disappoint you, Remingtons, but I can't confirm that we will be taking Mrs. Remington off the ventilator today. We're waiting on the radiologist to read the latest chest X-ray to be sure we see enough improvement in her pneumonia. Also, her ABG levels are close to normal, but still slightly elevated. As I said yesterday, we really don't want to take a chance on removing the ventilator, and her not doing well."

There was a collective moan.

"Of course, we all want the best for Jeanette. When will you know?" Adam asked.

"Early afternoon, I expect."

"Well, are you still seeing improvement?"

"Yes, Mr. Remington, slight improvement. We need to be sure it's enough before we take this big step." When no one replied, Dr. Marino continued. "I'll let you have your visit now. We'll call you, Mr. Remington, to let you know what happens later this afternoon."

After the doctor repositioned the tablet to the immobile Jeanette, everyone remained quiet. They were all so excited that Jeanette was getting better, and this felt like a setback.

"Jeanette, we're all here. Say hello, everybody."

After they all chimed in, Adam directed the conversation so that everyone updated Jeanette. Jerry sounded tense and irritated when talking about quarantining. "Mom, we hope to be driving out there to New Jersey soon. Why don't we coordinate? You have a few more days to get better. I can't wait to see you."

Alex talked about Baby Rem and the latest from his office. "Looks like I'm working from home for the duration. You know the baby is due in a few months. Oh, and don't forget I get paternity leave. So, Sue and I can visit with the baby when you get home."

A subdued Evie said work was going well, and they were sitting at home. "Mom, we're taking care of Lucy and waiting for you. Wake up and get better, OK?"

After more banal conversation, sometimes among the siblings, Nurse Amy once again pointed to an imaginary watch on her covered arm. Adam closed down the call. "Ok, Jeanette, that's our time for today. Listen, honey, it seems they need a bit more proof that you're improving. Why don't you show them?" Amid a chorus of "You've got this" and "Love you," the call was ended.

A few hours later, Dr. Marino was reviewing the most recent test results on the monitor. Her eyes crinkled on the edges as she smiled behind her mask and waved the purple pen excitedly. "That's it! Amy, begin the

SAT. Mrs. Remington's ABG is normal, and her chest X-ray shows improvement."

"Right away, doctor!" As Amy went about preparing for the procedure, she relished the positive atmosphere. The spontaneous awakening trial was the first step in removing Mrs. Remington from the ventilator. If all went well, she would be extubated within four hours. If that went well, she would be moved out to the COVID recovery floor within 24 hours. The ICU team were all seasoned medical professionals, and as such accustomed to both progress and relapses among their patients. However, the past several weeks of horrific COVID mortality rates had been absolutely demoralizing. Nearly 70 percent of their ICU patients did not recover. Every single patient that survived this virus was celebrated. And while the names of all her patients remained with Amy for weeks, she had real hope for Jeanette Remington. Amy prayed that this was the beginning of her recuperation. It sure looked like that.

"Mrs. Remington, can you hear me?"

Jeanette heard the voice from far away. She didn't recognize it, but it was very insistent. Her mind was quite foggy, and she didn't feel her body at all. *Where am I?*

"Mrs. Remington, it's time to wake up now. Can you open your eyes?" Amy coaxed watching closely.

Jeanette tried to comply, but her eyelids felt like sandpaper. It took several attempts. Even then she could only squint against the brightness.

Amy noticed the difficulty and adjusted the blinds on the window against the sun. "Oh, good. You're waking up. Hi, Mrs. Remington. Remember me? I'm Nurse Amy."

Jeanette blinked and moved her eyes to slowly scan the room. She was aware of the beeps and monitoring sounds from nearby equipment. *Adam?*

"Don't try to talk, Mrs. Remington." Amy pushed a button on the radio clipped to her white PPE and called for Dr. Marino, who came quickly.

"Mrs. Remington, it's Dr. Marino. Can you open your eyes and look at me?" Both the doctor and nurse waited tolerantly for Jeanette to comply.

"Good. You're doing great." Taking hold of Jeanette's hand, the doctor instructed her to squeeze it.

At first, Jeanette's hand was limp and wouldn't listen to her mind. She closed her eyes and would have drifted back to sleep, but once again Dr. Marino was insistent.

"Mrs. Remington, yoo-hoo! I'm holding your hand. Can you squeeze my hand for me?"

As disconnected as she felt, Jeanette was able to exert just a tiny bit of pressure.

"Fantastic! Good job, Mrs. Remington!" Both the doctor and nurse exchanged unseen grins behind the masks. "You've been under sedation, and we've just taken you off. You are still on heavy medication, so you probably don't quite feel like yourself."

Coherent thought escaped Jeanette.

"Don't worry, Mrs. Remington. As the sedative wears off, you'll be able to think a bit more clearly. But so far, so good!"

Maybe Jeanette dozed off again, or maybe she was just blinking slowly. It was impossible for her to tell. *Adam?*

"Mrs. Remington, you can't talk because you have a breathing tube in your throat. You've been improving. We'll be monitoring you closely for the next couple of hours. If all goes well, we'll be able to remove the breathing tube and let you breathe on your own, without the ventilator."

Ventilator? The nurse and doctor talked among themselves and updated the chart on the computer while Jeanette digested that. She realized that she didn't feel pain. Then she remembered how her chest had burned when she coughed and struggled for air. *Oh, God! COVID!*

A machine beeped faster, and they both returned their attention to Jeanette. "Mrs. Remington, you're okay. Trust us; we know what we're doing. Amy, why don't you remind Mrs. Remington about her family. They've been visiting you every day, Mrs. Remington."

Amy began retelling Jeanette about the short visits from her husband and children. While she didn't remember exactly what everyone had said, she remembered enough to distract Jeanette. She had trouble understanding the actual words Amy was saying, but registered that it was all about Jerry, Alex, and Evie. Her adult babies. She watched them grow up in her mind's eye.

She pictured them as infants swaddled in the bassinet. She pictured them as toddlers stumbling through the house. She pictured them bobbing in the neighbor's kiddie pool. She pictured them standing on the corner with their backpacks waiting for the school bus. She pictured them playing their sports. She pictured them at their elementary promotion ceremonies. She pictured them at their high school graduations. She pictured dropping them off at college. She pictured their college graduations. She pictured them driving off to meet their futures. She was lost in her thoughts of each child as the sedative was wearing off, and her mind was returning.

Jeanette had little sense of time, but eventually Dr. Marino returned to the room and announced that Jeanette was ready for the next step.

"Mrs. Remington, you're doing great! It's time for the spontaneous breathing trial. You're still on the ventilator, but we're lowering the oxygen level. As a result, you'll be breathing more on your own. We're going to test this for the next two hours. If all goes well, we'll remove you from the ventilator. Just relax and breathe, Mrs. Remington."

Her eyes widened in reply. *Off the ventilator? But don't I need it? Adam, where are you?*

Her mind spiraled again, and she thought of Adam. She pictured him on the first day she met him. She pictured him on their first date. She pictured him on their first break-up. She pictured him on their first trip to the Jersey shore. She pictured him proposing to her. She pictured him saying his vows at their wedding. She pictured him on the beach on their honeymoon. She pictured him in their first apartment. She pictured him in their first house. She pictured him encouraging her in the delivery room. She pictured him holding their children one by one. She pictured them moving into their current house. Before she knew it, Dr. Marino returned.

"Ok, Mrs. Remington, you've passed the SBT. We're going to move the bed so you're sitting up." Amy was using the arrow buttons to raise Jeanette's head. Another white-clad alien materialized from the corner of the room and helped hold Jeanette forward while the bed was folding. It was very uncomfortable for Jeanette to move; she was stiff and achy. It was difficult to hold her head upright without the gloved hand. "When we tell you, we want you to take a deep breath and try to cough. Are you ready?"

Jeanette felt a bit wobbly, but blinked her assent.

"Ok, deep breath and cough!"

In one fluid motion it felt as though the doctor ripped her throat out. Everyone was speaking at once, encouraging Jeanette to breathe and cough it out. The gagging reflex came first, followed by the coughing. Surely blood was spewing everywhere from some gaping wound. *Now I'm going to bleed to death!* A nose cannula was immediately placed over her ears as Amy lowered the bed to make Jeanette more comfortable.

"Don't worry about that squeaking noise," Amy was saying. "That's a result of the breathing tube. It'll pass."

That noise is me? Spent, Jeanette focused on breathing during the reflexive swallowing.

"Mrs. Remington, we need to call your husband with an update about your condition," the doctor was saying. She sounded clearer than before. "He'll be so happy to find out that you've been removed from the ventilator. Would you like to join the call with him?"

Dr. Marino asked Amy to place the call to Mr. Remington. He answered immediately.

"I've been waiting to hear, doctor. How is my wife?"

The sound of Adam's voice caused an exquisite mixture of relief and homesickness. *Adam, where are you?* Jeanette whimpered.

"Mr. Remington, I'm happy to report that your wife has been breathing successfully on her own, with the aid of 7 liters of oxygen, for the past four hours."

"That's wonderful!"

"We've removed her phone from her bag and plugged it in. Would you like to see her?"

"Oh my God, yes!"

"If you FaceTime her phone right now, we'll answer."

When Jeanette's revived phone rang, Amy arranged it and pushed the FaceTime button. The minutes seemed like an eternity; then the phone provided proof of life.

When Adam saw his Jeanette, he smiled and cried and nodded his head yes. "You're back! You came back to me! Oh, Jennie!" A wave of relief washed over him. She was looking for him; her eyes followed his voice, saw his face, and visibly relaxed. She leaned forward slightly in the bed for two beats with a ghost of a smile on her lips. Then she closed her eyes and leaned back into the bed. She was without her trademark spark and luster, but she was alive.

"Mr. Remington, if all continues to go well, we'll be moving your wife out of ICU to the COVID recovery floor tomorrow afternoon. Her test results show that she no longer has pneumonia, and she is functioning on her own. We'll continue to monitor for organ damage. She's very weak, and this novel coronavirus has lingering effects that may last months. However, her prognosis is very good."

The news was wonderful, yet seeing Jeanette was all he needed. Adam only had eyes for his wife. The change from this morning was remarkable; the huge mask covering her face was gone, and her face held expression again. He could tell that she was uncomfortable now by the pinched lines between her brows. She was obviously dazed and couldn't muster any other indication that she was aware of him. Still, he knew. Surely, he would get her back. Yes, he vowed, he would have his Jeanette once again.

After repeating the care plan, the doctor ended the call. Jeanette, groggy from having been sedated for a week, was also incapable of talking just yet due to the breathing tube. So, Adam did not say goodbye; he told his wife "welcome home" and that he would speak with her tomorrow. She gave no sign that she heard him other than that brief ghostly smile.

That was enough for Adam. He had taken Dr. Marino's call in his empty insurance office. Excitedly pacing from the front door to the windows, Adam placed a FaceTime call to Jerry, conferenced in Alex and finally Evie. He could not have hidden his huge smile, even if he tried, but of course he wanted everyone's anxiety to end. He shared the great news, and the whoops and hollers reverberated for some time. Then they all took to the WhatsApp once again.

JERRY: You did it! You hit a homeroom, Mom! #ComingHomeSoon 🩶

ALEX: That's it, mom! Winning! #Healing 🥀

EVIE: So proud of you! Lucy is, too! #LoveWins 🐶

ADAM: Jeanette, your favorite tea and blanket await! ☕🏠😌

SUE: Baby Rem says hi! 👶

KEVIN: Sunny days ahead! 😎

BETH: 🌻 🌼

Tuesday, May 5, 2020 - Day #23

Nurse Amy was updating Jeanette's chart on the laptop in the room when she heard the sniffling.

"Mrs. Remington? Are you in pain?" she asked.

After wallowing for several hours, Jeanette was able to find her voice and admit her overwhelming fear. "Will I die now?" Jeanette whispered brokenly.

Amy was surprised at the question. "Mrs. Remington, why would you ask that? You've made it! You're off the ventilator. You've done a great job healing, and you're holding your own. You're about to leave ICU."

"Sure?" Jeanette persisted.

"Honestly, other patients …" Amy unexpectedly choked up. She looked away and shook her head to dislodge the faces of so many victims that passed before her eyes. She took a deep breath and grasped Jeanette's hand with her gloved one. "You have survived COVID. Now you just need to recuperate. Relax. You've done it!" Amy's brown eyes were swimming. "We're all so proud of you!"

Jeanette turned her hand palm up to grasp Amy's. "Promise?"

Amy was confused. "Yes! Why would I lie to you?"

"Peace. So, I can die in peace," Jeanette rasped.

Amy gripped her hands tighter. "No, no, Mrs. Remington. No dying for you. Not from this horrible virus! We've all been cheering for you ... praying for you ..."

Jeanette stared deeply into the eyes behind the plastic face protector and exhaled. *Not dying.* She believed Amy. *How difficult it must be for this nurse to tend to all of us!*

"Mrs. Remington, may I ask ... what did you think about?"

Again, that ghostly smile appeared on Jeanette's face. "Family."

On cue, her phone pinged with a text message. Jeanette focused her energy and successfully read and answered Jerry's text with a heart emoji. *Thank you, God!*

Later that day, Jeanette began her journey home by moving from the ICU to the COVID recovery unit.

EPILOGUE

June 2020

Much later, Jeanette would wonder where the time went. Her memories, disjointed by medication and lack of oxygen, were somehow both foggy and exquisitely clear of her 16 days in the hospital and 10 days in the medical rehabilitation center. In her quiet moments, Jeanette reviewed the voice memos, texts, emails, and videos from her family. Her heart swelled with their tangible love, and she knew she would always treasure their precious words.

COVID had left its mark on her body. She was generally weak and slept a great deal. Sometimes she lost her train of thought, but Adam insisted that was "just Jeanette." She had lingering aches and pains, and a nightly cough that Adam was getting used to. While her ability to taste and smell was just beginning to return, her appetite was still diminished. Adam was constantly reminding her to eat to get stronger. Overall, she was exhausted, yet very happy.

Her school, after Adam contacted the principal, had put Jeanette on family leave until further notice. What a great relief it was to know another teacher had taken over and closed out her classes for the year. The idea of posting remote lesson plans online, grading the work, and following up was ludicrous; she simply didn't have the energy or will for the job. It was also too soon to make a decision about the next school year. The COVID lockdown continued, and it was still unclear if or how anyone would be returning to the classroom in September.

Dr. Roman had suggested Jeanette join a COVID support group set up through the hospital. She had dialed in to one Zoom meeting to hear how people were dealing with the haunting symptoms and survivor guilt. Others told about the inability to grieve for COVID victims due to lockdowns, and how some family members could only see the body of their loved one in the hospital parking lot on its way to the mortuary. Depending on the weather, some families were allowed graveside ceremonies, but no gatherings were allowed indoors. Jeanette couldn't imagine losing a loved one in that fashion. She knew she was blessed to have all her family members safe at home, and that her family didn't have to suffer such conditions because of her.

Jerry and Beth eventually arrived from Indiana. Fortunately, neither of them contracted COVID; unfortunately, both of Beth's parents did. They all recovered, but Jerry and Beth had needed to stay on longer to help out until everyone was healthy once again. With Beth's company abandoning the idea of opening the office, they were both free to work from home. When they arrived in New Jersey, they masked and quarantined as much as possible indoors for 10 days, which was worth the effort so that they could all be together. They were staying at Remington Central for the foreseeable future. Sue had set up her workspace in Jerry's childhood bedroom, and Jerry had claimed the dining room. Luckily, with summer in full swing, the family spent as much time outside on the deck as possible. At times Alex and Sue (with clearance from her doctor) stopped in, either for lunch or in the evening after dinner. It was wonderful to have everyone together, and the siblings and their partners became reacquainted with each other as adults.

COVID had also left its mark on her soul. It was still shocking and amazing to think of how close she came to death. Jeanette remembered several dreams about her mother, which were powerfully real. She spent most of the time recuperating outside in the backyard of her lovely home. Evie set up a cozy and welcoming outdoor space for Jeanette on the deck where she spent most of the glorious early summer under an umbrella, wearing her backyard blanket when needed, drinking her hot and/or cold tea with Lucy lounging at her feet. Sitting on the sunny deck, she thought about those dreams and decided that the strength of a mother's love was her legacy. Not only was her life a treasure, but the memory of a mother's love continued long after the life has ended. By supporting her family, a mother showed the way and encouraged more love. With the imminent birth of the first Remington grandchild, talk was generally about Sue and Baby Remington, who was growing big and strong within. And so, the legacy continued.

She heard the bustling in the kitchen through the slider, and Lucy lifted her head. It was noon. Evie and Kevin joined her on the deck with iced tea and peanut butter and jelly sandwiches. Jerry and Beth joined a few minutes later with heated leftover macaroni and cheese. Adam arrived home from the insurance office, which he was opening by himself from 9-11 and 2-4 on weekdays, and joined everyone outside. They munched and bantered companionably until Lucy's barking announced Alex's arrival. Sue also waddled in.

When they were all together, they talked about what Jeanette missed and her experience in the hospital. All expressed their joy at her recovery, and regret at not being able to be with her during that time. They were afraid, they said, that she thought she was alone. Sitting next to Adam, she noticed his silence and knew he still worried she felt abandoned. She reached out and took his hand, which he immediately covered with his other. Jeanette's answer was a slow smile and a simple truth. Looking around her deck at her children and their partners, Jeanette said, "You were always with me; I felt your love."

"I know the feeling," murmured Alex softly, holding Sue's hand.

"Here, here," added Jerry standing behind Beth.

"So much love!" sang Evie winking at Kevin.

ACKNOWLEDGMENTS

To my husband, my soul mate. I'm so grateful for our life.

To my children, their spouses, and my grandchildren. All of you fill my heart with joy and inspiration.

To my cousin Chrissy, whose medical expertise was instrumental to this novel. I'm so grateful for your love and support.

To Nicola, the magicians at The Unbound Press, and the Unbound Writing Community. I'm so grateful to be aligned with all of you.

To Dr. Kenneth Womack, Professor of English and Popular Music at Monmouth University. Thank you for encouraging me to visualize and craft this novel.

ABOUT THE AUTHOR

Carolyn Davis Cid is a wife, mother of three, grandmother of five, and school teacher who has long nurtured and shared her passion for literature. She joyfully lives in New Jersey with her husband, her chocolate lab Coco, and her tuxedo cat Sofia. Carolyn revels in her growing family and spends as much time as possible outdoors, walking with Coco and tending to her salsa garden.